J. ALISON COLE

EVERNIGHT PUBLISHING ®

www.evernightpublishing.com

Copyright© 2025

J. Alison Cole

ISBN: 978-0-3695-1261-1

Cover Artist: Jay Aheer

Editor: Stephanie Marrie

J. ALISON COLE

DEDICATION

To my family, for their unwavering support. My husband who inspired me, and my two sons who tell everyone that their mom writes dirty books. It's romance. There's a difference.

J. ALISON COLE

J. Alison Cole

Copyright © 2025

Chapter One

Four seconds seemed like forever. Bailey's willpower crumbled just like the stale donut she ate for breakfast, and her gaze beelined across the hall for another *accidental* sighting of Tony Shepard. The glass office partitions of Ajak's Signs provided her with an excellent view of her new boss, whether she wanted it or not.

"Ah, geez." The whispered observation resonated as more of a *'look at him'* while every muscle in and below her belly turned into a rock-hard quivering mess. The staggering response usually happened with every glance, gander, or sighting of the man. And thanks to her inept ability to control her wandering eyes, her core muscles were averaging a better workout than an entire day of sit-ups. Her cheeks ballooned with breath as she flopped onto the swivel chair in front of her desk and ran a hand across her aching stomach. How much longer would this nonsense last?

Wait—what if she was just hungry? Technically, her lunch did start ten minutes ago. Her brows lifted at the idea. Yes, let hunger be the culprit behind the nonsensical convulsions of her twisting belly.

Bailey grabbed her purse and retrieved the peanut butter and jelly sandwich she'd brought to eat. It was horribly misshapen from being shoved into the outer pocket, and the shiny clear cellophane had turned the bread a lovely shade of violet where she'd gone overboard with grape jelly. Peeling away the plastic allowed the purple gelatinous gems to ooze beyond the deformed crust.

After a quick lick of her fingers and a swipe over her jeans, she tugged her cell phone from her rear pocket and reread the text Quin sent earlier that morning.

Quin: **Call me, Bailey Alexandra Jazincski.**

Leave it to her dorky best friend to spell out her entire name. His phone was ancient so it probably took his big sausage fingers ten minutes to accomplish. Odds that the demanding message was for anything important—slim to none. When they became friends three years ago, he sent a similar text and even used 911 in the message. Frantically, she contacted him immediately, only to have him sing part of a song. Said he needed to know the title. Once her heart rate returned to normal, she forbade him to use the number 911 unless it was for a real emergency.

The song: *I Will Wait* by Mumford & Sons. It's sung throughout the entire song. How could he not figure that out?

A smile crept over Bailey's face as she took a hefty bite of her violet-colored tie-dyed clump and pressed his number.

It rang once. "It's about fuckin' time, Bailey!" Quin barked.

Only half of her laugh came out. The other half had a wad of doughy bread and peanut butter stuck to the back of her throat. She coughed the chunk down. "Really, Quin, that's how you're going to greet me?"

"Oh, come on, I thought I'd hear from you over the weekend. So what is this, day three of your new job? Hey, who helped you move?"

"Well, not you, obviously. But yes, this is magical day number three."

"Oh, magical, is it? And I would've helped you move, but the truck still needs a new alternator."

"You really need to get that fixed."

"I know. I only have to jump it every third or fourth time. So, how are you making out?"

"So far, so good. Not everyone can be their own boss like you, and it's busy around here. I'm trying to...you know, find my place and contribute where I can."

He snorted. "I'll bet you're making good money, but don't tell me. I guess it's still more than what I could've paid you."

"It's more than zero, so yeah."

"Still so bitchy." After a hearty laugh, Quin sucked in a quick breath. "Hey, do you remember the man who fixed the compressor at the old shop?"

"Oh...I think so." Bailey licked along the edge of the bread where jelly threatened to drip. "What about him?"

"Well, first off—"

Oh lord.

Bailey's head fell backward, and her eyes closed. All of Quin's long-winded stories started the same way, without fail. Around two minutes in, her chair swiveled from side to side, only—the last pivot twisted a bit too far, and Bailey's chewing all but stopped.

Leaning back into a plush leather chair, talking on his phone, Tony. He had one arm perched behind his head and his feet propped against the edge of his desk. The chair served him up like Sunday dinner—or Wednesday lunch. "Mm."

Quin's husky voice shattered her inner thoughts. "Bailey, Bailey? Did you just…moan?"

"What?" she scoffed, and her eyelids slammed shut. *Shit, shit, shit.* "I'm eating lunch, Quin, and it's really good. Go on with your story." She shoved a mutated corner of bread into her mouth.

"Okay, well, where was I? Oh yeah, he was the boy next door—"

Boy-next-door described Tony Shepard perfectly. Hands down adorable and unequivocally sweet, with an underlying appeal that made her think of those shadowy, sexy cologne ads for men. Physically, Tony stood a little over six feet tall, about three to four inches taller than her—the perfect height. What girl didn't fantasize about peering up into their lover's eyes? His dark brown, almost black hair was short on the sides but long enough on top for a good grip, and the teeny-tiny widow's peak right in the center of his forehead gave him the added appeal of what could be Clark Kent's younger brother. As for his age, her gut said he couldn't be more than three, four years older than herself, but definitely this side of thirty. As if it mattered.

Tony flexed his hips, shifting in the chair. Bailey's stomach clenched, and her mouth hung open mid-chew as the hand behind his head floated down and came to rest on his lap. Her gifted imagination had no problem conjuring a spectacular set of abs underneath his crisp white Henley.

"What do you think of that?" Quin paused, waiting for her reply.

"Wow." *Wow* sufficiently answered Quin's ramblings and her maddening assessment of Tony. *Shit, it's happening again.* She caught a blob of jelly before it fell on her pants.

"Yeah, that's exactly what I said. Anyway, he was an okay guy in school. That's where she knew him from, and—"

Guy in school. Bailey held out for a whole six seconds. A small victory, but two seconds of progress nonetheless.

Tony was probably the guy in school that everyone wanted to be friends with, most likely a sweetheart, one of the cool kids, but just enough of a smartass that people liked him anyway.

She knew the type. Her boyfriend Jordan, or more precisely—as of eight months ago, her ex-boyfriend, had the similar traits. *Has it really been eight months?* A numbing chill crept over Bailey.

Strange, how four seconds seemed like an eternity, yet eight months passed by like it was yesterday? The plan was to live happily ever after with Jordan. So much for the plan.

Just like she never planned to move back in with her parents. Sure, she wasn't the first twenty-four-year-old to find themselves in that position, but no one ever told her how different it would all be. First off, who were these people, and what happened to the mother and father that raised her? And exactly how many open jars of mayonnaise did her mother need in the refrigerator? The woman averaged three. Had it always been this way, and she just never noticed?

Then there were her friends who thought she needed to go out and find someone new, which was the last thing on her list. As cliché as it was, she needed to discover who she was as one and not half of a couple.

She didn't mind staying home, curled up on her parents' couch, and becoming an avid viewer of Turner Classic Movies. Humphrey Bogart may not have been remarkably handsome, but he had swag.

It took several months, but she finally learned to accept her mother's odd obsession with mayonnaise, being single, and the idea that she had a new normal. Was it great? Nope. Did it prepare her for the next upheaval life would throw at her? Not even close.

It was on a Thursday, right after lunch when Quin told her he was leaving the franchise sign company they both worked for to open his own shop. Somehow, puking her gourmet grilled cheese from the corner deli, didn't feel like the appropriate response to her best friend fulfilling his dreams. He'd talked about starting his own company for as long as she'd known him, and now he'd done it. Sure, she couldn't be happier for him, but once Quin left, the work that had kept her anchored wasn't the same.

But, things happened for a reason, and she believed that now more than ever, primarily due to the arbitrary decision she made four weeks ago. The decision to join her parents for Sunday brunch at her aunt and uncle's house in Haymarket, Virginia, almost didn't happen, but after three straight days of rain, the sun came out that morning. It felt like a sign from the universe.

Having slept through most of the two-hour scenic drive, she woke up when they turned onto Uncle Frank's road. His home, nestled in the mountains, is surrounded by towering oak trees and evergreens. Eastern redbuds and white dogwoods added the colors of spring along the stone driveway he shares with his neighbors.

It was because of the stones her father drove extra slow, trying to keep dust off his car. That was the first time she saw Tony and the very first time she found herself intrigued by him. He lives next door and just happened to be outside washing his truck. The sequence of events played out like a slow-motion commercial advertising sex appeal, and she got sucked in worse than Grandma Peg buying stretchy pants off of QVC.

Tony's wet shirt turned mostly transparent, clinging to every muscle along his shoulders and back as spray from the hose swirled tiny rainbows all around him, adding to the moment's mystical awe.

To this day, she has no recollection of what she ate for brunch, but she'd never forget what happened next.

Knowing Tony owned a sign company, Uncle Frank took it upon himself to introduce her to the neighbor. Fifteen minutes later, Bailey was standing in that hallway, right there, outside Tony's office, where he offered her a job, and she preposterously accepted.

A reflection of light bounced off the glass next to his door. Tony saw the same flash. A second later, his gaze connected with hers. What followed was a panty-melting smile and a quick wink. He always added the wink as if his gorgeous smile wasn't enough.

Bailey strained to unfurl her stomach muscles. *Means nothing.* Sure, she might be here for a reason, but he wasn't it. He couldn't be.

From the moment they met, it was clear that Tony liked to flirt. And—Bailey firmly believed those flirtatious gestures were the same to him as breathing and, most likely, perfected well before he hit puberty. Also, it couldn't mean anything—because his girlfriend was a dead ringer of a Kardashian wannabe.

Bailey was so *not* that.

Most of the time, wearing makeup was determined by her mood. Fair to say that over the last eight months, other than Carmex lip balm, she wasn't helping CoverGirl's stock any. Her long blonde curls rarely cooperated or stayed where she put them. Add any percentage of humidity to the air, and her massive locks could be two feet wide in every direction. On those days, Quin called it her Witchy-Bitchy hair.

Bailey nodded toward Tony—a clumsy nod that screamed of guilt for having been caught gawking—yet again. The chair squealed as she turned away, drawing ample humiliation to her self-inflicted lack of restraint. He probably thought there was something wrong with her.

Obviously, there is.

"Right?" Quin's rambunctious question severed her thoughts. "He said his boss was a real asshole. Hey, is your new boss an asshole? If he is, I'll come down there. Don't take any shit, Bailey."

She snorted outright. For the most part, Quin was a big guy with just enough redneck-ish-ness that people might perceive him as threatening. But, in truth, she'd probably do better in a fight than he would.

"He's not an asshole." Bailey steadied her tone. Quin had the knack of hearing things in her voice without having to say them. She quickly redirected the conversation. "But there's this guy named Dylan that works here. I managed to piss him off good this morning. I asked him to replace some vinyl on a van that was cock-eyed. It had to be at least a quarter of an inch off. He tried calling me a bitch under his breath, but I heard him."

"Well, sometimes, you can be a bitch.

"Don't you forget it, either." Bailey crammed more violet dough into her mouth. "There's another guy here, too, named Lazlo. He's old, like you."

"Ha, ha, ha. Thirty is not old."

"Relax, I'm joking, old man. Anyway, I think Lazlo's probably thirty-one or thirty-two. He does mostly busy work like weeding vinyl, sanding, and prep work, stuff like that. Kayla, the girl out front, told me Tony gave him the job after he'd been in a serious accident a couple of years ago. They both seem okay." She dropped the last bite into her mouth and licked her sticky fingers.

"So, how do you like your new roommates?"

"Yual." She groaned inward and outward. If she'd only taken up the offer from her aunt and uncle to live in the guest room for a while. *Should've, would've, could've.* Even though she'd almost doubled her previous salary, everything in northern Virginia cost twice as much as compared to home. Being able to afford a place on her own would be impossible. The main reason she found a place to live so quickly was that Tony's girlfriend just moved in with him, and the roommates needed to fill the spot.

Her new roommates were girly girls, club flies, super-skinny, overly perfumed yuppie professionals. Or, to put it another way, sophisticated upper-class whores. At least, that's what she really thought of them. Of course, with names like Desiree, Raven, and Shawna, how could you not think of strippers?

"Well, I don't have to worry about them stealing my food. I think they feast on the souls of unsuspecting men on a nightly basis."

"Bailey, are you sure you're going to be happy there? It all sounds…so different. Maybe I can borrow more money from somewhere. Make it work, somehow."

"Talk about an asshole for a boss." She covered her laugh with a mocking, harsh tone. "Come on, Quin, you can barely afford to pay yourself. Besides, I'm a much better artist than you, so realistically, I'd have to make more. Now, I don't own a sign company, but I would think the owner should make more than the employees.

"Okay, okay, enough. I got it. And I'm a pretty good artist."

"Yes, you are." An image of Quin came to mind, standing awkwardly and pigeon-toed in a Pirates baseball cap pushed back to the point of falling off, along with paint-splattered jeans and one of his many ratty Dave Matthews t-shirts. It brought a smile to her face.

Quin remained uncharacteristically quiet. *Uh.* He was either wallowing in undeserved guilt or reflecting on his bottomless pit of debt. The man deferred every student loan he had, and along with starting the new business from scratch, he was getting married soon and decided this was a good time to buy a house much larger than he could reasonably afford. By the grace of God, his fiancée Liz had a decent job teaching that provided them with other necessities like food, clothing, and health care.

"Hey, how are the plans progressing for the upcoming nuptials?" Bailey knew how eager Quin was to get married and start a family.

"Oh, Jesus, Bailey! It's crazy. Liz only let me pick some of the food. You know, I honestly think she might be colorblind. To her, there are only three shades of blue. Three! Can you believe that? She must have only had a small box of crayons as a kid." He paused. "Hey, wait, you're still coming, aren't you?" Wishful optimism filled his voice.

Yes, Quin's concern stemmed—not because she'd moved two hours away, but if she'd have a problem seeing Jordan. Sure, the timing sucked, but in this case, her taking a new job and relocating had nothing— absolutely nothing to do with the announcement of her former boyfriend becoming engaged. Adding to the bizarre twist—Jordan's fiancée was related to Liz.

Yes, technically, Bailey broke up with Jordan, but it was still odd to think that he met his soon-to-be wife because of her friendship with Quin. It all felt like an overly theatrical plot from *The Young and the Restless*.

Bailey caught movement from the corner of her eye. Tony veered into the hallway, heading toward the front office. "You know I wouldn't miss it. What did you want anyway, Quin?"

"Do I have to want something? God! Maybe I just wanted to hear your bitchy voice." He said it jokingly, but behind the bitchy part was sincerity. "It's not the same without you around, Bailey."

"I know."

The bond she had with Quin was tough to explain. Almost everyone who saw them together naturally assumed something more was going on. There wasn't. Still, labeling their friendship as brother-sisterly didn't work either. Sure, at times, he'd puff out his chest if someone looked at her the wrong way, and he flat-out refused to introduce her to any of his "dickhead" friends after her breakup. Not that she felt like dating. After spending the last seven years attached to someone, it only seemed right to have this time for herself, deserved it even.

"I miss you too, Quin." As the words left her mouth, the wavy curls along the back of her neck practically straightened. Her head swiveled, and sure enough, Tony stood in the doorway of her so-called office, his fist raised, ready to knock.

"I gotta go, Quin. I'll call you tonight. Bye." Bailey shoved her phone into a rear pocket and swiped at the gooey breadcrumbs stuck on the front of her shirt. *Seriously. Next time, less jelly.*

Tony's hand lowered. "I'm sorry, I didn't mean to interrupt." He crossed his arms and eased a shoulder against the doorjamb.

A tingly warmth hummed throughout her body.

Not because he overheard her tender goodbye but because of the way he stood in the doorway, so casual and all beefcakey. All she needed was some gravy—or whipped cream. Either would work. "Oh, you didn't. I just finished my lunch."

Tony eyed her with feigned curiosity. "So... Who's Quin? Sounded pretty serious."

"Oh, umm, Quin and I are just friends. We used to work together back home."

"Okay?" One of his dark brows lifted and curved into a tantalizing skeptic wave, clearly expecting her to offer more of an explanation which she did not intend to give. Explaining Quin wasn't necessary.

It wouldn't make a difference what Tony thought? Her spine stiffened, and she sat up straighter.

Midway through a reassuring breath, Tony's gaze roamed down her body in a slow, meandering evaluation. The heat swirling in her core flooded straight to her face. A second later, her nipples twerked for attention. *Traitorous little nubs.* Crossing her arms might hide at least one of those humiliating reactions. Her face, however, was probably three degrees away from spontaneously combusting. And it took two tries to cross her arms. How does one forget to do something like that? *Pay no attention to me. Just trying to cover up my titties and not burst into flames.*

Tony's head tilted sideways, clearly confused by her weird behavior. "Hey, I was wondering if you might have a different pair of work shoes or boots in your car." He exaggerated a glance at her sandals.

The air trapped in her lungs surged free. A boisterous laugh followed. He was checking out her shoes—not her. *Stupid. So stupid.* "Oh, I do, as a matter of fact." Inside her ragged-out Audi Quattro TT were three garbage bags of clothes; not all of them clean, but she was relatively confident that her work boots were among them. "Why, what's up?"

"Dylan called. He's not going to make it back this afternoon, and I need a second pair of hands to help with an install that I promised to get done today. Do you mind?"

"Not at all. I told you that I did a lot of the installations back home."

His brows lifted. "I remember. You'll be on a ladder. Are you afraid of heights?"

"Nope. Are you?"

His wavy brow straightened. "There's only one thing that scares me, and it's not heights."

For some reason, she couldn't imagine him being afraid of anything. "And what would that be?"

He didn't answer, but something, not quite a smile, flashed over his features. It said, *Wouldn't you like to know?* He pushed away from the doorway and straightened. "I'd like to leave in about ten minutes, if that works."

"No problem, I'll be ready." Bailey popped up from her chair like an overeager puppy, her nipples still beaming at full salute. Tony sauntered away. *Great.* Her chin and eyelids lowered, drowning in self-awareness. *Get the boots—Dork.*

Kayla Rosslen, the girl from the front office area, jumped from behind her desk and followed Bailey to her car. The young woman's petite frame and pixieish voice automatically conjured images of flowers and butterflies, not to mention that the tips of her dark-cropped hair were highlighted bright orange—today. Yesterday, they were lime green.

Bailey rummaged through the first plastic garbage bag with no luck. She started on the second bag.

Kayla made herself comfortable against her front

fender, slurping on a supersize berry red fountain drink. "He quit, you know?" She sucked on the straw until it screeched.

Bailey straightened and stared. "Who quit? Dylan?" *Shit.* "Because of me?"

Kayla simply shrugged, which looked more like a poorly disguised "yes." The straw screeched again.

"Oh, my God." The new girl rocked the boat and made someone quit. *Crap.* "What did Tony say?"

"Just that."

Guess Dylan couldn't handle the criticism. *Chalk up one more for the bitch.* Maybe the vinyl wasn't that crooked. Working with Quin for so long made it easy to forget how to play nice with others. *Shit, shit, shit!*

Kayla remained silent other than the slurping, and Bailey couldn't tell if she was happy that Dylan was gone or if she was one of those girls who feasted on drama.

Bailey would rather scrub toilets at a public gas station than deal with drama.

A stiff rubber sole scraped her knuckle. *Thank God.* Tugging the boots free, Bailey dumped most of the clothes from the bag onto the floor of the car. She snatched a pair of clean socks from the pile and headed back inside.

Stepping through the front door, Bailey had an unobstructed view down the narrow hallway—all the way to the back of the shop. The large bay door was open, and Tony was securing a second extension ladder to the bed of his sleek black F-350 Ford truck.

Her mind raced. *I should have checked the measurements before I said anything. I need to explain what happened.*

Just as she approached Tony, he grabbed the back collar of his white Henley shirt and yanked it over his head.

SIGNS OF LOVE

All she could do was gape.

J. ALISON COLE

Chapter Two

Bailey's mouth hung open—reprehensibly. Her greedy eyes scoured Tony's bare chest—the dark umber of his nipples, a set of spectacular pecs, rippling muscles on his stomach, as predicted, and the exact level of his tan line, barely visible from the fringed waist of his worn blue jeans. The drool-worthy scene had her jaw snapping shut before she did just that. Her earlier victory of six seconds—obliterated beyond repair.

Tony glanced at the boots in her hand. "Good, you found them."

"Oh yeah." Why was her voice so raspy? She cleared her throat and replied again. "Yeah."

Tony rummaged behind the driver's seat of the truck. Each subtle movement caused the hewed ridges along his back and shoulders to undulate.

Look away, look away, Bailey's mind warned futilely. Seeing Tony shirtless was the same as a forty-car pileup on the interstate. Only she didn't have to rubber neck because he was right here in front of her. And traffic is at a standstill.

He emerged from the truck holding a gray t-shirt, and began threading his arms into sleeves. "So, are you ready to go?" The shirt flipped over his head and ever so slowly unraveled over his torso.

Unsure of the actual look on her face, what color it was, or if she might actually have a string of drool hanging from the corner of her mouth, Bailey forced the new lump in her throat—down and swung the boots in his direction. "Ready as I'll ever be." *God, what is wrong with me?* She retreated to the passenger side of the truck, praying for this fixation, or whatever it was about Tony, would fizzle out soon. The sooner, the better. *I'm such an idiot.*

Once in the truck, Bailey kicked off her sandals, mindful to keep her feet off the seat and away from the dash. Tony's truck looked new, loaded with all the bells and whistles. Leather interior, inlaid wood dash, backup camera, full navigation, and an excellent sound system. Easily a seventy to eighty-thousand dollar truck, or more. Just another piece of the puzzle.

Tony didn't come across as some kind of secret millionaire. From what Bailey had seen in her three days, his business appeared steady, with relatively standard clients. Yet here he was—younger than most, running a successful business, driving an expensive truck while living in an enormous home nestled in a spiffy wooded community of Northern Virginia. She narrowed down her theories to three things. He had won the lottery, had a rich relative somewhere, or was in more debt than Quin.

Bailey finished tying the laces of her boots and leaned back into the seat. "Kayla told me that Dylan quit."

His laid-back chuckle filled the cab. "So that's what's got your panties all knotted? I figured something was bothering you. When I was changing my shirt, you had the most bizarre look on your face."

Bailey's eyes widened. *A bizarre look?* "Oh, that…really, huh. God, I didn't, I mean... well...I wasn't, umm ...." *Mumble much?* "I was going to say, I could call Dylan if you want, maybe explain or apologize." He didn't mention drool. *There had to be drool.* "And my panties aren't…by the way."

Tony squinted before glancing in her direction. Apparently, clarifying the condition of her underwear surprised him. "Do you mean they aren't knotted or that they're not panties? Are you wearing a thong?"

Her thoughts momentarily crashed. "What?" His

chuckle conveyed that he was only teasing. Bailey tried not to laugh but did—a big ole girly-girl laugh. *Ugh.* "No, I'm serious." She was about to reiterate her offer to contact Dylan when a different sight waylaid her already muddled abilities to behave like a normal human being around her new boss.

Tony had his left wrist casually draped over the steering wheel. The pose was identical to a month ago, the first time she rode with him. For whatever reason, she found it so incredibly sexy.

Exchanging glances between her and the road, the always-lingering smile from his lips filtered into his eyes. "Before I get myself in any kind of hot water, I'd just like to say, don't worry about Dylan. If it was crooked, I'm glad that you caught it. He probably figured it was close enough, and I don't want that type of work representing my company. I have a feeling that he'll come back around when he's ready to do it right."

Bailey turned away. Even though she was vindicated, his logic and understanding were as appealing as the rest of him. Staring out of the window, she suddenly became aware of the heavy traffic on the highway. This wasn't a road she'd been on before. One thing was for sure: she needed to watch where she was going, or she'd get lost—in more ways than one. Maybe working alongside Tony would be easier if he was an asshole.

Her gaze snagged onto Tony's reflection in the side passenger mirror. His gorgeous smile slowly faded. A second later, he broke the stalwart silence.

"So, tell me about your friend Quin."

"Okay, umm, like I said, we used to work together back home. Then, about four months ago, he left and started his own sign business."

"Oh. How come you didn't go to work for him?"

"Well, he's just getting started, and money's tight. Plus, I think this is something he wants to do on his own. Make his own mark on the world."

"I can respect that." He sniffed. "So, did things ever get complicated?"

Something in his tone made her turn and address him directly. "Complicated?"

"You know, working side by side, he's a guy, you're a girl." He lifted his chin, suggesting a different kind of…you know.

Of course, she knew what he meant. It was what everyone thought. "It's not like that between Quin and myself. In fact, he's getting married soon."

"Well, now, that would make things a bit complicated." Tony's fetching smile returned, and Bailey succumbed to a soft laugh.

"Don't you think men and women can be just friends?" she asked, genuinely curious to know what he thought.

"Sure, I mean…I guess it's possible." His drawn-out glance skimmed over her entire face. "But, I think it's also reasonable to assume that some guys would want to be *your* friend just to get in your panties—or thongs or whatever it is you're wearing." A glimmer entered his eyes as he rededicated his focus on the road.

"What can I say? Quin isn't like most guys." *Are you?* The question popped into the far back regions of her brain, causing a phantom pain. She blinked hard, forcing it away. "What about Kayla? Would you consider her a friend?"

"Hell no." When her jaw fell open, his grin broadened. "Kayla is my sister."

"O-oh…oh," Bailey stammered. "Wait, isn't her last name Rosslen?"

Tony adjusted his wrist and gripped the wheel.

"She got married right out of high school, but her husband Jason died in a car accident."

"That's horrible. I'm sorry." She wanted to ask if that was the same accident that Lazlo was in, but the hint of sadness in his voice kept her from doing so.

After a moment of silence, Tony took a solemn breath, and his jovial persona returned. "So you and Quin—have never…?"

"No, not ever, and what's this obsession you have with Quin?"

He straightened in his seat and let his wrist fall back onto the steering wheel—where it belonged. "Frank told me you were in a serious relationship a while back, but it was over now."

"Oh." *Thanks, Uncle Frank.* Her gaze shot back out of the window. "That was someone else. His name was Jordan."

"I didn't mean to make you uncomfortable. I'm just wondering, that's all." His sweetheart of a grin made it impossible to be upset. The man really was too hot for her own good.

"No. It's not that." The urge to let him know she wasn't seeing anyone threatened to explode from her lips. As if that would matter to him. She chuckled, mostly at herself. "It's just—my love life is not that interesting."

Tony's impressive features scrunched with half a smile. "In all seriousness, I don't believe that for a minute, but let's talk about something else. Let me tell you about the party your aunt and uncle threw last summer. I had no idea that Frank played the guitar. He's a regular Lynyrd Skynyrd."

Bailey readily welcomed the chance to talk about something other than her panties and past relationships. "He thinks he is."

After ten minutes of praising her uncle's musical

talent, Tony turned and entered Glendan Square Shopping Center.

The thick odor of new asphalt hung heavy in the air. Across the parking lot, landscapers shoveled fresh mulch around newly planted trees, adding to the already pungent aroma. At the far end of the L-shaped building, tarps covered the sidewalk where painters were nearly finished with a fresh coat of paint on the overhead façade. From the looks of it, the facelift on the aging structure was a vast improvement.

Tony parked along the curb in front of a storefront located near the middle of the longer section of the building. He pointed toward the lighted box running overhead. "See, it's not too high. All we have to do is swap the old bookstore sign face for Nadine's Nail Salon."

"You mean the 3' x 10' acrylic panel we've been walking around in the shop all week?"

"That's the one."

Bailey stepped from the truck, taking mental notes of the other businesses. On the left was a franchise greeting store. It had the only professional-looking sign there. To the right of what would be Nadine's, was a karate dojo. It had an overhead sign made on rough plywood. The letters were crooked, and the spacing was off. A few doors up was a tax prep business. The plain block lettering was too small, and the light gray color got lost on the glass from the inside light.

At the opposite end of the shopping center was a Mom-and-Pop pizza joint and a place selling antiques. The pizza sign looked old and dirty. Cockroaches came to mind, unfairly perhaps. The inside could be crystal clean, but that was the vibe she got from the sign.

The antique shop might sell lovely antiques, but from here, the sign looked chintzy and made her think of broken junk. There's never a second chance to make a first impression.

As for the other five storefronts, brown paper covered some of the windows, and the sparse number of parked cars suggested those spaces were empty.

Tony unloaded the two ladders and placed them into position while Bailey readied a DeWalt cordless drill to remove the end cap from the lighted box.

He seemed pleasantly surprised, hefting the tool from her hand. "You have done this before, haven't you?"

"Yeah. But I don't know what tip you'll need. It could be a Phillips, flathead, or a star bit. Or even a hex-head *nut*." Why did she emphasize the word *nut*?

Guys have nuts. Tony is a guy.

With nuts.

Stop!

Tony suppressed a smile and rooted in the toolbox. "Got it. I'll just take a variety with me."

A few minutes later, he leaped from the third rung of the ladder to the pavement, holding the drill in one hand and the metal end cap in the other. "It was a Phillips. Now, the old face isn't super heavy, but it is a little windy. Once the sign is out of the box, it could catch like a sail. Be ready."

The slight slope of the parking lot had one ladder extended as far as it would reach. Tony's added height made it clear he'd be using that one.

Bailey climbed up the ladder closest to the sign box and tugged on the ten-foot piece of acrylic. More cumbersome than heavy, she shimmied the sign face toward Tony in a series of jerks and pushes. Once free of the track inside the sign box, they rested the acrylic against the ladders and climbed down. Easy.

Tony gave her one of his toe-curling smiles. "Not

bad."

The smile on his lips triggered the same quiver that usually turned her into a glob of girly-goo. So, instead of suffering through another round of awkward grins and pointy nipples, she steered her gaze away from his face.

She made it as far as his smooth, round shoulders. They were magnificent. She wanted to run a finger along the curve where it connected to, oh, impressive biceps. He wasn't even flexing. Cords and tendons made up his sinewy forearms, shadowed with a spattering of dark hair. His hands, broad, with long fingers—fingers that lift, grip, pull, caress...

"Before we carry the new face up there, I want to compare the size of the two faces."

Her ogling bubble popped, and she ran a hand over her lips checking for drool. At least this time, he didn't catch her.

She took one end of the new sign, and they stacked the two faces back to back. "Looks like yours is slightly bigger and a smidge thicker."

Someone please cut out her tongue. *Slightly bigger and a smidge thicker. Good god.* She glanced sideways, hoping it was just her warped mind that made it sound kinky.

His eyebrows lifted, and mischief danced in his eyes. "Okay. Yeah, it's bigger, but I think it'll fit." He snickered and shook his head. "Go ahead and get your end."

One horrendous snort escaped before she could stop it. Did that noise come out of her? Bailey picked up her end, and together, they hoisted the new sign face up the ladders the same way they brought the old one down. It wasn't so much heavy as it was cumbersome for its size.

At the top of the ladder, Bailey carefully aligned the acrylic into the track inside the box. It slid about three inches when, out of nowhere, a gust of wind slammed against the panel, which still protruded.

"Hold on, Bailey. Be careful," Tony warned, even though he held the bulk of the sign from his end, as the sign face bowed from the wind.

If it curved too far, it might chip the corners already inside the frame or snap at the bend. Acrylic sheets weren't cheap, and if that happened, and they needed to remake the sign, they could say goodbye to any profit margin. Bailey tightened her grip on the front edge, ignoring the other lingering danger. If the wind blew hard enough, the sign wouldn't be the only thing that could end up broken. Twelve feet off the ground may not seem like a lot, but landing on her feet would be fifty-fifty at best—with splintering shards of acrylic to land on. No thanks.

Her struggle eased when the rogue gust vanished as mysteriously as it came. She nodded. "Push. Push now." The sign moved another two feet but refused to go any further. "Hold on. It's hitting something." Bailey brushed bits of debris and buildup out of the track. She spotted the problem. "There's a set screw." She tried lifting up on the new, slightly bigger sign, but there wasn't any extra space.

"See if you can take it out." A slight strain pinched Tony's voice.

She checked to see what tool she would need. "Yeah, it looks like one of those star tips." Bailey scurried down the ladder and rummaged through the toolbox. "Where are all the tips?"

Tony snorted from above her. "In my pockets."

"You took all of them?"

"Yeah, what can I say?" He readjusted his grip on

the sign as leaves from the roof churned into the air. "You're going to have to come and get it. I can't let go of the sign."

It didn't seem that windy when they started, but she looked around and checked the sky for flying monkeys.

On the fourth rung of his ladder, reality sunk in. She was going to put her hands in Tony's pants. She stopped two rungs below him. It put her face just above his butt. "Which pocket?" Her voice squeaked.

"Front and back."

Great, now his voice is squeaky.

"Really?" *Screw it.* If Quin were standing here, this wouldn't be a big deal. She would've already checked his pockets and been back on her ladder.

Bailey held onto the ladder with one hand and gently brushed over Tony's rear pockets with the other. Sure enough, she felt what could be a couple of pellets below his right cheek.

Her hand eased into his rear pocket just as a hefty wind rammed her from behind. Instinct tightened her hold on the ladder—and a handful of his ass.

"Sorry." *Oh my God.* She quickly scooped the contents, and successfully gathered one straight bit and three sizes of Phillips's—no star bit.

"It's not here. Maybe I can get a Phillips to work?"

"I doubt it. I know I grabbed some. The others are in my front pocket—the left one.

Bailey stepped higher to the next rung, which inevitably brought her closer to him but gave her hand a better angle.

"But be careful, it—goes to the left." He covered up a shaky laugh by clearing his throat.

It? Oh, Hell, no! A stupefied, indistinguishable

sound fumbled through her lips. "What...? No way. Let me hold the sign, and you get it yourself. Or we can start over."

"No way, I'm not pulling it out."

It took her mind less than half a second to dirty up his words. *I'm going straight to hell.*

Tony adjusted his grip on the sign. "Look, you can't reach the sign, and you're right here." He wasn't wrong. "It will be fine. Just—get it." Maybe she was making a way bigger deal out of this than it needed to be?

Bailey took a huge breath and tried positioning herself in a way that kept her body from touching his. Which was totally impossible. Two grown people sharing one ladder are going to touch. *Here goes nothing.* Her left hand snaked into his front left pocket.

The firmness of his thigh became instantly apparent through the thin, as in, nearly nonexistent pocket fabric. Who knew pocket fabric was so gauzy? Not her, that's for dang sure. Her fingers shimmied along the outer seam, safely away from—it. Bailey identified the leather key fob of the truck keys, but changeable tips were smaller and probably mingling near the bottom.

Her hand crept deeper... Pain stabbed into her middle finger. Bailey shrieked, Tony jerked—making her foot slip off the rung. Latching onto whatever she could grab, she flung herself against his backside to regain her footing.

Tony rushed an apology. "Sorry, sorry, Bailey. Are you all right?" He peered underneath his raised arms.

"I'm fine."

"You sure?" A moment passed before another smile budded on his lips.

Bailey released her grip on his pelvic region. "There's something sharp in your pocket."

"Yeah, that was probably one of the screws from

the end cap." The innocent grin on his face grew. "Is your finger bleeding?"

She checked. "No, but that's still two for flinching."

"I'll give you that. Let's see if we can get this done before I lose my—grip—on everything."

Why did he say it like that? "Okay." Her hand dipped into his front left pocket again, and by some bizarre chance, her focus landed on his exposed waist and the frayed edge of his jeans. Where was the band of his underwear?

They could be below his jeans or—*he wasn't wearing any.* Wouldn't she be able to feel his underwear?

No, don't. Just get the bit. Get the bit, get the bit.

What if he's going commando?

She reached the bottom of his pocket and scooped everything her timid fingers could safely gather.

Her triumph was nearly in hand, so to speak, but at the top of his pocket, her balled fist required some added maneuvering. *Just one more twist—*

Something firm nudged the backside of her hand right before her fist popped free. *Wtf?* Her mind started to reel—until the subtle intake of his breath offered one likely explanation.

No way. She climbed down the ladder in a mindless stupor and scattered her pocket loot over the tailgate. *Don't jump to conclusions. It could've been anything. The keyfob!* The skin on the back of her hand began to itch.

"Is it there?" he called from above.

"I'm looking." *Maybe it was the seam next to the zipper. Oh lord, how far was my hand in there?* The star tip revealed itself like the Hope Diamond, and it was the most beautiful thing she'd ever seen. "Oh, yes, I found it, thank God." Bailey scrambled up her ladder. *It had to be the keyfob.*

The rusty, dirt-covered set screw came out after a few twists, and the sign slid the rest of the way into the box with ease. *It was definitely firm, whatever it was.*

"Hey, just stay up there." Absorbed in her delirium, she shifted her ladder as Tony climbed up, seemingly unfazed.

Of course, he's unfazed. It had to be the key fob. Me and my dirty thoughts.

Tony's presence hovered behind her, more visceral than ever. Boy, how the tables had turned.

He handed her the drill. "Here."

"Thanks."

"Do you want me to hold the end piece in place?"

"No, I got this."

"Okay. Here, you'll need these." He handed her the four screws from his pocket.

They were warm.

Cradled next to his crotch, of course, they're warm.

"Oh my gosh."

"What?" he called from below.

"Nothing." It took her less than a minute to reattach the end piece and demonstrate that she could handle power tools. She hopped clear from the bottom rung and then headed for the rear of the truck. Tony was already walking toward the far ladder.

The storefront window acted like a mirror, and she just happened to glance up and see him tug on the front of his pants—and shift things around the way guys do.

She almost dropped the drill.

It was his—

A woman in her mid-fifties burst from the salon. She stepped beyond the curb to inspect the new sign.

"Oh, it looks wonderful, Mr. Shepard."

Tony leaned the ladder against the tailgate and greeted her with a friendly handshake. "Please, Nadine, call me Tony. I'm glad you like it."

"Absolutely. When you finish putting your stuff away, come inside, and I'll get you paid. And if you have a couple of minutes, I have a few more signs I'm going to need inside."

"Sure thing."

After the second ladder was lowered and secured on the truck, Tony grabbed the folder from the dash holding Nadine's paperwork. That's when Bailey looked up. "I might be a few minutes."

At least that's what she heard him say. The wry smile on his face said—*Yeah, Bailey, that was my dick.*

Bailey gulped down the *'Oh my God!'* clawing at her throat before climbing into the truck. Her hands landed on her lap as her mind raced.

Was it his dick? Her left hand slowly slid toward her hip. For it to reach her hand, it would have to be— "Oh, crap. I can't sit here."

She grabbed a handful of Tony's business cards from the center console and hopped out of the truck. It never hurt to exchange business cards, plus it allowed her to focus on something else besides the burning skin on the back of her hand.

Ten minutes later, she returned with a few prospects. Tony was leaning against the fender, waiting for her with that same, *yeah, that was my dick,* smile on his face.

In fact, it stayed on his face for the rest of the day.

Chapter Three

Bailey's head hit the pillow. Her eyelids lowered, but sleep was nowhere to be found. It turns out that trying to pinpoint her exact obsession with Tony was a horrible idea. She committed the first few hours of tossing and turning to his overall physicality. She'd seen him shirtless, groped his butt, and had first-hand knowledge of the firmness of his thighs. She knew lots of attractive, healthy people. What made him so special?

She pinched her eyes closed again and tried some deep breathing. A minute later, the back of her hand tingled, and her eyelids popped open. *Could his dick actually reach that far to his hip?* Bailey sat up and flipped on the small lamp sitting on her desk. She rummaged inside the drawer for a ruler. This probably wasn't the same way the detectives on CSI would reconstruct the *incident*, but it was all she had. Sitting on the edge of her bed, she held the ruler like a penis and angled it toward her hip. But it was one of those rubbery kinds, not wood, and the more she moved it around, the more it kind of flopped, bringing more questions to mind. How accurate could her experiment be?

Where was her hand actually positioned?

Was he fully aroused or just partially?

Her head sagged forward as the ruler bobbed up and down. "Oh my god." This was the same ruler she used in elementary school. "Gross."

It's the middle of the night, and she should be sleeping. She tossed the ruler onto the desk and turned the light off. "Ugh! This is crazy?" She flopped onto her back, rehashing what she already knew.

Tony's attractive, in great shape, and seemingly well-endowed. All obvious traits that anyone would find interesting. A stillness settled over her as she stared into the darkness. From the surrounding quiet, a voice in her head whispered.

What about the other stuff?

The stuff she kept tip-toeing around. The stuff that didn't make sense or go away.

For example, whenever she was around him, the air vibrated from something just beneath the surface. Some people might even refer to it as "Chemistry." It consumed her.

Maybe she just needed more time. She turned on her side and tucked her hand under the pillow. If there was really some kind of chemistry there, wouldn't he feel it, too? Sadly, yesterday afternoon was probably just another Wednesday for him. No doubt, he was used to women fawning all over him and making idiots of themselves.

Bailey wasn't used to making an idiot of herself. It seemed like her body had a mind of its own, responding to him, regardless of what was going on in her head. So, how does she stop that from happening?

Checking her phone, she had two hours before her alarm was set to go off. "Dammit." It wouldn't be worth it to fall asleep now.

Bailey crawled out of bed, showered, dressed, and headed out the door long before her roommates—or what she now mentally referred to them as, *The Witches of Eastwick,* and whatever random men they managed to lure home for the night—stirred.

On her commute, the roads were bare of the typical morning traffic she had recently dealt with, and the industrial park felt more like a ghost town. Sure, a few delivery trucks and a sparse gathering of cars from the night shift were changing over, but for the most part, the rest of the world still slept.

Bailey parked in a spot not too far from the entrance of Ajak's. The sun had yet to breach the horizon, but the dawn sprayed the sky a flame orange with bright streaks of yellow and pink, hemmed along the edges with a rich teal and satiny blue. She sat for a moment to admire the vivid array of colors. It was all very sobering.

She had to do better today.

Tony gave her a key on her first day. She didn't expect to use it, but now it came in handy. It was barely five-thirty when she stepped through the door and deactivated the alarm using the code written on a purple Post-it note taped inside the drawer of Kayla's desk.

In her workroom, Bailey sorted through the business cards she collected yesterday afternoon and jotted down a few simple ideas. An hour later, she had a series of workable thumbnails for three of the businesses that seemed interested. She sat them aside and headed into the shop.

She flipped the switch to the overhead mercury lights, and a dim blue sheen slowly filled the room. The lights buzzed and crackled in the quiet space, slowly warming into a more pure light that sprayed onto the thick coating of white paint covering the cinderblock walls.

The shop was basically one big open room separated into designated areas. The back wall was split in half by a large overhead door. An eight-foot Panel Saw was mounted on the left-hand side, and Lazlo's workbench ran along the other.

On Monday, Bailey made an offhand comment about the shop being in disarray. Tony said she could rearrange things any way she wanted. *Hope he meant it.*

Aside from not letting Tony be a distraction, Bailey's goal for today was to sort through the unruly pile of old signs and scrap lumber stacked beside the saw. The larger pieces could be saved and used for other projects, but the rest could be tossed or recycled. She rolled a mini dumpster across the room and got started.

Halfway through the stack, clumps of sawdust covered the floor and stuck to her clothes like burs from a weed patch. She'd have to find the vacuum, but for now, she brushed off her clothes and pushed what she could into a neat pile with the side of her foot.

Further back, wedged against the wall, was a thick piece of redwood wrapped in cardboard. A quick yank on the dried-out tape revealed a hand-drawn, partially carved—unfinished sign for Tony's business. She had no clue what Ajak's stood for, but overall, the sign had potential. It was a decent size and way more interesting than the generic *Helvetica*, red letters on the plain white rectangular sign hanging above the front door now. If anyone should have an eye-catching sign, it should be a sign company.

Bailey shimmed the sign away from the wall and dragged it toward the middle of the room. Halfway across the shop, the bell above the front door clanged. Looking up the hallway, she expected to see Kayla. Only it wasn't.

Her eyes connected with Tony's, and his face lit up with his boy-next-door grin. In that one single moment, he made and ruined her day simultaneously.

Bailey glanced over her shoulder, according to the Miller Lite neon clock that hung above Lazlo's workbench. It was ten minutes before eight. For the last three days, Tony didn't show his handsome face until closer to ten. Granted, he stayed later than the rest of them, and he was the boss. So why not sleep in?

An image of Tony sleeping manifested in her mind: him sprawled across a king-sized bed—possibly naked.

Her gaze shot to his crotch involuntarily. "Ah,

wow."

"What?" Tony's chin lifted, questioning.

"I mean, uh, I didn't expect…it to be you. Boy, you're here…early."

His green eyes brightened along with his smile. "I didn't get much sleep last night."

"Ha, ha." Oh, the irony of his statement. "Hey, I found this really cool sign behind that pile beside the saw. Is there a reason you didn't finish it?"

Tony shrugged, not overly concerned. "Boy, I haven't seen this in a while." He knelt beside the sign and brushed his fingers over the dust-covered wood grain. "Why don't you finish it? You can surprise me."

The bell on the front door dinged again. Kayla had a foam cup clamped between her teeth as she wrestled with the door while carrying a large box. Tony raced to help her.

Once she was relieved of her burden, Kayla propped her hands on her hips. "Umm, thanks." Her gaze bounced from Bailey to Tony. "What the hell are the two of you doing here so early?"

Bailey wasn't about to share her reasons.

Tony pointed to the box. "What's in the box?"

"Oh." Her pixie voice shifted from the distraction. "I thought since you're letting Bailey get the shop in order, she could help me with the front. It's never been much of a reception area."

Tony looked around. "Why, what's wrong with it?"

Kayla glared at Bailey for support. "Tell him…it sucks."

First impressions meant a lot, and Bailey had to admit the first time she walked in, other than Tony, nothing "wowed her." A small round table with three tired-looking barrel chairs was crammed into one corner.

The walls lacked any color, painted the same white throughout the shop. The sample signs displayed on the wall were too few and overly simple, not accurately representing the company's full potential. Even Kayla's desk was positioned in an unusual spot right in the middle of the room, too far from the door, leaving clients baffled about how far they should enter.

Kayla took Bailey's silent observation for the corroboration she wanted. "See."

"Wait a minute." Tony sat on the edge of Kayla's desk and pretended to polish the corner with his palm. "You can't have her." His gaze practically gobbled Bailey whole. "She's all mine."

The winky thing followed, and Bailey's heart ricocheted inside her ribcage like a lottery ball waiting to be drawn.

Kayla's hands flew off her hips. "Fine. I'll just wait until next week when you and Candice are away on your little love retreat."

Love retreat? The ricochets flying in Bailey's chest sank like a lead weight from the nice, hefty reality check. *Ding, ding, yes, folks, we have a winner.*

Tony rose from the corner of the desk, and the playful sparkle in his eyes wilted away. "Do what you want. I've got some calls to make." He disappeared around the corner, and the door to his office closed with a resounding clunk.

Kayla's arms landed around Bailey's shoulders. "Oh. I love having you here. I knew it was a good sign when you showed up."

****

After cleaning up the mess she had in the shop, Bailey emailed the three thumbnail sketches she'd worked on that morning. It never hurt to try. Sometimes, people just need a gentle push in the right direction to see new potential. It was almost lunchtime when she and Lazlo finished ten double-sided realtor signs—ahead of schedule.

She slid a protective sheet of brown paper between the last two signs and bundled them with the rest. "Hey Lazlo, is there any place nearby to get something to eat?" All her peanut butter was gone, and she hadn't found a grocery store yet.

Lazlo finished counting out ten metal realtor frames. "Eight, nine, ten. There's a chuck wagon that comes through the development, and then, there's Brindles."

"What's Brindles?" she asked.

Lazlo limped toward the table, carrying two frames at a time. Apparently, the accident damaged his entire left side, restricting his movement and hampering his strength. A nasty scar marred the skin above one eye, and sometimes his speech slurred, and tremors shook his hands. But it didn't take a genius to realize that he resented being treated differently. So Bailey made it a point not to.

"Brindles' is a bar at the other end of the complex. Every Friday, we go down for Happy hour and have a drink. It's kind of a tradition. Tony makes sure we always go. Hey, you'll get to meet my girlfriend tomorrow. I've told her all about you."

"Can't wait. I can always use a new friend." Bailey wasn't exactly bonding with all of her roommates. "What kind of food does Brindles serve?"

"Just put it this way: if it's deep-fried, you're probably safe, but you might want to stay away from things like egg salad."

"Noted. So what about this roach coach? Where does it park?"

He snickered at her slang. "It's usually parked

along Hyson Avenue, near the park entrance."

"Yeah, I know where you mean. Do you want me to grab you a sandwich? I, myself, am starved. I'm out of peanut butter, and I skipped breakfast." Asking her co-worker, who just happened to be a guy, to have lunch felt innocent enough—as it should. Nothing inappropriate, no tension, no big deal. Why couldn't it be this way with Tony?

Lazlo rubbed his belly. "Thanks, but I had the egg salad from Brindles yesterday. I'm not ready for solid food yet."

Bailey offered him a sympathetic smile. "Okay. I'll see you in a bit." She ducked into her workspace, grabbed her iPod, and shoved a twenty-dollar bill into her pocket. Turning to leave, she almost collided with Tony. "Whoa."

"Whoa, yourself." Tony looked and sounded so chipper. "Where you headed?"

"Um," Yeah, where was she headed? "The... chuckwagon."

"Know where it is?"

She barely opened her mouth before he cut her off.

"Never mind, I'll come with you." He backed into the hallway—and waited—for her.

Going through the front office, Kayla's gaze bounced away from her keyboard. The rice cake wedged between her lips bobbled up and down. "Hey, hey, where are you guys going?"

"Getting something to eat. Hold down the fort." Tony raced ahead and pulled the door open for Bailey. He signaled for her to go through first with the tilt of his head. But Bailey only took half a step forward before an incoming presence forced her to stop.

Candice Martin struck a runway pose at the

threshold. "Hi, everyone." The shrill voice of Tony's girlfriend jabbed into Bailey's spine like the sharp, jagged scrap pieces of aluminum she so carefully sorted through that morning.

Bailey stepped away from the door, giving Candice's awesomeness the space it needed.

Tony visibly balked with surprise. "Candice, what are you doing here?"

"Hey, baby. Aren't you glad to see me?" Candice draped her manicured fingers over Tony's shoulders before slathering his lips with an over-the-top, voluptuous kiss.

Bailey should've looked away, but the candid forces of nature wouldn't allow it, like that forty-car pileup, with her smack dab in the middle of the wreckage.

Tony stifled the kiss and stepped away from Candice. It was the first time she'd ever seen him so uncomfortable. Perhaps he didn't like the PDA. "Yeah, sure I am."

"I had to come by and tell you about this guy Shawna met." Candice laced her arm around his elbow and slowly dragged him up the hallway.

Tony mouthed Bailey a silent apology.

"No problem. Hyson Ave, I'll find it." Bailey backed out the door with the vivid image of Candice inserting her tongue into Tony's mouth. She wanted it burned onto the forefront of her memory. How much more of a sign did she need? This would definitely help.

Bailey tromped across the parking lot, opting to take a shortcut through some pine trees. The narrow gap and wispy limbs looked harmless enough. But midway through, the branches closed in, and the sharp needles clawed at her arms. There was no backing out. Pushing forward was her only option. *I got this.* Emerging to the other side, she brushed the prickly remnants away and took a fresh breath of air. Now her path was clear—of pine trees and, she hoped, her senseless infatuations.

On Hyson Avenue, a crowd gathered near a conventional silver trailer parked along the curb. Only, this was no roach coach. She took her place in line and scanned over the handwritten menu and specials of the day—smoked turkey with pineapple salsa, honeydew melon ham wraps, and stuffed Italian pitas. Spreads and sides included marinated chopped olives, Asian kimchi slaw, and southwest corn and bean relish. Back home, they were lucky if the food trucks had Dijon mustard.

The need to devour a mammoth-sized sandwich might be considered emotional eating, but after what she just witnessed, screw it. Bailey's turn came, and she stepped closer to the window. "I'll have the pastrami with Swiss, brown mustard, onion—" She wasn't kissing anyone anytime soon. "—and just a little lettuce. Oh, you wouldn't happen to have pumpernickel, would you?"

The woman inside the trailer gave her a "no worries" look.

"Now that sounds like a good sandwich."

Bailey politely smiled at the older gentleman standing behind her. His round belly and balding head gave him a cute and cuddly grandfatherly vibe.

He gruffly called to the woman through the window. "Make it two, the same way." His round cheeks nearly pushed his eyes closed from a boisterous smile. "You're a young woman with a formidable palate, my dear."

She offered her hand. "Bailey Jazincski."

"Bill Porter." They shook hands. "I don't believe I've seen you around here before. Where do you work?"

"Ajak's Signs. This is my first week."

"Tony Shepard's place?"

"Yes, sir."

"He seems like a very determined young man. From what I understand, he had a lot thrown at him at a young age. Nevertheless, he's built a solid business. That to be admired."

She couldn't comment, not knowing Tony's circumstances.

After a few minutes, the woman set their sandwiches on the counter. "Nine-fifty—each."

Bill handed twenty-five dollars through the window before Bailey even had a chance to reach into her pocket.

"I got this. Join an old man for lunch?" He pointed toward a few benches under a row of maple trees that ran along the curb.

"I'd be glad to, and next time, I'll buy. Thank you, Mr. Porter."

"And manners to boot. I told my grandson there were still good women out here. But knowing him, he'd probably mess it up anyway. All he's worried about is blogging and those other things...pods or podding casting. He's in his late twenties and has never had a real job. I don't understand it." His bushy white brows nearly reached the spot where his hairline should be.

Bailey swept away a few leaves from the bench, and they sat down. Peeling away the waxy paper from her bougie sandwich, she took a moment to admire the three-inch stack of lean pastrami, which explained the cost. Bill mimicked her silent appreciation.

Bailey hummed as the first bite practically melted in her mouth. "This is so much better than an over-jellied peanut butter sandwich. Do you want to know what else might be good? Liverwurst. Liverwurst on a panini with thin-sliced Bread-and-Butter pickles."

"That sounds delicious," he chuckled. "I haven't had Liverwurst in years. I might have to call my wife and tell her to go out and get some."

Bailey agreed with a shake of her head. "Not everyone likes liverwurst." She was about to take the next bite when a nagging question invaded her mind.

Does Tony like liverwurst?

Chapter Four

Friday morning, ten o'clock came and went, and still no Tony. Not that Bailey was waiting for him or anything.

She and Laz were almost done with the first of three complex signs for an ice cream shop getting ready to open about two miles up the road. "What's your favorite flavor, Laz?"

"I'm partial to rum raisin. How 'bout you?"

"Well, it's not Rum raisin. Raisins don't belong in ice cream, just cookies." Bailey snickered playfully. "But, I guess if I had to pick just one, I'd go with Moose Tracks."

"Because of the peanut butter."

"And the chocolate."

Kayla entered the shop. "Hey, guys, the arcade job is all set for one o'clock."

Just then, the metal rear door of the shop swung open, and Tony stomped inside. His gorgeous smile—MIA. And instead of his everyday well-fitted work polo, he had on a plain navy t-shirt that needed ironing—badly. He trekked past the three of them without looking up once.

"Wow! You look like shit." Kayla offered the observation as he zoomed by, heading toward his office.

"Leave me alone, Kayla. I don't want to hear it today."

"No problem. Gumphole." Kayla laughed away his comment before offering Bailey a timid smile.

Another hour passed, and Bailey was just about to apply a section of vinyl listing the flavors when the pesky hairs on the back of her neck tingled. She set the vinyl in place and then peeked over her shoulder.

Tony stood on the other side of the work table with his arms crossed—brooding. "I need you to come with me, Lazlo. Bailey can finish these."

A wave of anticipation swept through her. "Wait, is this for the window lettering—the silver foil for the arcade?"

"Yeah," Tony answered—still no eye contact.

Right next to her, Lazlo's mangled brow scrunched with confusion. "Wouldn't you rather take Bailey? I mean, she might be able to help you better, plus she fixed the design on her first day here."

So true. Using an iridescent film instead of plain silver added a layer of depth and an element of sci-fi to the logo. She was somewhat excited to see the job all put together.

It took Tony an eternity to answer, at least seven seconds, and the bitter edge in his voice practically sliced her in half. "No. She can help you gather what we'll need to take with us."

"Sure thing, Tony." Lazlo waited for their boss to walk away. "I'm sorry, Bailey. He seems pissed off about something."

"Maybe it's about Dylan."

"Nah, that ain't it."

"Well, Laz, can you take a picture for me when it's all done? I want to send it to Quin."

"Sure thing."

Five minutes after gathering the materials they'd need to install the vinyl, Lazlo and Tony were gone, and the shop felt cold and empty, leaving her somewhat deflated and hollow inside. Her stomach even growled.

Bailey tossed her squeegee aside, grabbed a banana off her desk, and headed to the front office. Maybe now was a good time to hear Kayla's ideas for jazzing up the reception area.

When she entered the front room, Kayla was discussing a past-due bill with a client on the telephone. So, she sat in one of the barrel chairs and began peeling her banana.

Removing the disgusting, slimy strings in the groves of the fruit was a must. For some reason, they grossed her out. Quin would purposely fling the strings on her, knowing how much she hated them. A mini quiver coursed through her limbs just thinking about it.

"Listen, sir, I gave you two extra weeks, and that's not counting the net thirty you agreed to." Kayla's lips perched while listening to the other end. "Yes, I have already verified with your bookkeeper that the invoice is still outstanding." Her brows lifted. "Well, that's between you and your bookkeeper."

Today, Kayla wore lime green pants and a shirt with wings printed on the back. Her bill-collecting voice totally contradicted her appearance. She rolled her eyes and made an obscene gesture to the phone and the unseen person on the other end.

"Yes, I'm sure it was just an oversight, but if it isn't paid today, I'll have to send it to collections. Excellent. I'll send you a confirmation as soon as the payment is received. Uh, uh. You're welcome." Kayla ended the call and reached into her desk drawer. "Well, that was fun." She pulled out a full-size Three Musketeers bar. "Go ahead and ask?"

"Oh, okay. I didn't know if you had some specific ideas in mind for up here because I have a few. I thought we could paint these two walls a vivid color unless you just wanted to rearrange stuff now and paint later. Lazlo even said he has an old bar we could revamp and use as a counter that could go closer to the door." One of the banana threads broke loose and landed on her leg. A hollowed-out gag nearly choked her. "Ack."

"No, I'm not talking about the office," Kayla wiggled her nose. "I meant about Tony. He tied one on last night, can't you tell?"

The strand stuck to her leg was all but forgotten. Bailey shrugged, pretending she hadn't noticed Tony at all.

"He stayed with his best friend last night. You'll meet Max soon enough." Kayla's free hand swirled in the air sporadically. "Max thinks he's God's gift to women." Her eyelids fluttered. "Well, he kind of is. The bad thing—he knows it. Anyway, apparently, Tony and Candice had a bit of a spat yesterday."

Bailey's mind blanked, not knowing how to respond, so she shrugged again. "Couples fight."

Kayla feigned shock. "Not Tony. If something's not working, he just moves on. Like his last girlfriend, he lived with her for about four months, and then Candice came along.

Bailey forced a long pause, trying not to sound overly interested. "Oh, so how long have they been together?"

"About two months."

"What!" Bailey scoffed louder than intended. "I mean, that's all? And they're already living together."

Kayla licked at the chocolate smears on her fingers. "Tony always has a girlfriend."

"Uh." Bailey was a little bit disgusted by that, but she could add this to the growing list of reasons why she shouldn't be "attracted" to Tony. Apparently, Mr. Perfect wasn't so perfect after all. He was one of *those* guys.

Bailey took a big bite of banana, strings and all.

****

The overhead door in the rear bay clanked and rattled as it lifted, signaling the return of Tony and Lazlo. Sunlight flooded the floor and bounced off the glass walls surrounding Bailey's workspace. *Don't look up. One-thousand-one, one-thousand-two...* Tony's cheerful laughter thwarted her efforts, and her gaze latched onto him like a heat-seeking missile. Her jaw clenched, resenting how much she missed seeing him. And how much she liked that he was in a better mood. Why should she care?

Walking through the open bay door, he stopped mid-stride to fish his cell phone from his rear pocket and answer a call. With the phone to his ear, he made his way over to Lazlo's workbench, leaned against one end, and crossed his ankles in what appeared to be a jovial conversation.

Then, he twisted over his shoulder to lower the volume on the radio. The motion lifted his shirt, giving her a glimpse of his bare waist. Sure, she'd seen him shirtless, but seeing the light play with the shadows on his flat exposed belly felt extra-racy, like a scandalous peek underneath the sheet. She could almost imagine running her hand down that indent of the "V." Well, she kind of already had. She felt thirsty and sweaty at the same time just thinking about it.

As Tony twisted back around, the brunt of his focus barreled straight at her. It was an arrow that might've knocked her over if she hadn't already been sitting.

The whopping gulp of air she took pumped her veins full of adrenaline. Overly exposed in the glass box workroom, she quickly buried her attention in the paperwork on her desk. *What was that all about?*

His cheerful voice echoed in the shop, threatening to distract her again. *Fight it. Don't look.* She checked the blade's position, selected the next graphic to be cut, and sent it to the plotter. The cutter twisted and turned with an electronic symphony of movement but failed to drown out the sound of Tony's voice—growing louder. *He's coming up the hallway.* Goosebumps broke out across her skin as her fingers hovered above the keyboard. *He's right outside the door.* But then, his voice faded and disappeared into his office.

Bailey exhaled long and slow. "Shoo." The mouse pointer was still frozen on the screen until she clicked on the graphics to be cut next. Content with her small victory, she readied the plotter for the next job.

Above her head, a loud tap on the glass practically launched her to the ceiling. Her hands landed on her knees. "Oh shit!" She exhaled and looked up.

Standing on the other side of the glass, Tony. "I need to see you in my office." The glass barrier muffled his voice *but* allowed the serious look on his face to come through crystal clear.

Twice in middle school, she'd been called to the principal's office, and this had that same *Oh crap* feeling. "Be right...there." Her voice dwindled into—nothing.

Maybe he'd had enough of her and the weird way she was always leering at him. She couldn't deny it or blame him.

Walking into Tony's office, Bailey was struck by how different he looked seated behind a desk. Part of his youthfulness was replaced with the presence of a well-seasoned businessman. *Reason 216 to be impressed. Damn.*

"Close the door." Tony sounded way more serious than Principal Holcholm ever did. Even the time in fourth grade when she punched Jacob Wilcoat for picking on her best friend.

Bailey pushed the door closed and turned, ready to accept her fate. Whatever it was.

"I just got off the phone with a new client." He stated matter-of-factly. "And two others before that." His shoulders lifted as his forearms came to rest on the surface of the desk. "Is there anything you want to tell me?"

New clients? Her mind tripped, and her gaze made a mad dash around the room. How would she know anything about new clients—

Finally, it clicked. "From the shopping center? I sent sketches yesterday, but…"

His extraordinary smile ignited. "Yeah, the antique shop, the karate place, and the guy who owns the complex. They were all quite pleased with the designs you sent and wanted pricing."

The adrenaline racing in her veins shot straight to her head. "Oh my gosh. That's great. I sent thumbnails hoping we'd pick up one, but three—and so soon." Her lips perched, trying to hide her excitement—and relief.

Tony's office door flew open, and Kayla barged inside, completely flabbergasted. "There's a gentleman out front that would like to go over some truck lettering."

Tony shook his head. "Have him make an appointment?"

"No." Kayla lowered her voice. "It's William Porter."

Bailey recognized the name and peeked into the hallway. Sure enough, standing next to the front door, Bill Porter gave her a modest wave.

Tony jumped to his feet. "What the hell?"

Bailey didn't quite understand their reaction, so she strolled toward her lunch buddy from yesterday. "Did your wife get the Liverwurst?"

"She did, and I'm ashamed to say I ate most of it last night on a full sleeve of saltine crackers." His guilt was nowhere close to genuine. "I've already sent her out for some more. She had to go all the way to a little deli in Berkleyville. I'll find out the exact name for you because

I've been told that they have the best peppered corned beef around."

"Since I'm not from around here, it's good to know where I can find a nice deli. I love Reuben's, and who *doesn't* like peppered meat?"

Tony appeared beside her. "Mr. Porter." He offered his hand. "I'm Tony Shepard, and it seems you already know Bailey. What can we do for you?"

"You can call Bill for one."

"Yes, sir. How about the three of us go into my office to discuss this truck lettering."

Bill Porter stayed for nearly an hour. The plumbing company he owned had six new trucks that needed graphics. The logo was typical, a plain font spelling out *Porter Plumbing*, no gadgets or goofy symbols, which made sense to Bailey. Bill was an older man, appeared to be a little conservative, with what she guessed was traditional values. However, he did seem excited and open to the idea when she offered to jazz it up a tiny bit.

"Thank you for stopping in today. I'm sure Bailey will put together a design you'll love." Tony extended his hand.

"Don't doubt for a minute." Bill shook Tony's hand. Thanks for meeting with me, Mr. Shepard." He shook Bailey's hand next. "Bailey, I look forward to hearing from you."

"Of Course. And don't forget to find out the name of that deli."

"You better believe it. Have a good rest of your day."

Bill was barely out the door before Kayla burst into a semi-spirited celebration. Tony hoisted his sister's small frame off the floor and spun once.

Bailey had no time to prepare when he swept her

into his arms and did the same, only she lost count of how many times they twirled. Even after her feet landed on the floor, she still needed a few more seconds to float back to Earth.

Tony squared off in front of her. "Jesus, Bailey, do you know who that was? Do you have any idea of what you've done?" His radiant smile only added to her lightheadedness.

"Not really." She could barely speak.

"God, I could kiss you. Bill Porter is one of the biggest merchants in the area and known for being a tough businessman."

"His plumbing business is that big?"

"It's not just plumbing. He's an industrialist, a tycoon. He has hundreds of businesses. I think one of his corporations even owns this entire complex, as well as several others. You just got our foot in the door, something I haven't been able to do since we've been here and believe me, I've tried. Oh, the hell with it." Tony's hands captured either side of her face.

Oh shit!

His warm lips landed on her. The voice in her head shrieked. *It will be okay, just a quick peck over in an instant.*

And *instant* it was. Every cell in her body quickened from the underlying attraction she had for him. Time—slowed, or perhaps it was her subconscious trying to preserve this memory for all time. His head drifted to one side with a hint of persuasion, and right before it ended, she felt an ever so light, gentle pinch from his lips on hers.

Five extraordinary seconds. Bailey's lashes fluttered open. Boy, she must be delirious because Tony looked as dazed as she felt.

"Holy shit!" Lazlo stood in the hallway entrance

with a goofy grin plastered over his face. "I'm going to assume that I missed something."

The sparkle in Tony's eyes sputtered away, and he gobbled her up with more of his excitement. "Bailey just got us the honey pot. Get your stuff, Lazlo. We're going to Brindles early."

Lazlo squinted at his watch. "It's not even four yet."

Kayla danced behind her desk. "This calls for a celebration."

****

The light from outside barely penetrated Brindles' tinted glass doors. Light fixtures resting on twisted brass arms resonated a soft glow overhead, and rope lighting framed a large U-shaped bar. The booths and barstools were all made from dark wood. Faded green, plastic upholstery clashed against the burnt orange color of the walls. The outdated decor teetered between diner and nightclub and had definitely seen better days.

In a way, Bailey found it comforting. Didn't every town have a place like this?

Bailey followed Kayla and moseyed up to the bar, conveniently choosing a spot as far away from Tony as possible. Four shots of Patron Tequila landed on the punched copper surface, along with four wedges of lime and a single salt shaker. She eyed the clear liquid cautiously.

In general, drinking could instill a sense of courage or even loosen inhibitions. The flip side of drinking—too much could rob you of common sense and make you do very irresponsible things—the type of things you can't take back. Put Tequila into the mix, and someone was sure to be puking before the night was over.

Bailey would much rather hold onto her inhibitions, not do anything irresponsible, and leave puking to the drunk people. If she were to lose her wits, she might do something really stupid and admit how much she liked that kiss, or even more ridiculous, imagine that Tony liked it too. *Which*—he wouldn't, he couldn't. *Of course, he didn't. It was just a stupid, flirty kiss. It meant nothing—to him.*

"You okay, Bailey?" Kayla asked her.

The temperature inside the club was either a stifling ten degrees warmer, or she had turned into one big, sweaty mess. "Um… Is it hot in here, or is it just me?" Bailey's traitorous gaze lifted to the far end of their group. Her single-minded focus zeroed in on Tony licking the back of his hand. *Stop looking at his tongue.* He covered the wet spot on his skin with salt before passing the shaker to Lazlo. "Feels like an oven in here."

"I'm fine. I guess it's just you." Kayla took the salt shaker from Laz.

"Huh." When it was Bailey's turn for the salt shaker, her tongue was as dry as the Sierra, and because she was last in line, everyone's eyes fell on her. One pair specifically.

In a silent salute, Tony raised his glass before speaking aloud. "To Ajak's and to Bailey."

Bottoms up.

Salt coated her tongue, liquid burned her throat, and the wedge of lime added the citrusy punch. Her mouth hollowed to cool all the sensations simmering inside.

"Let's do another!" Lazlo bellowed.

"You guys can. No more shots for me." Bailey didn't need any more help corrupting her decision-making skills.

Tony left his end of the bar and planted himself right next to her. "You got someplace to be?"

His presence smacked her the same as the Tequila

heating the walls of her stomach. She redirected her eyes onto the mangled piece of lime in the empty shot glass. *Focus, I'm not drunk yet. Yet? I'm not getting drunk.* "I have somewhere to be early tomorrow morning."

"Tomorrow morning is a good way off. The evening is young. We have the whole night."

The invisible pull started, and her self-control, or lack thereof allowed her to look up. Whether he meant it to be there or not, his potent charm was amped to full power, shining off him like a one-hundred-watt bulb. Now, her entire body felt swampy. Panties included.

The way Tony flirted was never offensive or over-the-top. He probably wasn't even aware that he was doing it or its effect on her.

"Stay and have at least one beer. Enjoy yourself, Bailey. You had a good first week. This celebration is all for you." His sage green eyes sparked with sincerity—and just sparkled in general.

She found the lime in her glass again. Realistically, if she put aside her Tony-related struggles, it was a "good" first week. Getting Bill Porter as a client seemed like a big deal and sure sounded like something to celebrate. One beer might help her relax and put everything back into perspective.

"Okay, I'll have one before I need to leave." She could do this, maybe even use this time to rebuild her defenses.

"What do you drink?"

"Miller Lite is fine."

Tony lifted his eyebrows. "Good choice." He signaled the bartender. "Four Miller Lites, please." He took a deep breath before smothering her with his easy smile.

For those few moments, she fell victim to his charm and could not look away. Especially when his gaze dropped from her eyes to her lips. Perfect recall of the kiss made her lips tingle. *Lord, help me.*

"Hey, is that you, Shepard?" A tall man wearing an all-beige uniform called for Tony from the opposite side of the bar.

Tony raised his hand toward the man. "Be right there." With a swanky grin, he handed her one of the beers, clinked his bottle against hers, and then strolled away.

Saved by the Jolly Beige Giant.

By five o'clock, happy hour patrons began filtering into the club. Bailey recognized a few people from the custom cabinetry shop two doors down from theirs. Right behind them was another group of people wearing teal-colored scrubs. She didn't know of any medical facilities in the park, so she figured it was probably some kind of lab. Two women from that group screamed and hollered when Lizzo's *Good as Hell* came over the sound system. The empowerment of the lyrics wasn't entirely lost on Bailey. TGIF was in full swing.

Tony had long since moved on from *"beige guy"* and was talking to two men wearing navy chinos and white collared shirts. How did she know where he was? Well, it didn't matter where Tony stood or who he was talking to—her unconscious surveillance consistently tracked him down.

Like now, he smiled—looking directly at her. Static filled the air like raw electricity, forcing Bailey to lower her gaze. The label on her bottle was her default go-to.

4.2% ABV, brewed with pure water, barley malt, and Galena and Saas hops. She'd read it enough by now to know it by heart.

"Bailey." Kayla tugged on her arm. "This is Sherry, Lazlo's girlfriend."

Thank God, a distraction.

"It's nice to finally meet you, Bailey. Lazlo tells me you've made quite an impact."

"Oh, I hope in a good way." Besides keeping up with the workload and cleaning up the shop, how much of an impact could she have had? *Unless she meant the situation with Dylan?*

Lazlo released a deep chuckle. "Just wait 'til I tell you what happened today." Bailey hoped he was referring to Bill Porter's visit. With his scar, it was hard to tell if he was smirking or smiling sometimes.

It didn't take long before she solidified two new friendships. She already got along with Kayla. Everyone needed a quirky friend who always said what was on her mind. And Sherry represented the quintessential hippy who resonated with a peaceful calm like a cool older sister, which she didn't have being an only child.

But the three somehow clicked, and Bailey was eternally thankful to have them both. Maybe covens weren't such a bad thing.

"Are you going to order another beer, Bailey?" Kayla motioned toward her almost empty bottle.

After the shot of tequila, she'd cautiously nursed her one beer for all it was worth. The two sips she had left were as warm as bathwater.

"No. I'm good." Better safe than sorry. She squeezed into the gap beside Kayla and placed her bottle on the bar.

Before she had time to turn around, two giant hands landed on her hips from behind and trapped her against the bar. A man's deep, raspy voice and warm, minty breath brushed over the back of her neck.

"Hmmm. How about I give you a screaming orgasm? We can both have one. You'll love it, I promise." The hands on her hips inched further around her waist, pulling her closer to a brick-hard body.

Beside her, sitting on a barstool, Kayla scoffed and rolled her eyes.

Bailey wiggled and spun far enough around to find herself staring into the face of an extremely handsome man. Sandy brown hair, slim regal features, and velvety brown eyes—God's gift to women. Kayla's warning helped. "You must be Max."

Despite his perfectly fitted tailored suit and the enticing smell of expensive cologne, he had *Player* written all over him. She planted her hands firmly on his chest and politely pushed free of his clutches.

His shapely brows lifted. "And you must be Bailey. I heard all about you last night."

What?

He leaned closer. "My god, your hazel eyes really are stunning."

"Max." Tony appeared like the woodsman, saving her from the big, bad, sleazy wolf.

"You're supposed to be my best friend, dude," Max said accusingly. His gaze bounced from Tony back to her. Then he bit at his bottom lip. "Unh, uh, uh."

Tony's eyes pivoted toward hers. "Pay no attention to him."

No problem.

Max veered toward Kayla, licking his lips. "How about me, you and Bailey do a 'Suck, Bang and a Blow.'" Kayla blinked extra slowly, feigning boredom. "What? It's a drink, that's all."

Kayla huffed with disgust and offered him the back of her shoulder.

"Oh. Come on." Max uttered before swinging his attention back toward Bailey. "How 'bout it, darling?"

"Sorry," Bailey said, equally repulsed. "I was just leaving."

Something flashed over Tony's features. *Was that...disappointment?* It happened so fast, she couldn't be sure what she saw. Probably wishful thinking. Why would he be disappointed that she was leaving?

"Oh, don't go yet." Max's jaw lowered in exaggeration. "I just got here."

Tony placed his half-empty bottle on the bar next to hers. "Most of the businesses are closed now. I'll walk you to your car."

She was about to say "no," but his hand landed ever-so-softly on her lower back. The innocent yet thoughtful gesture halted her words, making that her first mistake of this juncture. The second was acknowledging how natural it felt. It was so natural, in fact, that once they made it outside, her fingers twitched to reach for his hand. She would've died right then and there if that had happened.

She could hear it now. *How did Bailey die?*

Pure embarrassment, the looney girl tried to hold his hand.

She sucked in the cool evening air, hoping to clear her mind. It kind of worked. What she got was a hefty whiff of the fryers from Brindles.

Tony walked beside her the entire distance from the club to the rear of Ajak's Signs without saying a word. An open space separated her car from Tony's truck. It all seemed very cozy and blossomed into her third faux pas of the evening. Standing here with him, like this, strangely felt like the end of a date.

Which was crazy. Bailey scoffed out loud while rooting inside her purse for her car keys.

"Are you okay to drive?" He sought her gaze, genuinely concerned.

"Yeah, yeah, I'm good. I only had that shot of tequila and the one beer. But, I'm hitting the first fast food joint I come to. I'm starving, and all I can smell is French Fries."

He chuckled softly. "Look, Bailey, about earlier...this morning...I was never upset with you."

How was it possible for someone to look shy and sultry at the same time? Trying to figure it out, she realized she was staring at him for what a normal person might consider a really long time.

His eyes stayed glued to hers. "I guess I need to say that it's been a good first week, Bailey. You're really good at what you do. And I'm lucky—Ajak's is lucky to have you." When his smile waned, the tip of his tongue moistened the inside edge of his bottom lip. The street light hit that spot just right.

This isn't a date. He's not going to kiss you. He has a girlfriend.

The odious reminder allowed the keys to slip right through her fingers. "Dammit."

Tony snatched the keys from the pavement before she had time to bend over. "Maybe I should give you a ride."

Snickering, her mind quickly redefined the innocent offer. *Yeah, sure, that's all I need, a ride from Tony.* "No! God, no. I'm fine, positive." She plucked her keys from his hand and unlocked the car door.

From the safety of being behind the steering wheel, Bailey rolled down her window. "Goodnight, Tony, and—thanks for everything. Have a good weekend."

"You too." He took four slow steps backward before shoving his hands into his front pockets and turning around completely.

Bailey stuck the key into the ignition, watching him gather distance. But then—he blew out a full breath like people do when they just somehow dodged a bullet.

Wtf was that about?

Chapter Five

Candice lay face down, passed out, across the end of Tony's king-sized bed. It would take a herd of elephants to wake her, not that he wanted to. She'd all but forgotten their tiff, so she stayed out late and invited her friends over. With all the noise they were making downstairs, he didn't get any sleep. Ironically, this was kind of what started their argument in the first place. It was somewhere between three and four in the morning when her friends finally left.

He'd deal with all that later because right now, he had another issue to take care of. He climbed out of bed and waddled toward the bathroom, bent over like an old man with a sore back. This made three mornings in a row that he woke with the same engorged affliction. But this wasn't typical morning wood. It didn't sprout because of the woman draped over his bed or the need to take a piss. No, no, this chunk of timber belonged to the same sassy individual who'd invaded his thoughts and surroundings for the past week.

Something about Bailey fascinated him more than it should, but damned if he could figure it out. He could barely talk to her without smiling like a jackass. And sometimes, he had to catch himself from making it into something more.

Ever since that day on the ladder, his perspective of her had shifted considerably. Her roaming hands made it too hard to ignore, literally. And he couldn't stop thinking about that stupid little kiss yesterday. She tasted like honey.

Fucking honey.

Tony reached inside the shower and twisted the water handle.

Sure, he'd hired Bailey because she was Frank's cute niece and a breath of fresh air. Her personality, along with her looks were refreshing and so natural. It was nice to see a girl who wasn't smothered in makeup, like most of the women he knew. Bailey didn't really need it.

Yeah, she was definitely growing on him in ways he hadn't counted on—this being one of them.

Her talent impressed the hell out of him. As a graphic designer, she had inspiring ideas and clever designs. Plus, the shop had never been so clean or arranged so efficiently. Everything had a place and purpose. She also worked at a pace twice the speed of others and had enough knowledge and versatility to help with everything, including installs, a huge bonus since Dylan quit and Lazlo had limitations.

Not to mention that in one week, Bailey brought in several new jobs and acquired a prestigious client that could anchor the growth his business needed. He absolutely liked having her around. She's amazing, and Quin should have sold his soul to hire her.

As her boss, there were lines he couldn't cross. However, if she didn't work for him, he'd be willing to admit that Bailey's a well-toned, curly-haired vixen, "make any dick rock-hard" kind of girl.

But she did work for him.

Steam curled over the shower door, and Tony stepped under the hot stream. Water pummeled the center of his chest as the image of Bailey's wild curls and soft peach lips developed in his mind. His dick jumped for attention. A smirk landed on his lips as he braced one hand against the tile and gripped his shaft with the other. He hadn't masturbated this much since eighth grade, but if this was the only way he could throttle Bailey Jazincski from his thoughts. So be it. Or, in this case, so beat it.

****

Tony threw on a pair of shorts and jogged down the stairs. In the stillness of a quiet morning, the hum of a car coming up the shared driveway drew him closer to the glass wall that defined the front of the house. A silver Audi drove past.

Bailey said she had to be somewhere early. Curiosity held him at the window, watching and hoping to catch another glimpse through the trees. A few minutes later, Frank and Trish rode by in their Tahoe. The last time he talked to Frank, he mentioned taking Trish to Williamsburg for a weekend getaway.

Tony put two and two together. Bailey was babysitting her younger cousins for the next two days. He eased away from the window, smiling. Why that made him smile was a mystery.

Upon entering the kitchen, the smile vanished, and the lightness in his step came to a thudding stop. Stemware covered with cloudy fingerprints and half-empty beer bottles littered the antique oak table he inherited from his grandmother.

On the counter next to the sink were three empty wine bottles. One was knocked over, hanging partially off the edge. A puddle of wine had dribbled onto the floor. Tony grabbed a handful of paper towels. The floor was light ash. If it stained, he'd be pissed. He soaked up the mess and tossed the soppy towels into the sink. He'd never been a so-called "neat freak," but *come on.*

"Screw it. I'm making coffee." This was Candice's mess, and she could clean it up. He wanted to head to the garage first thing to make a few adjustments on his '73 Ford Convertible Mustang for the upcoming car show. And that was what he was going to do.

By 10:30, Tony rolled out from under the car and wiped a smudge of grease from his hands. He let the engine run for a few minutes, satisfied with the smooth hum, before turning it off. Mission accomplished.

Children's laughter drew Tony from the garage, and he headed toward the back of his house. Just then, a fluorescent green Frisbee came sailing over the split-rail fence that separated his yard from the neighbor's. He jogged to retrieve it for Vivian. She was around seven years old and the younger of Bailey's two cousins.

"Hey, stay there, Viv. I got ya." Tony retrieved the Frisbee and casually scanned their backyard. Bailey was nowhere in sight.

"Hey, Mr. Tony," Carter, Vivian's older brother by a couple of years, called to him from the opposite side of the lawn.

Every time they called him "Mr. Tony," he felt way older than twenty-eight. "Hey, Carter. What are you guys up to?" Tony leaned on the railing first but then decided to climb over.

"We're getting ready to take a hike." Carter caught a wobbly throw from his sister. "Catch this one, Mr. Tony." The Frisbee came straight to him.

"Nice throw, buddy." Tony gave Carter a thumbs up. "A hike sounds like fun." Just then, the sliding door on the deck above him rumbled open. A second later, Bailey appeared at the railing. The sun beamed through the ringlets of her hair, making a halo of sorts around her.

Her expression launched into a series of changes the second she spotted him. He couldn't tell if she was happy to see him or if she just swallowed a bug. That happened a lot.

"Tony?"

"Bailey." A flashback of his early morning condition fueled his smile. "Thought I'd come over and say hello since I saw you drive by this morning."

She chuckled skeptically, making her way down the side stairs to the yard. "Wow, that was like 5 a.m. I didn't mean to wake you."

"I wasn't sleeping." He tossed the Frisbee to Vivian.

"What were you doing up that early— Oh, god, never mind." Bailey's face turned beet red.

What did she think— Oh. She must've thought he was getting his rocks off with Candice. She was right about the first part—only he was in the shower by himself. What color would she turn if she knew he was thinking about her when he did it?

She started clawing on the back of her left hand. "Did you get bit?"

"What?" The scratching stopped. "No. Just had an itch." She shoved her hands into the rear pockets—of jeans that fit her ass perfectly.

Vivian threw the Frisbee, but it sailed about five feet over her brother's head.

Tony returned his attention back to Bailey. "Carter said you guys are going for a hike. Do you know where the trails are?"

"Aunt Trish told me about the one that goes down toward the creek." Bailey glanced at him briefly before pointing in the general direction of the hills behind them.

Tony knew of a better place, but she'd never find it without him. A flash of color entered his peripheral. He snatched the Frisbee out of the air right before it dwoinked Bailey in the head. She flinched away from him and the Frisbee.

He grabbed her arm with his free hand to keep her from falling. "That was close. I didn't think you saw it coming."

She regained her balance and looked around nervously. "Yeah, that's for sure."

Carter raced toward them. "Hey, why don't you come with us, Mr. Tony, you and Ms. Candy?

Tony chuckled to himself. Candice hated the woods. Heck, she hated grass. "Ms. Candy's still asleep." She'd sleep for the rest of the afternoon—if he was lucky. And then, she had a mess to clean up.

Vivian chimed in. "But if you come, you can protect us from bears. We're going to have a picnic too."

Bailey knelt in front of her young cousin. "Now, Vivian, I'm sure Mr. Tony is busy, and besides, I'm mean enough to protect us from bears." She bared her teeth and growled, making the girl laugh.

He was on the cusp of declining when a gnawing feeling hit the pit of his stomach. This felt like an opportunity he shouldn't pass up. Maybe spending time around Bailey outside of work would make his mornings a little easier to handle. "You know, I happen to know of a perfect spot." *Yeah, what could it hurt?* "Give me ten minutes. I'll be right back."

Tony changed into jeans and swapped his flip-flops for sneakers. He met Bailey and the kids along the ridge of trees that bordered the rear of both properties.

"You guys ready?" Everyone nodded except Bailey.

****

It'd been at least a year since Tony hiked up the mountain. As far as he knew, no one else knew about his secret place. And this would be the first time he shared it with someone.

Dry, older leaves, remnants of the season before, carpeted the ground and crunched under his feet. Overhead, new life made of bright greens filled the canopy. The crisp mountain air was like no other. If anyone could appreciate the beauty of this place, it would be someone like Bailey.

Ten minutes into the hike, Vivian and Carter attempted several versions of birdcalls. The tiny birds chirping in the trees overhead echoed their chatter.

Bailey had been quiet up until now. "Whose property is this?"

"I'm not sure to tell you the truth. Why? Do you think we're going to get into trouble?"

"No, I just want to make sure we don't stumble into some backwoods, banjo-playing survivalist nightmare."

He chuckled. "Well, I'll holler if I hear the twang of the banjo."

"Holler or squeal?"

He loved the mischief in her smile. "Well, if I'm squealing—it's too late."

Ahead, Carter tried wrapping his arms around a massive red oak tree. "Hey, Mr. Tony, this tree is almost as big as the one that used to be in your front yard, isn't it?"

"Yeah, buddy. I'm surprised you remember that. You were just little."

Bailey shot him a curious glance. "How long have you lived here?"

"Seven years," he answered Bailey, then called the kids. "Hey, wait up, you guys. We'll take a shortcut over those bigger rocks ahead."

"Wow!" Bailey sounded truly surprised. "I thought you were going to say two or three."

"Well, I moved in right before your aunt and uncle bought their house." He and Bailey approached the kids waiting by the rock formation. "Oh, and watch out for snakes. They like to hide in the crevasses."

"So, bears *and* snakes." Bailey grimaced playfully.

"Yeah."

The gathering of indigenous rocks resembled an oversized staircase that just happened to be built by nature. And just like nature, the first step was often the biggest. Tony scaled the waist-high bolder and hoisted the two kids with ease. They darted on to the next level. Turning around, he offered Bailey his hand. Hesitation was written all over her face. True, she could probably get up without his help, but he felt like king of the hill when her slender hand landed on his.

Once they scaled the remaining rock steps, the so-called trail became easier to detect, with trees edging the sides as if someone had planted them for just this reason. Heck, for all he knew, maybe they did.

Carter and Vivian trailed several yards behind as Bailey ambled next to him, her brows pinched near the center of her forehead.

"So…" She broke her silence. "What does Ajak's stand for?"

Tony snickered and swatted at some low-hanging leaves. "Augh, that was all my older brother Aaron's doing. He started the sign company eight years ago. Ajak's. The first 'A' stands for Aaron, the 'J' Jason, his best friend. The second 'A' is me." His face scrunched. "Anthony, which I hate, so never call me that, and the 'K' is for Kayla. I didn't come up with it." Bailey giggled, but her gaze remained on the path ahead, making it easier for him to continue.

"You see, Aaron had it all figured out. He was the artist." Tony purposely bumped against her shoulder. "He had that spark, like the one you have." His hands rose into the air to mimic a crazed Dr. Frankenstein. "You see things the rest of us don't." A bashful smile touched her slender lips. "The sign you found in the shop the other day was one that Aaron started but never had the chance to finish. I'm glad you found it, and I know you'll come up with something amazing."

"I'll do my best."

"I have no doubt." Tony filled his lungs with another big breath. "Jason. Man, he was a real talker, the perfect pitchman. He could sell anything to anyone. Sales were going to be his forte." An unexpected pain twitched in his gut. "Jason was married to Kayla." His throat grew dry, causing him to swallow hard. A quick cough cleared it away. "And I was there to do everything else. But, not what Kayla does. Thank God, because I hate paperwork as it is." He snatched a small twig from the ground and cracked it up into smaller pieces. "Aaron and I were close, but he was more than just my brother. You see, my dad took off when we were young. From what I remember, he was pretty much a shitty father. And in my book, there's no such thing as a part-time dad. You're either there, or you're not. I'll never understand how a man could consciously decide not to be there for his kids? So it was Aaron who stepped up and watched out for us, my mom, my sister—me."

A long shuddering breath followed. He hadn't talked this openly about Aaron in—years, not with any of his girlfriends, not with Max, not anyone. Truth be told, only two people in the whole world knew how hard this was for him: Kayla and his mom. They carried the same grief. Only Kayla had twice the loss.

"I guess that's what big brothers do." Bailey nodded toward Carter, helping Vivian over a fallen tree.

"Yeah." The need for Bailey to know the whole story kept him talking. "It was right after we signed the lease that Aaron and Jason were killed in a car accident. A truck driver fell asleep and crossed the centerline. My mom filed a wrongful lawsuit, but fighting a large corporation wasn't easy, and our lawyer wasn't the greatest. The settlement covered the rent just long enough for the business to get on its feet."

Tony swung around a small tree that split the

path.

"I'm so sorry, Tony." Bailey's tone held compassion but no pity. He never wanted her pity. "Was Lazlo with them in the accident?"

Tony grimaced. "Lazlo was with them but came out of the accident without a scratch. Surviving is what messed him up. He handled Aaron and Jason's deaths by excessive drinking and getting mixed up with all kinds of drugs. About two years ago, he hit a pole and flipped his car into a ditch. When he was released from the hospital, I made him come and work for me even though he was still in physical therapy. That's where he met Sherry. So, now he's her problem." He scanned further ahead. "Ah-ha. Come on guys." He wiggled his brows to lighten the somber mood. "We're almost there. It's just ahead."

He emerged from the dense canopy of trees. Sunlight landed on his face. The hilly terrain leveled, creating a meadow of sorts. Tony spread his arms. "Ta-dah!" He coaxed Bailey and the children into the knee-high grass. "I recall someone saying something about a picnic." He rubbed his tummy. "I'm getting a little bit hungry."

"Can we roast hot dogs?" Carter begged, stretching his bottom lip.

"Well." Bailey's head tilted to the side. "How about instead of lighting a fire that could burn down the mountain, we pretend that bologna is an oversized hot dog, just sliced thin, served cold, and eaten on bread? Will that work?"

"Ah, man. Whatever," Carter grumbled. "I'm going to look for salamanders."

"I want ketchup on my bologna." Vivian chimed in right before a swallowtail butterfly flew past her nose. "Oh, look." She chased after it.

Tony surveyed his surroundings. For the first time

in a long time, remembering Aaron filled him with more pride than sadness. The weight on his chest hadn't felt this light in years.

Chapter Six

Now that Bailey knew what Ajak's stood for, it certainly defined just how important the company was to Tony. *Reason #323*, he loves his family very much.

Tony had wandered a few steps away. Staring off into the distance, he seemed to be in his own little world. She had no siblings, so trying to imagine losing one was impossible. Guilt trickled down her spine. She was merely curious about the name of the company. The last thing she meant to do was stir up painful memories for him.

"Tony?"

He turned. "Yeah."

"I didn't mean to…"

He shook his head, somehow knowing what she was trying to say. "Nah, I'm good. Trust me." His smile returned. "And don't worry, I like bologna. Just hold the ketchup on mine."

He seemed okay, and that made her feel better. "Okay. Come on, guys." She called for the kids. "Bologna sandwiches all around. And yes, Vivian, I brought ketchup for you."

A downed log in a shaded area gave them the perfect place to sit for their picnic lunch. After they finished eating, Bailey started collecting their trash and put it in an old paper grocery bag she'd brought.

"Carter, are you done with your juice box?"

"Not yet. Hey, I found one. Take a picture of me and my salamander."

Bailey pulled a camera from her backpack, but the salamander ran off before she could get to Carter. "See if you can find another one."

She raised her camera and snapped a few pictures

of her surroundings. The mountains in the distance made the perfect backdrop for the bright pink blossoms of mountain laurel and bloodroot. The rest of the landscape comprised a palette of colors. This place was remarkable.

She returned to the log to go through them when Vivian bounced in front of her.

"Can I take some pictures?"

Bailey wavered for a fleeting moment. The camera was older, and she could go through her pictures later tonight once the kids were asleep. "Sure." Vivian took the camera and immediately aimed it toward her and—Tony.

"Get closer together." Vivian waved them toward one another. Tony leaned closer from his side of the log.

Bailey heard the digital click. "There you go."

"No, wait." Tony jumped up and crouched behind her. His hands came to rest on either side of her hips. "You ready, Viv?" His closeness wafted onto her like tiny ants crawling over her skin. "Let's say—star bits."

Bailey burst out laughing and glanced over her shoulder. "Oh, my God." The twinkle in Tony's sage green eyes pierced straight into her soul. The camera clicked again.

"Wait, you guys weren't looking. Let me take one more." Vivian raised the camera again, but Bailey scampered to her feet, buzzing from head to toe.

"No, no, that's enough of us. Go take some pictures of your brother. Or see if you can find another butterfly." Vivian ran away with the camera.

Chances that Tony was grinning when she turned around were through the roof.

And boy, was he.

"Come on—don't tell me you've forgotten." He flattened his lips to look bleak.

Kind of hard to forget. The memory came

flooding back along with a heatwave of embarrassment. But she could play, too. "Oh wait, I think vaguely…oh yeah, I was looking for something small in your pockets."

Tony clutched his chest in an overly dramatic fashion. "Oh, that hurt. You wound me, Bailey."

She giggled involuntarily. Gawd, it was that girly laugh—again. Where did that even come from? When the laughter skidded away, a peaceful quiet replaced it. Tony snagged her sweeping glance—caught it and held it. Bantering with him like this was so easy and enticing— and dangerous. So very, very dangerous, for her at least.

An ear-piercing screech shattered the warm fuzzy moment. Bailey raced toward Vivian. *Please don't be a snake.*

Tony got to her first. "What's wrong, Viv?"

"Something moved by the trees over there." Vivian pointed.

"It might be a bear?" Carter thudded to a stop behind his sister.

Bailey's gaze searched in that direction just as a doe with a fawn stepped into view.

Tony's concern dissipated, and he took a semi-serious stance, bracing his two hands on his knees. "Bambi over there is not a bear, but let me tell you something you need to know about bears. You don't have to run fast."

Carter gave him a puzzled look. "I thought you weren't supposed to run at all."

A roguish grin scoured Tony's face. "Normally, that's right. But, if you're with other people, you just need to run faster than them."

Carter shoved his sister. "Ha, ha, ha. I get it. Viv, you'd be in trouble."

"No, no, no," Tony said. "You see, I'm fast and strong enough to carry Vivian. Carter, you're speedy like a bullet, so—" he pulled his lips down and lifted his eyebrows. "That just leaves…" His words trailed away, and his head tilted toward Bailey very conspicuously.

"Oh, I guess." Bailey rummaged in Carter's backpack and pulled out the Nerf football. "I'll show you how fast I am. It's on."

Chapter Seven

"Let's do shirts and skins. I call shirts." Tony grinned over the top, and *over top* of Vivian and Carter's heads.

Bailey's chin lowered in effect, squashing his offer. "I don't think so. How about boy-girl, youngest-oldest?"

Tony was having the best day ever. "Fine. Viv and I are going to crush you guys."

What started as two-hand touch football quickly progressed to light tackle and one heaping pileup at the end of every play—every time.

Carter and Bailey were losing by one touchdown.

Tony had to give Bailey credit. She was way more athletic than he thought, given her artistic abilities. And she knew the game—strategy, plays, and her spiral was probably tighter than his. He lined up across from her. "You think you're going somewhere."

"Who, me?" Her spirited answer issued the challenge. "Nah, Carter told me to stand here. He's going to rush past Vivian. I'm supposed to block you."

"Liar."

"We'll see." Bailey nodded toward Carter, and his count started. On Omaha four, Bailey stepped back, took a lateral pass, and then crisscrossed behind her teammate.

Tony counted to three and then rushed forward—but Bailey flicked the ball back to Carter and dodged by him on a diagonal slant. *Oh shit!* After ten yards, she checked over her shoulder, searching for a high arching pass.

And damned, she actually had him by half a step when the ball landed in her hands. He barely managed to snag her waist, and they tumbled together onto the thick cushion of grass.

When the rolling stopped, Tony found himself braced on his elbows hovering over her. She was breathing hard. Heck, they both were. A curtain of hair covered her face, so he pushed it away. Their eyes met, and that line he couldn't cross suddenly felt precariously thin. All he wanted to do was kiss her, right here, right now, a real kiss—one as sweet as honey. Heat flooded his body—quickly followed by acute awareness. Not only was he lying on top of her, his thighs were fortuitously nestled directly between hers. *Holy shit.* Her eyelids lowered, and her warm breath touched his face. If he didn't move soon, he was going to find himself with another hard predicament. He shifted his weight to his knees, leaning away from her. "Are you all right?"

"I'm fine." She bent her knees and scooted back enough to sit up.

"I guess we should probably... you know, head home soon. I'm sure the kids are getting tired."

Between two long breaths, Bailey agreed. Her eyes stayed on the ground by her feet. "Yeah, we should do that."

Carter and Vivian found them in the grass. "She caught it. We tied," Carter cheered.

Tony climbed to his feet and offered Bailey his hand. Only this time, she ignored it and stood up on her own.

Marching away, she barked at the kids. "Carter, Vivian, gather your souvenirs and backpacks. It's time to get going."

Tony looked around sheepishly. "Yeah, back to the real world."

Chapter Eight

Climbing over the split rail fence into Uncle Frank's backyard, Carter started waving to someone. Bailey followed his line of sight—and instantly wished she hadn't. Across the way, standing on the upper level of Tony's deck, Candice. Her attire consisted of boy shorts and a severely cropped t-shirt—no bra, evident by the amount of underboob on display.

Really? Barf.

Instinct, or just a glutton for punishment, Bailey's gaze shifted in time to witness Tony's reaction to seeing his girlfriend. His expression blanked like a zombie, ogling the goddess on the deck.

The gurgle in Bailey's stomach erupted in the form of a bologna burp. *Uuh. Serves me right.*

"I'm thirsty." Vivian handed Bailey her backpack.

"Can we play Warcraft now?" Carter piled his backpack with Vivian's and raced his sister toward the stairs up the deck.

She didn't get a chance to reply before the children ran up and entered the house.

"Hey. You okay? Are you going to have enough energy left to handle those two?" Tony asked.

"Oh, I can handle them." *Just not you.*

"Well, thanks for letting me tag along."

"No problem. Thanks for showing us your mountain."

"Well, it's true that I like to think of it as mine." He glanced over his shoulder toward his house. Candice had disappeared from his deck. "Hey." Tony took a few steps backward, the same way he did the night before. "You know that thing about the bear?" Bailey shook her head as every part of his face lit up. "That'd be one lucky bear." The wink followed. Then he turned, hopped over the split rail fence, and disappeared around the corner of his garage.

She couldn't move. It was like she'd grown roots into the soil.

Means nothing.

****

Monday morning came, and the rain soured Bailey's mood even more. After Tony walked away from her Saturday afternoon, she didn't see him for the rest of the weekend. He was probably too busy packing for his romantic getaway with Candice.

Bailey walked into her office and tossed her purse beside her desk. No matter how much fun she had with Tony, it couldn't be more than that. She shouldn't feel this miserable, but had no one to blame but herself.

Kayla stuck her head through the door frame. "Hey, lady. How was your weekend?" Did you do anything special?

Wallowing in self-pity wouldn't change reality. Bailey plastered on the best smile she could muster. "Um, kind of. I spent the weekend watching my cousins. How about yours?"

The bell on the front door chimed. "Uneventful, for the most part." Kayla's gaze shifted toward the front. "My—Oh my god. What are you doing here? Shouldn't you be knee-deep in chocolate-covered strawberries about now?" Tony stopped at the doorway of his office.

At the mere sight of him Bailey's spirits lifted like he was her very own ray of sunshine.

He cleared his throat, and his gaze bounced toward her briefly. "I just didn't think it was a good time to be away. Do you have a problem with that?"

Kayla gave him a lazy giggle. "No, of course not. What did you do this weekend?"

His chin lowered, concealing a smile. "I worked on the Mustang some. Then I went on a hike. It was—a perfect day." His gaze shifted to her. He didn't elaborate beyond that. Like it was a secret they could share.

Bailey couldn't keep her lips from curving up. Even if she set aside her struggling infatuation, it was still impossible to ignore how well they got along. They could be friends. Right? It didn't have to be more than that.

But what if it was?

The voice in the back of her mind screamed the warning. *Don't go there. No what-ifs.*

****

Two days later, Bailey used a small window of time to start the renovations in the front office.

"The deep purple is a bold choice. I love it, and you're right. It really makes a statement." Kayla bubbled with excitement. "I can't believe how different it looks already."

"I'm glad you like the color?" Tiny flecks of purple paint landed on Bailey's arm as she rolled the "accent wall" in the front office. "I figure that I can work on this until the blank banner gets here this afternoon."

"Yeah, it should come in today. The shopping center guy paid extra for the quick turn-around. Since Tony will be around, it can be up by the end of the week. It's all working out so fabulously."

"I'll help you carry the rug in later, and hey, did you see the old bar Lazlo brought in? He suggested recovering the top with a piece of brushed silver aluminum, and I think if we paint the base this color, it will look great."

"I can't wait, Bailey."

An hour later, she and Kayla unrolled the new rug along the wall where the table and chairs were.

"We need to slide your desk over here, at least."

Bailey boxed her hands where she thought the desk should go, around four feet deeper into the room.

"I'm not sure that the wires are long enough."

Bailey checked under Kayla's desk. The dust-covered tangled mass was almost the size of a basketball. "Hold on, I think they just need to be untangled. I'll get it." She crawled onto the floor under the desk. "Good grief, Kayla, when was the last time you ran a broom under here?"

"It's been a while. Most of the time, I just let it blow away when the door opens."

Bailey traced the phone line and the power plug to the printer. They were easy to identify and the main culprits for the snarled-up mess. "Here, hold these." She handed Kayla the disconnected wires. "I need to unloop the printer cord. Then we should have plenty of slack."

The bell above the door dinged. From under the desk, Bailey could only see Tony's shoes when he entered the room to greet the person who came in. "Hi, can I help you?"

"I think I'm in the right place. I'm looking for Bailey Jazincski."

Bailey knew that burly baritone voice anywhere. She scrambled from under the desk, smacking her dusty hands over her pants.

Quin stood on the welcome mat just inside the door. His expression perked up, and his arms opened wide.

Bailey raced into the husky embrace. "Quinten." She squealed like a ten-year-old girl getting her first iPhone. "What the hell are you doing here?"

"I've got a big surprise for you." Quin looked as happy as she'd ever seen him.

"Okay. That's great, but hold on a minute." Bailey composed herself enough to introduce him to everyone. "Quin, this is Kayla and Tony. Lazlo is in the back somewhere. And you guys, this is Quin."

Kayla, still holding wires, waved with two free fingers. Quin gave her a nod and then extended his hand toward Tony. "You know if you mess this up, I get her back." Quin may have said it jokingly, but his underlying tone was dead serious.

Tony's gaze shifted toward her. "Not planning on it."

Bailey checked the clock. "Come on, Quin, I'll take you to lunch. I'm still waiting on a delivery." She grabbed his sleeve and pulled him out the front door. Not only was she happy to see a familiar face—but her best friend. She needed this more than she could say.

Quin took in the surroundings of the industrial park. "I didn't see your car, so I wasn't sure if this was the right place."

"I started parking out back to leave room for the customers. Now tell me, what the hell are you doing here? What's this surprise?"

His smile beamed. "I got us in Bailey, 'The Reever's Art Show.'"

"Reever's? The elite art show you've been entering for as long as I've known you."

"And then some. I signed us up again like I do every year. Turned out that someone messed up the notification. They called me because they hadn't heard from us. So, of course, I told them we'd still do it. And I came straight here with the news. How many pieces do you have?"

"Like three, maybe four, that are okay. How many do I need?"

"I told them you had nine."

"Nine! Good grief, Quin."

Bailey used the same route to the food truck as

she had the week before. Quin barreled through the pine trees, snapping branches right and left. A herd of buffalo would probably have done less damage.

"Yeah, I've got seven and I won't have time to do anymore. I *am* getting married, you know." His face ignited with another smile.

"When is the show? How much time do I have?"

"It's the week before the wedding, so you have a little less than three weeks."

Bailey stopped dead in her tracks. Her head flopped back in disbelief. It was so like him to just spring something of this importance on her. But how could she be mad at her best friend? "I'll see what I can do." She pointed toward the chuck wagon. "My treat, and before you ask, I think they may even have pimento loaf."

"That's my favorite."

"Yeah, I know."

Quin gave the menu a thorough going-over before deciding on Virginia-baked ham and Swiss. Bailey ordered the cajun turkey panini.

"Jesus, Bailey. Who the hell pays twelve dollars for a ham sandwich?" Quin only splurged on beer.

"Stop your complaining. You spent more than that on gas just getting here. Come on, there's a bench over here."

"When I told Liz, she said, *'Oh, that's nice.'*" He tore into his sandwich, dribbling a few hunks of the thinly sliced ham down the front of his shirt. Quin shook his head, nibbling at the pieces. "I knew if anyone could appreciate what this means, it would be you. So I think that it was worth it."

Nothing against Liz, but if Quin had a white whale, the art show was it. Sure, she was supportive, but Bailey did understand how much this accomplishment truly meant to him, not just as his best friend but as another creative right-brain artist.

"It *was* worth it. Good job, Quin. I'm proud of you. You never gave up." She took a bite of her sandwich. The turkey all but melted in her mouth. "God, this is heaven in a sandwich." She finished chewing. "Did you get a haircut?" Like real friends, it was easy for them to pick up where they left off.

"Liz did it last night. What do you think?"

"Honestly?"

"That bad, huh?"

"Nah, Dutch boy is a thing, right?"

"Shut the fuck up. Hey, you want to see my toe?"

Two nights ago, a little past ten o'clock, Quin sent her a picture of his big toe minus the toenail. "No thanks, I'm eating." He laughed at her. "So tell me, Mr. Business owner, how's business?"

"Not too bad, if I do say so myself. A couple more months, and I'll be out of the garage, if not sooner. Damn, I wonder what kind of glaze they used on this meat. This is a good sandwich."

"Told ya," she snickered.

"So, what's happening with you? Any new developments I should know about."

"Nah, not really. Just working. But I have been in a groove lately with some interesting designs. The clients in this region spend money way easier than back home. I'm able to push uniqueness without worrying so much about the dollar sign attached."

"I liked the pictures you sent using that iridescent vinyl. That's some expensive shit, but it gave it a really cool effect. He gave her a penetrating stare before shoving another bite into his mouth. After a thorough chew and swallow, his piercing stare lessened. "I guess it's too early to grab a beer somewhere."

"Actually, there is a place, but it's the middle of

the workday and might be frowned upon by those who actually work for someone else." She swatted at the bill of his ball cap. "Speaking of which, how long are you planning on hanging out? Maybe we could grab one after work?"

"Nah, I gotta get going. I didn't tell Liz I was coming down here. She thinks I'm installing signs at the golf course. But I'm doing that tomorrow."

"You lied to her."

"No. I didn't lie. I just didn't tell her. Hey, I don't need her permission."

Bailey shoved his shoulder. "Dork. Oh, I mean Dutch boy Dork. Come on."

On the trek back to Ajak's, Quinn fell into one of his quiet-thinking phases. He was trying to figure something out, and Bailey didn't know whether to go on high alert or prepare for one of his infamous long-winded stories.

They walked up to his old Dodge pickup. He started picking at a spot of rust on the red hood. "So, what's the deal with you and the pretty boy in there?" He nodded toward Ajak's.

Oh, Shit! It's high alert. "Who? Tony?" *Be calm.* "There is no deal. He has a girlfriend, and if you must know, he thought there was a deal between you and me."

Quin snorted. "That's hysterical, but I know what I saw." After a long pause, the smile on his face faded away. "Great, he *is* an asshole. Christ almighty Bailey. I'm not blind."

Bailey scoffed. "I don't know what you're looking at. You heard me say he has a girlfriend, right?" Her scoff was more of a snort. "Nothing is going on. Absolutely nothing." *Maintain eye contact. Don't blink.*

Quin's eyes narrowed. "I guess you missed the look on his face when you jumped into my arms. I thought he was about to punch me, which probably would've hurt. He looks like he could throw a punch.

"Unlike you."

"Shut up," he whined, acting offended. After another long pause, his eyes widened. "Wait a minute. It's you. Holy shit! You got a thing for him, don't you?" He pointed at her with an accusing finger.

"What?" Bailey swatted at his finger. "Why are you talking so loud? And get your finger out of my face, or *I'm* going to punch you, and don't make me use your middle name, Quinten." Who other than her best friend could figure everything out so easily? No sense in lying. "It's nothing. I'm...handling it." Quin grimaced. He didn't believe her. "Hey, I'm going to be too busy getting ready for this art show, so don't worry."

He released a nasally sigh as a brown delivery truck zoomed into the spot next to them.

"Well, that's the banner that I've been waiting on. I should probably get back to work." She stepped closer and gave him a hug. "Shoot me a text when you get home. I'll see you in a couple of weeks. We'll grab that beer."

Quin added an extra squeeze before letting her go. "Start painting, Bailey." He looked toward the door of Ajak's. "And be careful."

"I will. Thanks, Quin."

****

Thursday midday, Bailey stepped back from the banner, admiring her hand-painted color rendering of the shopping center's new upscale façade which she'd painted yesterday after the banner arrived. The owner of the strip mall was excited to get it up as soon as possible. All she had left was to apply the vinyl lettering. And since Tony was here instead of some island love shack with Candice, the banner would be ready for installation tomorrow.

Bailey carefully positioned the painted part of the banner over the worktable and unrolled the remaining eighteen feet of the thick material across the shop floor.

"Here you go." Lazlo handed her a barrel-sized roll of bright red vinyl lettering, all weeded and masked. "I didn't realize that these letters were so tall."

"Only the words 'Commercial Space' are twenty-eight inches. The phone numbers are only half that. It won't be too hard."

"I can help you after my doctor's appointment. Sherry is coming to pick me up. I shouldn't be more than an hour."

"Don't worry. I have a few tricks to get it started. I'll split the copy and only do a couple of letters at a time to make it easier."

Sherry emerged from the entrance of the hallway and waved.

"Hey, Sherry." Bailey waved to her new friend. "Don't worry, Laz. I got this."

"Okay, well, don't work too hard." Laz shuffled around the banner covering the floor and disappeared with Sherry.

Bailey kicked off her shoes, hoping to keep everything as clean as possible. The first four letters of the word Commercial transferred with ease. At this rate, she might even have this done before Lazlo made it back.

She finished peeling the transfer paper away from the second "M." An undercurrent in the room sent a ripple coursing through her limbs until it reached her center. Glancing over her shoulder, Tony was three steps into the shop. Max was with him. They stopped on the other side of the banner to inspect her progress.

Max leaned over the part she'd painted. "You did this? Freehand from a photo?"

"Yeah." He didn't have to sound so surprised.

His suave brow lifted. "With everything in today's market being digitally printed, this is impressive. Not bad, sweetheart." His lips curved into a grin. "Not bad at all."

Tony's chin lifted as one of his pristine smiles oozed over her like warm gravy covering a pile of mashed potatoes. "Yeah, and she did it quicker than we could've had it printed. Bailey's talents are what set us apart from our competition. There's no one else like her. At least not around here." He added his trademark wink. "Look, I came back here to tell you that Kayla went to the dentist, which I didn't know was happening, and I'm not sure when Lazlo will be back from his doctor's appointment. Max and I were supposed to have lunch, but if you want me to stay, I will. Max and I can try to have lunch another day."

"Nah, I should be alright. Go, have a nice lunch."

"Really? You sure?"

"I am."

"Okay. And hey, it looks great, Bailey. We shouldn't be too long, promise." Right then, the phone rang. "I'll take care of this call real quick. You keep working." Tony jogged up the hallway. Her gaze trailed after him until he disappeared from her sight.

The man had a nice butt.

Bailey inhaled, effectively resetting her frame of mind back to work mode. She lifted the next set of giant letters away from the carrier and carefully aligned it in place. Her hand went for the squeegee in her rear pocket, but—it wasn't there. Checking her immediate surroundings, she didn't spot it anywhere. "Where in the world...?" She must've laid it down, or it accidently stuck to something. Lucky for her, Lazlo kept a box full of squeegees on his bench. She'd grab one of those and look for the other one later.

Unlike the rest of the shop, Lazlo's area was still a wee bit dirty and messy. But after upsetting Dylan, she chose to tread a little more lightly. Plus, she liked working with Laz, and to be fair, he was entitled to his space.

She spotted the dusty box next to a jar of screws and a lazy Susan holding Sharpie Markers, a few ink pens, and some grease pencils. Bailey grabbed a newer-looking squeegee and checked the edge.

However, when she turned, the belt loop of her jeans snagged on a piece of wood barely hanging over the edge. The four-foot-thin piece of trim sprung like a mousetrap and landed against an old coffee tin and two eight-foot fluorescent lamps that just happened to be resting against the end of the workbench. The day before, Lazlo changed several bulbs, so now they matched. No more warms and brights together or that one bulb that flickered in that annoying way.

However, Lazlo used the coffee tin to drown his cigarette butts. It reeked of stinky water and now wavered at a forty-five-degree angle, threatening to spill all over the counter and possibly splash onto the floor.

Bailey grabbed for the can, but the drastic move caused the lamps to shift away from her. She reached but could only snag one. The second tube was at least an inch beyond her reach—and was still sliding. Ever so slowly, it cleared the front corner of the bench. When it smacked the floor next to the banner, shards of glass covered the area like a ground sparkler on the Fourth of July—and she was barefoot.

The flimsy piece of wood jabbing into her hip still bowed from pressure. Holding one fluorescent tube and the stinky water can, she tried nudging away from the trim, using her elbow to keep it from causing any more problems.

But—instead, the troublesome scrap of wood flipped upward and knocked over a small can of red paint. Helpless, Bailey watched the can roll off the shelf. It landed on the counter and bounced, causing the lid to pop off, shooting a blob of paint the size of a tennis ball directly onto the center of her shirt.

Bailey relinquished the yucky can of brown cigarette juice, let go of the first lamp, and yanked the hem of her shirt away from her body. She leaned forward just as it started to ooze down her front.

Tony charged into the shop. "Jesus, what the hell is going on in here?" He did a quick assessment. "Holy shit! Is that blood? And where the hell are your shoes?"

"No, it's not blood, just paint. I was trying to keep my shoeprints off the banner. Oh crap, it's dripping."

"Here, let me get you." He raced around the banner, intending to lift her out of the glass.

"No, wait, paint will get everywhere." Bailey did a quick inspection of the banner. She'd blocked the initial splash. "It's only on my shirt for now. Oh man, I hope I didn't get any on my jeans. They're my favorite."

"Mine too."

"What?"

"Nothing. What do you suggest we do?"

A puddle of paint had formed between her feet. She stretched the fabric further away from her body. If she moved, it would drizzle everywhere, and there was no way she'd ever be able to take it over her head and come out clean. "Cut it off."

Tony laughed. Actually, it was more of a chortle. "You want me to cut your shirt off?"

"Yes, yes, it's an old shirt." She snagged the shirt from the clearance rack at Target two years ago, but the jeans she'd had since ninth grade. She only wore them today because she figured she wouldn't be around paint. The shirt was a no-brainer, but she wasn't ready to sacrifice her favorite pair of jeans into true work jeans just yet.

"Are you sure?" Tony questioned, and she shook her head. "Okay. Let me find some scissors."

Was it her imagination, or did he sound vastly more excited than he did a second ago?

Bailey peeked down the inside of her shirt. "Oh shit." Figures, her last clean bra was her Victoria's Secret bra. The skimpy black lace accentuated her cleavage and barely covered her nipples. She really needed to catch up on her laundry. *Great.*

"What, did it get on you?" Tony hurried across the room with a pair of orange-handled scissors.

"No." Bailey closed her eyes briefly. "Umm. You do know—this is no big deal, right?" Her voice fluctuated. "I guess I'm trying to say that a bra is very much like a bathing suit."

Broken glass crunched under his shoes as he maneuvered to stand directly behind her. "Yeah, I get that." He leaned closer to whisper in her ear. "And it's okay because I've seen bras before too."

She distinctly heard the smile in his voice without having to see it. "I'm sure you have," Bailey said more to herself than him.

First, Tony gathered her thick hair into a makeshift ponytail. Then he tugged the back of her shirt free from the waist of her jeans and smoothed his palms over her back. "Are you ready?"

What was I thinking? "Yes, yes—just do it." This couldn't get any worse.

But then it did. Cold metal touched her skin. "Auh!" She jerked backward.

"Shit." Tony grabbed her hips. "Don't move your

feet." He yanked her backward against his—front to steady her balance. "Watch the glass."

The scene in her mind played out in real-time: Tony holding onto her hips from behind, her bent over, and a whole lot of pushing and pulling. "Oh my gosh."

"What happened?"

Her eyes closed from the absurdity of being semi-turned on. "The scissors were—cold."

"Okay, hold on." He rubbed them against his jeans. "That's still two for flinching, but I'll wait until we're done." He brought the scissors back to the base of her spine. "All right. Let's try this again." The scissors traveled up her back, slicing the jersey material in a rhythm of brusque chafing. He made it to her bra. "Whoa, or should I say, wow?"

"Just hurry." She blurted.

"Don't worry, I'm almost...done." Tony snipped through the collar and tossed the scissors onto Lazlo's counter. Her daisy yellow crew neck peeled away from her shoulders and landed in the puddle of paint in front of her.

She had barely uprighted before an arm circled her bare torso, and her feet left the floor. Tony was carrying her away from the paint and the sea of broken glass.

Her half-clad body buzzed when his warm breath fanned over her skin. Cradled in his arms, his smooth, spicy scent floated under her nose. She could drown in that scent.

Tony reached the other side of the shop and stopped. His Adam's apple dipped right before her bare feet landed on the cold concrete floor.

Being this close to him, her attention-seeking nipples had already firmed up like little berries, and her stomach was probably wrapped around her spine. Any chance of modesty she may have had was lost the second her shirt came off.

His gaze raked up her body. "Well…" He tried—unsuccessfully to hold back a smile. "That's one hell of a bathing suit." He reached for her chin. "Hold still. You have one little speck of paint right here." He rubbed it away with the side of his thumb. "I think you may have actually come out of this unscathed." A warm gleam entered his eyes.

"Whoa! What the hell?" Max stood in the middle of the hallway, gapping. "You guys need a couple more minutes?"

Tony grabbed her shoulders and whirled her around, shielding her from his friend. "Christ, Max. I told you to wait in the car." He whipped his navy blue t-shirt over his head and started shoving it over hers. It fell onto her body with the warmth of his skin still in it.

"Here, you can keep it. I'll grab another shirt from my office." He jogged across the shop and retrieved her tennis shoes beside the banner. "You may need these." He offered her shoes, then tapped her shoulder twice. "Let's get this cleaned up."

Bailey shook her head. "No, I'll clean this up. You should go. Really Tony. You and Max go have lunch."

"You sure?"

"Of course I am."

"All right, like I said, I won't belong." He took several steps backward before turning away. In all, probably about three seconds. But they were the longest three seconds of her life.

Chapter Nine

The banner looked great on the side of the building. The installation went smoothly, with no clothing mishaps or desperate searches for missing tools. Thank goodness—just a regular install with a not-so-regular guy.

Bailey fidgeted in the passenger seat. The awkward silence didn't help, nor did the memories from the night before. Against her better judgment, she did something unbelievably foolish and wore Tony's shirt to bed. Reveling in his luscious scent fueled her imagination—and fingers.

"Is everything okay? You seem kind of quiet today."

Bailey could barely look at him without getting all tingly. *Oh, I'm just an idiot with no one to blame but myself.* "I've just got a lot on my mind." Bailey kept her focus directed out of the passenger window. They passed a billboard for Hobby World. "Hey, how close are we to Hobby World?"

"It's up here on the left. We can stop if you want. Kayla said you and Quin got into some art show."

Bailey sat up straighter, surprised that he knew anything about it. "That's right, but you don't have to stop. I just need to know where it is so I can come back after work."

"It sounds special. Congratulations, by the way. I guess you do have a lot on your mind." Apparently, he mistook her silence as worry over the art show and not unrequited sexual tension. At least she had that working in her favor.

"Thanks." Bailey leaned back, humbled. Technically, the art show was special.

"We can stop now." His blinker clicked on, and he made the turn into the shopping center before she had time to argue. He parked the truck in the middle of the lot and turned the engine off. Then his door opened.

Panic rushed her words. "You don't need to come in. I'll be fast, I promise."

The corners of his lips curved up. "I don't mind."

"Oh, okay." What harm could it do if he came inside? *Don't make this weird.* She and Quin shopped together in stores like this a million times.

So why did walking into the store with Tony feel…couple-ish? And to make it worse, he insisted on pushing the cart.

Bailey beelined for the paint section. She grabbed a few new brushes and a variety pack of acrylic paints, then headed for the canvases. She already had a few ideas of what she wanted to paint, and she would use the photos from last weekend for reference.

Tony sorted through a stack. "You said you're looking for a big one. How 'bout one this size? It's probably, what, four feet?"

Bailey eyed the canvas for a minute. "Yeah, that might work, but I don't think it'll fit in my car."

"I guess it's a good thing that we're in the truck."

"Hey Tony, do you think it would be okay if I worked on these at the shop? My room at the apartment is small, and I like to spread my stuff out."

Tony shrugged. "Sure. You have a key. Just keep the doors locked. The park tends to be empty on the weekends."

"Thanks." Bailey liked the idea of paintings at the shop. Plus, it would get her away from the coven. "I think that will work for me."

Near the end of the day, Bailey inserted the memory card from her camera into the printer.

Fun memories from the previous weekend rekindled in the form of 4x6 inch snapshots. The first photo Vivian took of her and Tony chugged out of the printer one-quarter of an inch at a time. Then came Tony's "star bits" picture.

The first half of the image revealed Bailey in all her lovesick glory. One little unguarded moment and her true feelings had gushed like a river after a heavy rain. It was unnerving to see it so plainly. Her gaze bounced from the printer to the shop, where she found the bane of her misery plugging in a small jigsaw.

Tony's an excellent craftsman. Reason #375

Bailey's gaze dropped back to the printer as the finished photo spat out. *What the hell?* She snatched the picture from her desk to examine it closer. Seeing all the longing beaming from her eyes, hopeless and indisputable, was a given and completely expected. Seeing that same look on Tony's face—was not.

Confused, she squinted harder. Eyes twinkling…a glimmer of admiration. God, if she didn't know any better, she'd say that was a man who was–smitten. But sadly, she did know better. *Wishful thinking and nothing more.* Bailey stacked the picture with the rest.

Her imagination had run amuck long enough.

This fruitless infatuation needs to end. Today.

****

Happy hour at Brindles was packed with a variety of people. Plumbers, electricians, and mechanics wearing the complete spectrum of Dickies uniforms raised a mug to salute the end of the workweek. The girls from the lab were back, and a couple of guys from the cabinet shop were playing electronic darts with a construction crew. One of these days, Bailey would have to drive around to see where all these people actually came from.

About an hour into TGIF, Candice, Desiree,

Raven, and Shawna entered the bar. Since moving in with her roommates, Raven was the only one who made any effort to get to know her. She wasn't as bad as Bailey first thought.

Candice sashayed up to Tony. Desiree and Shawna pounced all over Max. Raven headed straight for the bar.

"Hi, guys." Raven squeezed between Bailey and Kayla. "I just had the shittiest day ever." She leaned further across, looking for the bartender. "I, for one, need to get drunk tonight."

Kayla was curious and wanted to know more. "Why, what happened, Raven?"

The bartender placed a goblet of white wine on the bar for Raven. "Oh, thank you, Stephon. You're a dear." Of course, Raven knew the bartender by name. Raven gulped most of it down and signaled him for another. "I fucked up, that's what." Talking more to herself, her head dropped, swirling the remaining wine in her glass. "I let myself fall. I knew the bastard was married." She emptied the remaining liquid from the glass and swapped it for the full one on the bar before looking at them. "I know. Let's go out tonight, the four of us."

Sherry and Kayla did a really poor job hiding how ridiculous the idea sounded.

Raven immediately picked up on their reaction, glancing toward the femme fatales she'd arrived with to offer an explanation. "The other girls are going to a bar outside Alexandria, and I don't want to go there." She waved her free hand. "It's a long story, but this jerk works there, and we fucked once, okay, maybe twice. Anyway, they all just love him, but I don't want to run into him again. Look, while I go take a whiz, you guys talk about it, and when I get back, you can let me know."

Raven skipped away with a hopeful spring in her step.

When Raven was far enough away, Sherry spoke first. "I can't go. I have to take Lazlo home."

Of course, Bailey thought it was crazy, but oddly enough, she could relate to Raven's woes. Tony, although not technically married, was still unavailable.

Scoping the crowd happened more like a reflex at this point. She found Tony not too far away, sitting on a bar stool with his knees spread open, giving Candice a place to stand. Bailey's chin twisted to suppress a wave of jealousy. Of all things, being jealous was doubly—infuriating and pathetic. She can't keep torturing herself like this.

After a calming breath, her brows lifted with a questionable grin toward Kayla.

Kayla shook her head. "Any other time I would go, but I have to be at the dentist's office by eight o'clock in the morning. I can't show up hungover."

A shrill laugh smacked Bailey from behind. Candice had such a stupid laugh—way beyond girly-girl. It was more like a hyena getting tickled. It took a lot, but Bailey courageously and proudly refrained from looking.

Raven returned from the restroom. "Well? What's it going to be?"

"Okay, I'm in."

****

"You look great, by the way. That outfit looks so much better on you than it did on me. The navy blue goes perfectly with your complexion." Raven sat on the opposite side of the pub table and gave her a nod of approval.

"Thank you, but I didn't expect you to lend me your new clothes. It still had the tags on it." Bailey pinched at the hem of the skirt. It was flared and hefted by a delicate layer of tule. The top was the same navy blue, only cropped with a silvery lace accent. At least the silver hoop earrings were Bailey's.

"Yeah, good thing we wear the same size shoes. You didn't have any high heels that would've gone with this. No offense, Bailey, but most of your wardrobe is covered in paint. Although, as pretty as you are, you could probably get away with wearing anything." Raven leaned forward on her elbows. "Thanks for coming out with me tonight. And humoring me. I felt like your fairy godmother getting you ready for the ball."

Bailey snickered. By the time Raven finished dressing her, fixing her hair, and applying a delicate but tasteful amount of makeup, she did feel like Cinderella— and *Pretty Woman* minus the whole prostitute thing. "Honestly, I haven't gone out in a while. What's the name of this place again?"

"Jabbers. The lights are lower, the music is loud, and it would appear that the ratio of attractive young men far outnumbers the women here. I'm feeling lucky. Just look around."

Bailey scanned her surroundings. For a brief moment, she felt like a lamb in a den full of hungry wolves—like Max.

The first gin and tonic went down smooth, a little too smooth. "I better pace myself."

"What for? We're here to have fun, Bailey." Raven arched one of her perfect brows. "I want to drink, dance, and if I'm lucky, maybe find a man that doesn't belong to someone else. I deserve that."

"We both do," Bailey said without thinking. No one but Quin knew about her misguided attraction for Tony, and she wanted to keep it that way. "Let's finish this drink, and then we'll dance."

And dance she did. The lights flashed, the tempos changed, new songs and old songs, one after the other, and Bailey danced. If she knew the words, she sang along. As loud as the music was, no one could hear her. Quin kindly told her she did not have the voice of an angel but one that sounded more like a sick cow. Uh, friends.

Raven grabbed her arm. "Let's take a break, Bailey. We've been dancing for like an hour."

"Okay. I could cool down some." Bailey swiped the sweaty curls away from her neck.

Raven signaled the waitress with a swirl of her wrist over the table. "Bailey, don't look now, but there are two guys at that end table next to the dartboard. They may have some potential. Wait…wait…okay, look now, tell me what you think. What are they doing?"

Bailey "causally" peered over her shoulder. "Well, if one of them is wearing a dark green shirt, they're coming toward us."

"Okay. I'll take the guy in the dark green. He kind of has a young Brad Pitt thing going on. You think? You can have the guy in gray, although he's cute too. Damn."

The loud music stomped all over Young Brad Pitt's suave introduction. But Raven gobbled up the attention like a starving lioness.

The second round of drinks followed. Now, Bailey remembered why she hated going to clubs, single or not. The smile plastered on her face made her jaw ache because it wasn't real. The image of a cooing Candice standing between Tony's legs was somehow messing up her night.

She downed the next drink in one continuous gulp. Don—Dan, shit, whatever gray shirt's name was, didn't seem like such a bad guy, and he could dance. *Doug! His name is Doug.* There was something likable about a guy with good moves.

Bailey's monumental level of dancing energy

came to a screeching halt when Ed Sheeran's *Perfect* took over the dancefloor. Slow dancing was meant to be with someone you know, not the guy you just met. "Oh, I think I need a break."

"You sure? It's a great song." Doug extended his hand.

Bailey eyed his hand. *Definitely sure.* "Yeah." She fanned her face and headed to the table. He followed her. "My gosh. I haven't danced this much in a long time." Her small talk was a little rusty. "It's gotten crowded, hasn't it?" She scooped a piece of ice from one of the empty glasses and popped it into her mouth. All she needed to do now was ask him about the weather. *Augh.*

"Yeah." With the music so loud, Doug leaned closer to speak in her ear. "Bailey, if you want, we can get out of here. Maybe go somewhere else that isn't so loud."

His thumb stroked the side of her wrist, triggering a warm sensation in the pit of her belly. *Whoa, whoa, whoa.* Warning bells kicked in. Bailey eased her hand away from his. "I should find Raven."

"Your friend is gone, sweetheart. She and Mitch left ten minutes ago, but she made me promise to give you a ride home. I don't mind, really." A spry smile lifted either side of his lips.

Even at her current level of inebriation, Bailey felt that he was telling the truth. *Of course Raven left.* "Listen—Doug, I need to use the restroom."

"Yeah, sure." He turned sideways, giving her room to squeeze around him. "I'll order us some more drinks."

"That'd be great."

The lights in the bathroom were stark white and a huge contrast to the subdued lighting in the club. They hurt her brain. Two girls stood in front of the mirrors, dabbing fresh lipstick onto puckered lips. They wanted to be here and had probably looked forward to it all week long. Excitement bellowed off them in waves.

Bailey stepped up to the mirror and eyed her reflection. The club was packed with people, but she'd never felt so alone. Fishing her cell phone from her clutch, she called Raven. *Just to be sure.*

After four rings, the phone picked up. Instead of the expected greeting, Bailey caught a muffled grunt, a man's groan, and then clumsy handling of the phone before the call dropped.

"Well, that was disgusting." *Great, now what am I going to do?* Kayla! *Yes, yes, yes.* It took three frantic swipes to locate her number in contacts.

"Hello?" said a voice laden with sleep.

Bailey had no idea what time it was. "Raven picked up some guy and left me here."

"Bailey?"

"Oh, hey, yeah, it's me. I'm at Gitters, Jeepers, Jammer's, something like that, and Doug—Doug is friends with a young Brad Pitt, the guy Raven left with– and Doug wants to take me home. I…I mean, he offered to give me a ride home. Not that I'd do anything stupid— I just don't know him, and well…you know, I've seen Dateline. I wouldn't go home with a guy I just met…and… and I don't want him coming to the apartment. What if he doesn't want to leave? What if he expects something? Then what? He'd know where I live. He could even be a pervert. Not that he looks like a pervert, he's actually kind of cute, but he's not who I— want, I…mean, I don't want him. I should probably call an Uber."

"Are you done?"

"Rambling—yes, I think so."

Kayla released a long, slow breath into the phone. "Okay. Don't call an Uber. Just stay where you are."

"You're coming? You know where I am?"

"Yes, Bailey. I'm pretty sure you're at Jabbers. I'll get there as soon as I can."

"Yes, Jabbers, that's it. Thank you. Thank you so much, Kayla. You're fabulous."

"Yes, yes, I know."

"And sweet. I'm so glad you're my friend. I can't wait to see you. Goodbye." Bailey crammed her phone back inside the clutch, dangling from her wrist. Everything was going to be okay now. Kayla was coming to her rescue. Bailey entered a stall and peed for a really long time. Her relief was twofold.

Leaving the bathroom, Bailey's eyes took a few seconds to readjust to the different lighting. A sea of people made a wall in front of her. But Bailey maneuvered her way through and made it back to the table…and…a waiting Doug.

Handsome Doug, wearing a perfectly pressed gray shirt and navy slacks, beamed with delight when he spotted her. And as promised, he'd ordered more drinks.

"You mentioned that you liked tequila. I hope this is okay."

Knowing that Kayla was coming gave her permission to be a little reckless. "As a matter of fact, I do like tequila." After the second shot, she ordered another gin and tonic. "Oh, I love this song. Let's dance." She took Doug's hand, feeling rambunctious.

Two, three, or maybe it was five songs later, the dance floor became overly congested. She felt like the ball inside a pinball machine.

"Hey, it's—" Doug gripped her elbow, pointing over his shoulder toward the table. His mouth continued to move, but she heard nothing.

"I can't hear you, but let's sit down for a while."

At the table, she hopped onto a stool like she was playing a game of musical chairs. *Safe.* A group of people parading past forced Doug closer. His hip pressed against her knees as they shimmied by. Warm fuzzies settled over her. If he stood between her legs, there'd be more room. *Take that, Karma.* Doug's hand landed on her outer thigh as two more people squeezed by.

She looked at his hand. *At least he wants me.* How long has it been? "I must be horny."

Doug leaned closer. "What? Did you say something?"

Shit. "No, no, don't mind me." Her impaired gaze landed on Doug again or tried to. His lips were thick, and his smile—was vaguely attractive. He was tall with interesting eyes and dark hair. If she squinted real hard, he'd look just like, *No, don't go there.*

Too late, the drunken blur took hold.

…and Bailey let it.

Doug's face slowly transformed into the features that she wanted them to be. Fictitious, *Tony* lowered his head, seeking her lips.

Fueled by the fantasy, Bailey's hands landed on his shoulders, and she delved into the kiss—then— nothing. The body against her—gone. Replaced by some kind of bizarre commotion in the space right in front of her? What was going on?

Doug reappeared beside the table next to theirs. "Whoa, man. What's your deal?"

How did he get over there? Bailey was so confused, and her view was semi-blocked.

"Bailey, honey, come on."

Bailey recognized that pixie voice beside her. "Kayla!" Her magical friend appeared from thin air. "You came."

"Of course I did." Kayla helped her down from the barstool. "Okay, I think she's got all her stuff. Let's go."

The obstacle blocking her view spun and took her other arm. She must be drunk because this person also turned into Tony. Only this version held his arm up in front of her like a protective barricade from the crowd as he shuffled her toward the exit.

The doors opened, but the brisk night air did nothing to help clear her head. She was beyond that. Her brain stumbled and tripped almost as much as she did.

Halfway across the parking lot, Bailey wiggled or—squirmed from their grip. "Wait, wait. You are Tony?" She planted her feet. "Why, why are *you* here, in actual, in person?" The ground shifted, and she countered with two steps forward and one back. It wasn't so much to remain standing, but to find her balance on the moving ocean of blacktop.

Tony crossed his arms. The stern look on his face made three little lines across his forehead. *Damn.* Bailey dubbed this as his serious face. She had the urge to run her finger over the lines to soothe them away.

His brows gathered more. "She called me."

Bailey's gaze bounced toward Kayla. "Why? Why would you call *him*?"

"I didn't want you puking in my car. I just had it cleaned."

"I...wouldn't puke in your car." The statement contained a hefty amount of confidence, even though Bailey guessed—that they knew it was a promise she might not be able to keep. The countdown for that event clocked in at least two hours ago. Her dizzy gaze ricocheted back to Tony's. "So, you want me puking in your spiffy expensive truck, or is it your fancy car. I'd feel really bad if I puked in your car."

"No, Bailey." His chin wavered, full of disappointment. "What the fuck are you doing?"

A bubbly laugh escaped. Bailey hadn't heard him drop the "F" bomb before. Her laugh garbled, wondering why that was so funny. And why was he so upset? Pinching her brows, she also tried putting serious lines across her forehead. *Is it working?* Her fingers trailed over her forehead before pushing back her hair. There, now she could see him better—and drink him in.

Tony had on dark jeans and a navy zip-up sweatshirt. A tiger's eye necklace dangled on his bare chest. Either he was wearing a V-neck, or he wasn't wearing a shirt underneath the hoodie. Yum. He looked as tempting as she'd ever seen him.

The resonating music from inside the club thumped inside her head. *Damn you, Tony.* "This...this is your fault." Bailey shook a finger at all three Tonys.

"Me?" he said defensively. "Jesus, you are so drunk."

"Maybe I am." *Thanks to you.*

Kayla offered him a sympathetic look. "I'll follow you to the apartment."

"No, I got this. You can go home."

Bailey shooed her away with both hands. "Yeah, you go on. You go ahead and leave in your just-cleaned car."

Kayla disappeared in between the parked cars with an elfin laugh. "Have a good time. I'm sure she's not the only drunk you'll have on your hands tonight."

"Come on." Tony steered Bailey toward his truck. Opening the passenger door, he practically hissed through clenched teeth. "I didn't think you were like this."

His words slapped Bailey in the face the same as a cold, wet rag. She didn't have to be completely sober or drunk to know *what or who* he was talking about. "Like this? You mean like them?"

"Just—just get in."

"No, no, no, you mean those prima-donnas… Shawna, Desiree, Raven—and…" the name formed on the tip of her tongue, and if she had been sober, she might've been able to stop, but she wasn't. "Candice."

His shoulders flexed. "No, that's not what I said. And you barely know Candice."

Bailey guffawed—openly; it grew into a giant boisterous laugh. "Yeah, sure, she's nothing like her friends." The parking lot shifted under her feet again. She sidestepped the wave and regained her balance. "But, hey, whatever helps you sleep at night."

Tony's head jerked sideways. "We sleep just fine."

"Of course you do. Meanwhile, the bartender in Alexandria probably knows all of them."

"What?" he chided. "Never mind, Bailey. I should just leave your frisky little ass here."

"Do what you want. I'll just have Don, no wait," Bailey corrected herself. "Doug.

"Is that what you really want, Bailey, that guy in there?" He pointed to the bar.

Bailey's self-control, or lack thereof, flat-lined. "No." She teetered forward and ran the tip of her finger up the middle of his exposed chest, giving the precious stone on his necklace a little flick. "He kind of looked like you." She inhaled with a sigh. "God, you always smell so good." Reveling in his luscious scent, her lids lowered. *I could just lap you up.* Her eyes opened directly to his penetrating gaze. Did she accidentally say that last part aloud? "Oh, crap?"

"Bailey, I—"

"Aw crap." Scrambling by him, her body heaved beyond the front of the truck. She flung herself toward a row of bushes lining the curb as the first of many waves hit.

She vaguely recalled car horns blowing from the passing traffic as she shamefully and violently called for Mr. O'Roarke, "The puke man."

J. ALISON COLE

Chapter Ten

Early Sunday morning, Tony backed out of the garage. Candice was sleeping off her Saturday night outing. He had no reason to wake her. She made it clear she was not interested in going with him to the car show in Leesburg. He'd have a better time taking his best friend anyway.

Tony pressed the button to close the garage door and texted Max.

Tony: **Rise and shine, Mother Fucker, be there in fifteen minutes. Be ready**.

Max lived in a development of newer townhomes between Centreville and Chantilly. His phone pinged with Max's reply.

Max: **Ready as a fucking racehorse.**

He laughed to himself. "And we're off."

Driving due east into the morning sun, Tony donned his sunglasses. The mild overnight chill was almost gone, promising a beautiful Spring day for the show, which meant he could take the top down on the Mustang. What better way to show off a convertible? The chrome was shining, the interior was spotless, and the hum of the engine was like music to his ears. It was the coolest fuckin' car ever made.

Tony pulled into the space outside Max's house and tapped the horn. Only once because of the early hour. "Not much of a racehorse." After another two minutes, Max finally bounded out of his front door.

"Aw, man. I thought for sure, you'd have the top down."

"Yeah, we will. I need to stop by the shop to get the photo out of my office."

"The one of you and Aaron? I like that photo."

"Yeah, that's the one. I want to set it next to the sign that lists all the specs for the car."

Max rubbed his hand along the armrest. "I remember this was a real piece of shit when you guys first got it."

"Yeah, it was. Took some work to get it here, but it was worth it." Max had an appreciation for the car almost as much as him.

Ten minutes later, they turned into the industrial park and wove through the empty maze to get to Ajak's. Bailey's Audi was parked out front. Tony pulled into the space next to it.

"Looks like somebody is putting in for some overtime." Max pointed to Bailey's car.

"Na. Bailey has an art show with her friend. She needed the space." Tony glanced at Max. "Put the top down while I get the photo."

"You want me to do it by myself?" Max whined.

"Fine. We can do it when we get to Leesburg. Stay here. I'll only be a minute."

Muffled music thumped from inside the building. Tony unlocked the front door to the sound of classic Maroon 5. No way would she hear the front bell. Intrigued, he passed his office to sneak a peek inside the shop.

Bailey had three canvases propped against the back wall. She was painting and dancing on the large canvas in the middle. Some curly ringlets had escaped the pile on top of her head. And damn if she didn't look searing hot wearing a tiny orange tank top and cutoff jean shorts. Her weekend attire was way different from how she looked the other night, but equally sexy—but then, there was that one pair of jeans that fit the curve of her ass just right.

"What the fuck, dude?" Max joined Tony in the

center of the hallway.

"Are you ever going to learn to listen?"

"Depends." Max caught sight of Bailey and opened his mouth, preparing to yell.

Tony stopped him. "Don't. We shouldn't disturb her. She looks like she's in a groove." Subsequently, he rather enjoyed watching the way she *painted*. Each time she leaned away from the canvas, her shoulders rolled, and her hips swirled in time with the music. He'd seen how much she liked to dance the other night as memories from then surged to the front of his thoughts.

****

He pulled his phone from the front pocket of his hoodie. A text from Kayla wanting to know his whereabouts.

Tony: ***Yeah, I'm here.***

Kayla: ***Good. Do you see her?***

Tony: ***Thumbs up emoji.***

Kayla: ***Okay, I'll be there soon.***

Tony: ***Stop pissing around.***

Yeah, he'd spotted Bailey the moment he entered Jabbers. Frankly, she was hard to miss in a sexy little blue skirt and heels that showed off her legs. Her hair was down and a mass of shiny ringlets. It was also the first time he'd seen her in full-fledged makeup. It was a different look for her, even though she was pretty, with or without. He found a spot against the wall that gave him a clear view of her. Tipsy or not, the girl clearly liked to dance. He could have watched her for hours. But after the dance floor got crowded, she headed back to her table. A guy followed, sniffing after her like a dog. The sheer number of empty glasses and lime wedges explained a lot. She did say that she liked tequila. Thank god Kayla got there when she did because the guy from the club—the dick was making his move.

It might've been the lights, but at that point everything turned red. The son-of-a-bitch was all over her.

Once he shuffled her outside, it was worse than he thought. Bailey wasn't just three sheets to the wind. It was more like seven. After blaming him for her sobriety, she proceeded to retch, swear like a sailor, and laugh like a loon between dry heaves. It was hard to stay mad when she was throwing up her guts. Getting her in the truck, she kept mumbling something about kittens. He didn't understand what that meant until later, because by the time they reached her apartment, she found her second wind, hopping onto his back for a piggyback ride. It 'was' the easiest way to get her inside.

He trotted her into Candice's old room, to keep her from bouncing off the walls.

He set her down. "Okay, you should be all set now." Bailey kicked off her shoes—and shimmied out of her skirt quicker than Houdini. "Whoa, what are you doing?"

"I need to get changed." Her top was three-quarters of the way off when one of her earrings looped into the lace and trapped her arms with only her hands and the top portion of her curls showing.

She continued to pull. "Stop, stop. You're going to fall and...or rip your ear." He corralled her against the door. "Just stand still. I almost have it."

"Oh, you definitely have it."

He couldn't see her face but her laugh—very drunk. "Shush, maybe you shouldn't say anything else." The silver loop slid loose from the lace. "There. You're free." The next thing he knew, the lacy top smacked him square in the face. As he pulled the material away, Bailey paraded by him in a baby blue demi-bra with matching panties. Both had a tiny yellow bow right in the center. A sight which required a shower as soon as he got home.

Her arms angled back to unhook the bra. "Hold on now. You're...naked enough—and my well won't handle that." He grabbed a shirt off the end of the bed. "Hey, this is my shirt from the other day." It took him three tries to get it over her head, and for a second, he understood what mothers go through trying to dress toddlers.

Her hands ran over her breasts and down the front of the shirt. "I like this shirt. It smells like you." She fell back onto her bed, curled up, and—purred?

"Ah, 'Drunken Sorry Kitten,' got it." He finagled the covers over her, but she wrestled an arm free and looped a finger through his necklace.

"Aren't you going to kiss me goodnight?"

"Shush, just go to sleep now." She turned over on her side, purred again, and within minutes, she was out. It took him five minutes before he could move.

****

Tony would've given anything to kiss her. *Absolutely anything.* But it would have been wrong on his part for so many reasons. One, even though she was incredibly sexy and very appealing, she had just thrown up. Two, he was positive she wouldn't remember any of it, and three, technically, he *was* still with Candice. For now, at least.

"Come on, Max, we need to get going." He shoved Max toward the front door and started toward his office. The two steps gave him a better view of the large painting in the center. Broad strokes of blues for an open sky, purples on the distant ridge, and lush greens accented by the mixture of pinks and white—mountain laurel. He'd know his meadow anywhere. An odd feeling washed over him.

Tony snatched the photo of Arron from the wall

and locked the front door.

Max glared from the passenger seat as he climbed behind the wheel. "You're a real asshole. You know that?"

"Gee, thanks, Max."

"No, I mean it. If you're not going to hit that, then you should let me."

Max had been his best friend since sixth grade, but as far as he was concerned, that wasn't going to happen. Tony returned the glare with a sneer. "You stay the hell away from her."

Max fidgeted in the bucket seat. "Why?"

"Because if you mess this up for me, she'll leave, and she's really helping the business."

Max shook his head, laughing. "I call bullshit! Just admit it, This has nothing to do with your business."

"Of course it does."

"No. The way I see it, you want to fuck her, but you can't, so no one else can either?"

"That's not true."

"Oh yeah? You tell me, in all honesty, that you haven't thought about tapping that." Max straightened his legs and winced.

Tony offered Max a smirk and a tilt of his head. Max would never believe him if he tried to lie. It was kind of a given.

"See." Max planted his feet on the floor and lifted his hips.

"What the hell is wrong with you? Why are you so fidgety?"

"If you must know, my pecker started getting hard, and I think it's bent." Max fished for the tab of his zipper.

Tony turned the key to the Mustang, and the engine roared to life. "You pull that thing out, now or anywhere around Bailey, and so help me God, a bent dick is going to be the least of your worries."

Chapter Eleven

As Monday mornings went, Bailey had never dreaded one as much as this. She wouldn't have an appetite for real food for the next week. Which was fine since she'd be feasting on crow and making apologies. Her self-respect had never taken such a blow, debasing herself and her standards. She'd swapped spit with a stranger, whose last name she couldn't remember, openly insulted people who may not have entirely deserved it, and crossed the line that would be hard to come back from. *Damn, tequila.*

And those were things she *did* remember. Everything got fuzzy right after the parking lot. But there was one good thing to come from this. Tony would never look at her with the same twinkle in his eyes. He thought she was like—them.

She spent a good portion of the night before combing the internet for blue high heels like the ones Raven let her borrow. They didn't survive. For Kayla, she picked out a small planter to go on the corner of her desk. For Tony, car wipes and an air freshener. Of course, it was lame as far as apologies go, but at least it matched how she felt—lame.

Arriving at Ajak's well before eight o'clock, her penance launched the moment she pulled into the parking lot. Both Kayla and Tony beat her to work. "How? Damn it."

Bailey entered the front office and found Tony leaning against the newly revamped counter. His conversation with Kayla ended abruptly as he pushed away and straightened to his full height. Looking him in the eye required more fortitude than she could muster just yet. Kayla stood up from her chair.

Here goes nothing. "Since you're both here now, I'll do this together." Bailey took a shaky breath. "I don't normally drink to that extreme, but that doesn't excuse my behavior. Thank you for helping me the other night." She handed Kayla a gift bag holding the planter. She picked out the one with a tiny fairy sitting on the edge of the pot. "I know it's not much, but I'm sorry. It was late, and I probably could've just called an Uber. You didn't have to come, but you did. Thank you." She angled toward Tony but kept her focus fixed on the new tan Berber rug. Seeing his *disappointment* would level her. "Tony, I owe you an extra apology." She offered him the bag holding the air freshener and car wipes. "I'm sorry for...the mess I may have left in your truck and the horrible things I said about—Candice. You're right. I don't know her. I was completely out of line."

"Bailey, look at me."

She met Tony's gaze and expected to see disgust or resentment, even his serious face. Instead, he wore the crest of a smile and a glint in the sage part of his green eyes. *This is going to be so hard.*

Kayla maneuvered around her desk, holding something behind her back. Today, the hot pink highlights in her hair matched her leggings. "We got you something, too." After a fluttering laugh, she presented Bailey with—a mini bottle of *Tequila.*

Bailey's stomach gurgled from the lingering effects of her hangover. "Gee. Thanks, guys. This is— great and totally...unnecessary." Her voice flattened.

Kayla broke into a fit of laughter. "Hey, what are friends for?"

The smile on Tony's face nearly sent her to heaven. Then he cocked his head to the side and added a wink.

He stepped closer. "Now that that's out of the way, we can get to work. Bailey, I laid a few new work orders on your desk. When you get to them, come see me. I have a sample to show you." He walked away.

Kayla pushed Bailey's hair away from her neck. "No earrings today?"

"What?" Kayla had the goofiest look on her face. "No, why?"

Kayla's giggle sounded crazy as she walked back to her desk. "No reason."

Bailey released an extra-long breath. They may have forgiven her, but forgetting his smile and forgiving herself would take a bit longer. She strolled into her office and positioned the bottle of Tequila next to the monitor on her desk. It'd make an excellent reminder of how *not* to act. She spied the new stack of work orders and shuffled through them. From the looks of it, Tony must've attended a car show over the weekend. Four of the seven new work orders were for signs people used at events like that.

Bailey crossed the hall and tapped on the open door of Tony's office. "You said you had a sample?"

Tony had his back to her, hanging a photograph on the wall behind his desk. He adjusted the corner one last time before turning around.

Bailey had seen the photo before but had never really taken the time to examine it thoroughly. She stepped around his desk for a better look. Tony's pre-restoration Mustang with all the dents and rust. Leaning against the hood, a much younger Tony and a man with very, *very* similar features. "This is you and your brother."

"Yeah, that's Aaron and me." Tony touched the corner of the frame.

"You look like him."

"So, I've been told." He studied the image. "Aaron and I spent a lot of weekends together. You can't see it in the photo, but there are no tires on the rear of the car. He taught me all about engines and gave it to me when I got my license." Tony went silent for a brief moment before pointing to a sign on his desk. "This is the sign I use at car shows. It lists all the vehicle specs, besides the year, make, and model. You can use it as a sample for the others. If you find some of the information missing, let me know. I also have pictures for you to use. I'll send them in a bit."

"Jordan's brother, Alan, has a Mach 1 fastback. I made a sign like this for him a while back. He was working on a '72 GTO Shelby about a year ago, but I don't know if he ever finished it. He needed a carburetor, but original parts for those older cars are getting hard to come by.

"You sound like you know a little something about cars?"

"Out of necessity mostly, you've seen what I drive, haven't you? The TT is only a four-cylinder, and it's simple enough that I can change the oil myself if I have to—unlike the cars they make today. But that's about all I can do."

He huffed. "Aaron would have loved you." Tony raised a finger. "And just so you know, he had a thing for Tequila too."

****

She'd get to the drafts for the car show signs in a day or two, maybe sooner. She had all the material to prep for the Porter Plumbing vans and several signs for a local builder to put together first. Having Builders for clients worked out great. Builders usually had three or four developments in progress at any given time and always needed signage. Tony spent his day working in the shop with Laz, cutting, sanding, and painting the five, four by eight temporary entrance signs for Carson Builders.

The best part of being busy was that Bailey totally crushed her previous record—by two hours and thirty-six minutes. It came to a crashing halt when Tony strolled into her office. She'd just finished making the cut pattern for the antique store sign.

"Augh, that's exactly what I need. Hey, you wouldn't happen to have the pattern for the Karate Studio, would you?"

"Not yet, but I can make it now." Bailey opened the file on her computer.

"I'm glad that I caught you. I want to check one of the dimensions." Tony leaned over her shoulder and hit a few keys on the keyboard. "Could you make that thirty-six inches instead of thirty-eight?" He pointed to the screen at the cutout overlay of the abstract silhouette rendering of a flying kick.

A hint of Tony's masculine scent hit her like a drug. Being the addict that she was, she inhaled to secretly get her fix. "I can make it any size you want. Those two inches won't affect the design."

"Great, go ahead and make it thirty-six inches. I found an odd-shaped piece of sign material from that stack you salvaged." He sat on the edge of the table next to her. "Otherwise, I'd have to cut into a whole new piece. Win, win."

"That's great. The pattern will only take a few minutes." She clicked some keys on the keyboard as he hovered beside her. When she glanced up, she caught him eyeing the rear of the room.

"I see you got some painting done this weekend."

She'd stacked her paintings next to the file cabinet in the back of the room. "Yes, a few pieces." What's with the odd grin on his face?

"Mind if I take a closer look?" Bailey lifted her shoulders. "Sure." It didn't matter to her.

Tony carefully spread them out along the far wall before stepping back. Bailey had to admit, she was pleasantly surprised with her post-hangover paintings. The large canvas turned out better than she would've expected.

"How did you get it so perfect?" Tony pointed toward the big painting.

"I used photos for reference and then added—*the things the rest of you don't see.*" She chuckled, mocking the words he used to describe her.

Tony spotted her camera on the desk and the pile of photos next to it. He reached for the pictures.

"Oh, may I?"

"Sure."

He shuffled through the photographs from their hike. The snickering sound he made tickled a spot inside her torso. Overall, the day of the hike was in her top five of best days ever. He flipped to another photo and studied it longer than he had any of the others. He glanced at her with a condensed, quick inspection before scanning the last two pictures.

"Your paintings are wonderful, Bailey. I'm impressed. How much are you going to sell the big one for?"

"I want to keep it, but I have to take it to the show to meet my quota, thanks to Quin. I'll put some outrageous price on it so no one will buy it."

One corner of his lips lifted into a smile. "What if someone really wants it?"

"In all honesty, I don't expect to sell anything. I'm doing this mostly for Quin."

"You might be surprised. I don't think that you're

fully aware of your talents."

The respect in his voice caused her mind to go blank for a few seconds. "Thank you. Quin keeps telling me I need to learn how to take a compliment."

"Really? I'm sure you get your share and then some, and not only about your artwork." He slathered her with a double punch of his signature charm *and* charisma before topping it off with his not-so-innocent flirty smile. Her shields took a direct hit. Odds of surviving another— without making an idiot of herself, not so good. She bolstered her defenses. *Flirt all you want, means nothing.*

The operating hum from the plotter went silent when the pattern for the Karate shop finished. Tony took the pattern off the machine as she restacked her paintings.

Out of the three paintings she completed over the weekend, *The Meadow* was her favorite for a lot of reasons, but none she could readily share—with him, anyway.

When she turned, Tony was already headed back to the shop. He'd taken the karate pattern but left the one for the antique shop sitting on her desk. "Oh, hey." She didn't catch him in time.

Bailey grabbed the pattern and followed him to the shop.

Tony glanced over his shoulder and headed for the radio. He cranked the volume on "Payphone" by Maroon 5 and shimmied toward her in time with the music. She held the pattern toward him only to have it snatched from her fingers and tossed over his shoulder. His hand came back down and extended toward her. The music must've drowned out all the warning bells because her hand landed in his.

He danced them toward the stack of now dry, painted boards. She might've guessed Tony danced well, as in really well.

Reason #412.

Shit.

Completely in sync, he took one end of the board, and she took the other. With a few bumps and grinds along the way, they moved the first sign blank to the closet worktable.

Once the chorus started, he gathered her close for a whirling dip. Not once, but twice. The warmth of his breath washed over her face, and for a fleeting moment, it all felt so real. So right.

But then she remembered it wasn't.

"Let's see what else you got." She swirled and circled around him. "Are you up for a dance-off?" A little distance was probably safer for her.

"A dance-off? Really?"

"Hey, if you don't have the moves—"

"Oh, I have the moves."

Lazlo stepped onto two crates. "I'll be the judge."

Bailey went first and threw in some rag-time arm swings at the end, just for fun. Tony doubled over, laughing. But lifted his finger, determined not to be outdone. He shimmied, swayed, and rolled his hips, and for his finale, he added a pretend tap dance number.

He could be as silly as her. *Reason #413*.

She turned to Lazlo, who shrugged, refusing to pick a winner. Instead, he started lip-syncing with Wiz Khalifa. Midway through his rap, the music ended abruptly.

All eyes turned toward the radio. Standing beside it, Kayla, fuming with her hands perched on her hips. "I guess you guys have fun like this all day, and I'm out front all by myself. That's just great. Thanks a lot, guys."

Tony crossed the room and twisted the volume back up. Ignoring her protest, he circled around her, luring her to the center of the room.

"No, no, no, too late." The sound of her high-pitched giggles only fortified her fairy-like statice.

Bailey laughed so hard she could barely breathe, and she almost missed the sound of the bell above the front door. She darted up the hall and found a delivery man holding a relatively long skinny box. He shoved a clipboard toward her for a signature.

A florist?

Kayla and Tony entered the room just as the delivery man walked out.

"What is it?" Kayla asked, semi-breathless.

Bailey placed the box on the corner of the counter. "I don't know."

Tony plucked the card from the ribbon, but Kayla snatched it from his hand. "Don't be so nosey. I can almost guarantee that it's not for you." Kayla read the card aloud. "Bailey, I can't wait to see you again. It's signed, Doug Shellman."

"Shit." Bailey almost fell over.

Kayla handed her the card. "Looks like it's for you. Let's see what handsome Doug got you."

"That's okay. I'll open it later."

Kayla shoved the box toward Bailey. "Don't be silly." She yanked on the ribbon and pulled the top off. It was all Bailey could do to keep from dropping everything. "Augh, look! Peach and orange roses. You know what they mean, don't you?"

"They're pretty?" Bailey had no idea.

"Well, yeah, but different colored roses mean different things. Orange roses mean *desire,* and peach roses mean he wants to *seal the deal*, as it were."

"That's bull." Tony crossed his arms and leaned against the corner where the hallway started.

"No, it's not. If you don't believe me, you can look it up." Kayla gasped. "Oh, I know, maybe you could take him to your friend's wedding."

Bailey placed the lid back onto the box. "No, no, that's not going to happen. I'm going to Quin's wedding alone."

"Oh, come on, he didn't seem *that* bad."

"No, that's not it."

"Well, you still shouldn't go to the wedding by yourself. Maybe Max would go with you."

"No." Tony and Bailey blurted the response at the same time. Her gaze locked with his for a second.

Bailey scrambled to put the ribbon back around the box in a vain attempt to make the flowers disappear. "No," she repeated. "Here, you keep the flowers if you want." She shoved the box toward Kayla. "I've got some more work to finish up."

Kayla hollered up the hallway after her. "But Bailey, he desires *you*."

Bailey plopped into the chair in front of her computer. Her thoughts spiraled all over the place—until the stack of photos caught her eye. She remembered how Tony paused at one particular image. She grabbed the pile and flipped to the third picture from the back. Her gut twisted already knowing what photo it would be— and it was.

****

The next day, Bailey assembled three of the 4'x 8' signs for Carson Builders before lunch. With rain expected the rest of the week, Tony decided to get as many outside installs off his list as he could. She offered to help, but he took Lazlo instead.

In the shop, Bailey painted the first coat of dark green paint onto the 'Butler Antiques' sign. The distinct ding from the bell on the front door chimed. After a minute, dainty heels clicked against the concrete floor and grew louder.

"Hi, Bailey."

Bailey lifted the wet brush into the air. "Oh," an icy chill stabbed into the side of her head. "Hey, Candice." *Aw shit*. She'd said some nasty things about this woman and her friends, which he most likely told her all about. "Tony's not here. He should be back soon, though."

"Yeah, Kayla said." Candice took a cautious step forward, eyeing the wet paint.

As a pharmaceutical rep, Candice looked every bit the professional that her job required. She had on a burgundy pencil dress with coordinating heels. Free-flowing waves of dark brunette hair reached to her waist and shimmered like satin. The woman was absolutely stunning.

Bailey's attire, on the other hand, knowing that she would be painting today, consisted of a plain t-shirt and a pair of designated work jeans. Work jeans meant smears, flecks, specks, and paint splashes of every color on the paint chart. Standing next to Candice, Bailey felt like a vagrant.

"I'm going to wait out front, but I wanted to say hi." She paused. "Raven said the two of you had a wild time the other night. I should've come with you guys instead."

"Uh, huh." Bailey waited for the other shoe, or in this case—stiletto, to drop. But nothing happened, leading her to believe that Candice was either a great actress or Tony never mentioned the nasty things she said. And since Candice didn't seem the least bit catty, Bailey felt like even a bigger bitch for misjudging her.

However, no matter how much she tried, Bailey still found it incredibly hard to like Candice—even a little.

Twenty minutes later, Tony and Lazlo returned,

and Candice revealed the reason for her "surprise visit." She'd booked a short trip to Cancun to make up for last week's canceled plans, and the fight they had.

Tony would be gone for the rest of the week.

****

That night, Bailey entered her apartment door carrying two bags from the grocery store. She had a craving for Moose Tracks ice cream. To her surprise, her roomies were home, and they had company. *Oh yay.* Apparently, Candice wanted to show the girls her travel attire.

Every time Candice held up an article of clothing, the coven oohed and ahhed. Bailey refused to look up. Listening was bad enough. From the breakfast bar in the kitchen, Bailey went straight for the ice cream.

"And this is my new bathing suit."

Her eye twitched from the scathing octave of Candice's shrill voice. Heck, she'd rather have a brain freeze than endure that for any length of time. She ripped the lid off the Ben and Jerry's and grabbed a spoon from the drawer.

"It's so skimpy, Candy. Tony won't be able to keep his hands off of you." Shawna's voice had the astute sound of authority that made her doubly intimidating. Maybe that's why she worked for an attorney.

"I'm hoping this will heat things back up."

The spoon stopped halfway to Bailey's mouth. *What?*

"He hasn't been himself lately. It's been so long since we...did anything." Between the pitch and the pout in Candice's voice, her entire body twitched.

Desiree, the other roommate, was a beautiful African-American woman with short-cropped hair. She worked as an administrator for a hospital and modeled part-time.

Bailey's gaze begrudgingly lifted when Desiree pulled an olive green dress from one of the bags. "I'd tell you not to wear a bra with this, but then no one would be able to keep their hands off you."

Bailey shoved both grocery bags into the fridge, whether the contents needed to be there or not. The fridge, basically empty, had plenty of cauldron space. She left the kitchen to eat her ice cream in her room.

"I don't know what it is," Candice said. "It's like his mind is somewhere else."

Shawna and Desiree cast their evil eye on her as she walked by. Raven just sat there with a weird smile on her face.

J. ALISON COLE

Chapter Twelve

Without Tony's presence as a constant distraction, Bailey accomplished her work unfettered. She and Lazlo had the third Porter Plumbing van finished by three thirty.

"That's good news, Bailey," said Mr. Porter. "I'll have someone bring the other three vans, and I also have two older ones I'd like to have redone to match these. If that's okay?"

"That'd be fine, Mr. Porter."

"Call me, Bill, and if possible, is there any way you could have them ready by Friday."

"Do you mean two days from now, Friday—or next Friday?"

"Actually, I'd really like to have them by this Friday. That's not a problem, is it?"

The gauntlet fell. "No, sir. Friday, I'll have them all done."

"Great, I'll be expecting your call."

Bailey hung up the telephone.

Kayla's eyes widened. "Did I just hear you right? He wants you to re-letter two existing vans on top of the last three? By *this* Friday."

Bailey shook her head, unable to find her voice.

"There's not enough time. What happened to the extra week? I know you work fast, but what if you can't finish them? Oh my God, what are we going to do?"

If Mr. Porter was the mogul everyone said he was, they had to get them done. And since Tony wasn't here, this was all on her. "I'll stay late and get here early. We don't really have another option." She wasn't about to let Tony or his reputation down.

"I don't think we even have enough material to do that many trucks, and the earliest it could get here is noon tomorrow. You can't possibly have enough time, even with Lazlo and me helping. And what about your art show? Isn't that this Saturday? Don't you have more painting to do?"

Bailey had wanted to use the next two nights to create two more pieces. She had seven framed and ready to go.

Shit.

Lazlo plopped into one of the rejuvenated front office chairs. "Call Dylan. I know he's not working anywhere yet."

Kayla picked at a gold thread in her sweater. "I'm not calling him. He was a jerk."

"Lazlo, I didn't think you got along with him." Bailey took the other seat.

"I get along with everyone, Bailey, can't you tell? I think this is something Tony would do."

A plan slowly developed, but she'd need Dylan's help to pull this off. "Do you think Dylan would start tomorrow? And no more half-ass stuff. These vans need to be perfect."

Lazlo took a moment. "Dylan got his feelings hurt. He thought he was a real artist. Don't get me wrong, he's not bad, just young and stupid. He could learn a lot from you if he's smart enough to listen. I think all he needed was someone to crack the whip." Lazlo's smile tugged on the scar next to his eye.

Bailey wasn't sure, but it sounded like Lazlo just called her a bitch in the right kind of way. She took a deep breath. Dylan quit because of her, and since Tony was off somewhere, putting his hands all over a braless Candice—

"I can do it." Bailey's gaze bounced from Kayla to Lazlo. "We can do this."

Ten minutes later, after a carefully worded

conversation with Dylan, he agreed to come back. Then Bailey tallied up the material they'd need for Kayla to place the order. Quin was her next call.

He picked up right away. "Are you ready for this weekend?"

"Kind of. I have seven pieces ready, and that's all I can get done. Quin, I know you have a full plate too, but I was hoping you could meet me tonight, halfway, of course, to pick up what I have ready."

His end of the phone went quiet for a brief moment. "It'll cost ya."

"Yeah, I know. IPA or Stella?"

"Surprise me."

"Thanks, I'll be in Uncle Frank's Tahoe."

****

The last inch of tacky transfer paper peeled away from the final line of copy. The previous two days felt like a warped version of Groundhog Day, applying the same graphics again and again. But now, Porter Plumbing's eighth van—was done. And they looked great.

Bailey straightened, stretching her shoulders and flexing the ache in her back. Working past midnight and arriving by six, didn't leave for a whole lot of sleep. She couldn't risk disappointing Tony again—at least not when it came to her work.

Lazlo slouched against his workbench. "That's it, the last one."

Dylan tapped Bailey's shoulder. "I should've asked for more money. And, if I'm being honest, I didn't think we could do it."

She held onto her grin. "We couldn't have done it without you, Dylan, but the money end isn't up to me."

Lazlo took a huge breath. "Dylan, back this van out, and I'll start the cleanup."

Kayla pranced into the shop. "I just called Bill to let him know we're all done. Here, take this. I figured today's Happy hour would be a little different." She handed Bailey a foam cup.

"What is it?" It looked like orange juice.

"Just drink it."

Bailey took a swig. It *was* orange juice with a hefty shot of coconut rum. "Wow. So this is what you keep in your desk with the Three Musketeers candy bars."

Kayla wiggled her eyebrows and took a sip. "I just talked to my brother too. He's on his way back. I told him what happened."

The coconut smell from the rum summoned an image of Tony, tanned and shirtless. Bailey gulped half the glass to make it go away. "What did he say?"

"He was upset, of course, that we didn't let him know what was going on sooner. He also asked about your art show, but I told him you worked it out with Quin."

"Quin and I are supposed to have an early breakfast tomorrow morning, that is if I wake up in time. I'm pooped." This time, she took a sip. "I'm driving to PA tonight. So, cheers, and no more of these."

Looking around the room, Kayla's bright smile faded. "Bailey. Thank you for being here and doing this. I know he doesn't act like it or say a lot sometimes, but this business means everything to Tony because of Aaron. We both know how special you are. Thanks again."

Bailey lifted her drink and scraped her foam cup against Kayla's. "Hey, what are friends for?"

****

Being in Pennsylvania, and hanging out with Quin at the art show felt like old times. It made the whirlwind of a weekend worth it, but seeing a few of her other friends—not so much. Everyone eagerly shared everything there was to know about Jordan and Michele and the trouble brewing in their relationship. She could've done without the drama.

Monday morning couldn't come soon enough. What a stark difference from her previous Monday. Walking through the door of Ajak's felt right in so many ways. She belonged here.

Sure, getting over her unrequited attraction for Tony was taking longer than she'd hoped, but *maybe* she'd get there with a little more time. If by a little more time meant the rest of eternity plus a day or two, then sure, why not. She had to try.

Kayla peeked into her office. New sky-blue tints accented her short-cropped hair. "Good morning."

"Good morning, yourself." The incessant need to see Tony tugged Bailey's gaze across the hallway. A stern breath ushered the weakness away.

Kayla's eyes followed the path of her unruly scan. "Tony's going to be a little late this morning. Well, later than usual, he had to do something, but I expect him here by noon."

"Oh. He probably needs to recover." Bailey meant it, in general, but her Freudian subconscious went straight to topless beaches, round beds with red satin sheets, and nights filled with heated sex. *Ugh, gross.* "You know where I'll be."

In order to meet the deadline for the Porter Plumber vans, she pushed all of her other jobs aside. She looked forward to the busy week ahead.

Just after lunch, she headed to the shop to finish up the sign for the antique shop sign. Real gold leaf could transform an ordinary sign into something stunning and memorable. Working with the delicate, thin sheets required a steady hand and a soft touch. The slightest rush of air or any sudden movement could rip the leaves apart, sending flakes into the air like glitter in a snow globe. Only this was very expensive glitter.

Bailey carefully lifted another sheet of the precious material when the atmosphere in the room crackled and the hairs on her arms lifted straight up. Without turning her head, her eyes scanned to the side.

Sure enough, leaning against the large bay door, Tony. How long had he been watching her? The edges of the gold sheet flapped. Bailey held her breath and carefully lowered the gold onto the tacky sizing. His footsteps echoed across the floor as she finished burnishing the precious metal into place. A contradictory calmness settled over her just knowing he was here, like all was right in the world somehow.

"So beautiful."

She uprighted and fell right into his tantalizing gaze. Through no fault of his own, she could swim and or drown in the way he looked at her sometimes. Either way, she was still doomed.

His gaze shifted to the sign, and she was free to doggy-paddle all she wanted.

Tony was tan before, but now his skin glowed a subtle shade darker. "How was your trip?" *Yah. No, no, no.* Why would she ask that? Hearing about Candice heating things back up in her skimpy bathing suit and that sexy olive dress was not something she wanted to even think about. *Great!* Now, that's all she was going to think about.

"It was hot."

Yeah, I bet.

He studied the sign some more. "How was the art show?"

"It went well as far as I know. Quin called me last

night to tell me I actually sold four pieces."

"Four—that's great. Do you know which ones?"

"I don't, but I'm guessing it's probably a few of the smaller ones. I'll check the website when I get time."

Tony's features went from glowing to resolute. "You really got a lot accomplished last week. Good call bringing Dylan back."

She nodded and laughed. "Aw shucks, it was nothing.

He laughed too, at first, but then squared his shoulders. "But seriously, thanks for all your hard work." His gaze caressed her entire face before landing on her lips. They tingled like she'd just smeared cinnamon Red Hots all over them.

Then he just—walked away, and Bailey hardly saw him the rest of the day or the one after that.

****

Tony strode into Bailey's office. "Here's your camera. I took pictures as you requested. The installation went off without a hitch."

"I'll bet Dylan was glad of that."

Tony snickered. "No, I was glad of that." He propped his backside against the edge of the table close to where she was working. "I think it's safe to say that Mr. Butler has the sharpest-looking Antique sign in all of northern Virginia, thanks to you. He loved it, Bailey."

"It turned out well, if I do say so myself. I might ride by there this evening." She scanned through the different pictures he'd taken. "I want to send some of these pictures to Quin."

Kayla stuck her head into the room. "Bailey. There's a guy out front asking for you by name."

Bailey's gaze flickered toward Tony before she could stop herself. He pushed away from the table and stood to his full height.

She set the camera down. "Is it that guy Doug?" Her voice was no more than a whisper.

Kayla shook her head.

Who then? Other than handsome Doug and Bill Porter, Bailey didn't know that many people from around here. Maybe it was Uncle Frank? Bailey veered into the hall toward the front office, and her feet nearly turned into cinder blocks when she saw the person standing by the front door.

Not in a million years did she expect to see Jordan Wentz in the reception area of Ajak's Signs. Not in a billion, trillion years.

Jordan's glowing blue eyes landed on her, and with a toss of his dirty blonde hair, he crossed the room and consumed her with a hug. "Hey, Babe."

Beyond stunned, Bailey's arms never moved from her sides. After spending almost a third of their lives together, she knew a great deal about him. She knew that he loved tomatoes but never on his sandwiches. He'd only eat them cut up with salt and pepper. She knew his favorite movie was *The Notebook*, although he'd never admit it to another living soul. She knew the scar on his chin needed five stitches after he got kicked in the face senior year at their high school's homecoming game. In fact, she knew every square inch of his body. After seven years together, how could she not? Their sex life had never been—dull. But, the one thing she couldn't figure out was why he was here—now.

"Jordan?"

A laugh rumbled from his lips. "Don't look so shocked."

Chapter Thirteen

Tony followed Bailey from her office. When she came to a sudden stop, so did he. A moment later, she darted out the front door with the guy she evidently *did* know. Kayla pushed her way around him to get back to her desk.

"Hey, Kayla." Tony nodded toward the door. "Who is that?" He mouthed the words.

"What does it matter to you?" Her tone seemed extra snotty. "He is hot, and oh look, he's on a motorcycle. That's—kind of sexy."

"So, you don't know who it is?"

"I didn't say that."

Tony turned, ready to walk away, but halted mid-stride. The guy had parked two spaces away from the front door, and from this angle, Tony had a perfect view of Bailey and her mystery man. The way the guy moved and touched her was subtle, even comfortable. It confirmed they were familiar in every sense of the word. She never flinched when he reached to push a stray curl away from her eyes, probably something he'd done a thousand times. "That's her ex-boyfriend."

"It would seem so, huh? It's impolite to stare, you know."

Tony eased back to the counter and planted himself against the edge. "I'm not. Just trying to make sure she's okay." His glance ricocheted between the door, Kayla, and the pestering hangnail on his pinky. "Hey, did you call…um?"

Kayla snipped impatiently. "Who? Who did you want me to call?"

"Um…that lady from… uh…look how she's smiling at him."

"Yeah. He's kind of dreamy. Don't you think?"

Tony huffed. "No."

Jordan sat sideways on the motorcycle and took Bailey's hands into his, pulling her into space between his feet.

If Tony's jaw locked, any harder, he might break a tooth.

A minute later, Jordan stood and draped himself around Bailey in a tight, *loving* embrace. "Son of a bitch—"

"Whoa! Where do you think you're going?" Kayla snapped.

Tony had taken two steps toward the door without realizing it. "Uh, nowhere." He spun and drew a long breath to clear his head. Seeing Bailey with Jordan bothered him more than he could put into words.

Kayla stood up from her chair and slid a piece of paper over the counter. "Here."

Tony read the bizarre note. "Follow the signs." It was something Aaron used to say and Kayla's favorite and annoying comeback for nearly everything. She even had it tattooed on her left shoulder. "What the fuck, Kayla? What does this have to do with anything?"

"You tell me."

The motorcycle rumbled to life. The door flew open, and Bailey rushed inside.

Thank God.

She raced straight into her office—a second later, she came back into the front room looking—a little indecisive. Finally, she spoke. "I may have changed my mind about going to Quin's wedding alone. Do...you have Max's number?"

Wtf? "Max? Bailey, you don't—"

"Of course I do." Kayla cut him off, snatched the note from his hand, and wrote down Max's phone number on the back—for Bailey.

"I may not call him. I…just don't know what I'm going to do yet.

Someone must've kicked him in the head—and nuts when he wasn't looking. He stomped into his office. The first thing he should do is call his best friend and forbid him from going anywhere with Bailey. Of course, it'd be an asshole move since Bailey had the right to see whomever she wanted. Anybody at all. *But Max? No way!—Or that dickhead from the club.* "Dammit!"

Tony bit at the hangnail on his pinky. It started to bleed and hurt like hell. He grabbed a tissue as Bailey reentered her workspace. He eased into the chair behind his desk and scooted a couple of inches to the right to see her better. She shoved the note in her rear pocket and went back to work.

Yeah, she knows it would be a mistake. Tony breathed a sigh of relief.

After five minutes, the bleeding stopped and he *almost* convinced himself that she wouldn't call Max. Problem solved—but then she leaned away from the keyboard. *Wait, what is she doing? Shit.* She retrieved the note from her pocket and held it briefly before tossing it down. *Phew—wait. Oh crap.* It barely landed before Bailey plucked it off the desk and unfolded it. *Aw man!* She eyed the number and then turned the note over to see Kayla's message to him. *Follow the signs.* She rolled her eyes and chuckled.

"Thanks a lot, Sis, for that tidbit of irony." He spoke—to himself and the walls around him. "And damn, she's reaching for her phone—and now she's dialing— Max's *fucking* number." A low growl hissed through his clenched teeth.

Tony propped his elbows on his desk and placed his chin on the steeple he made with his fingers—

watching her. His knee started bouncing. *Maybe Max will say no. This wedding is this weekend. It's hardly any notice. He might already have plans.* His lips drew together with doubt. *Who would say no to her?* The call ended in under a minute. *Wait. That was quick.* Hope sprung in his chest. When she set her phone down, Tony dialed his "best friend."

Max answered right away. "Hey, there's my Buddy. You'll never guess who just called me."

"Did you say no?"

"Oh, oh, oh, I see what this is. Uh, Dude, I said yes. I wanted to say "fuck yeah," but I figured I'd keep it classy."

"Max, so help me, God. If you touch her... Remember what I said about your bent dick."

"Hey, have you ever stopped to consider that she has needs too? If she wants to sample the Max rod—"

"She doesn't want your dick, Asshole. She's doing this because her ex-boyfriend was just here."

"Well, weddings aren't normally my thing, but hey, I'm not above being used, especially by someone like her. So if you want, I can pretend not to like it too much." Max paused to gloat.

"You're going to mess this up for me."

"I promise not to mess anything up. I'll be a perfect gentleman," he added with a chuckle. "You just need to chill and remember that Bailey works for you. She doesn't belong to you. Besides, you have a girlfriend, or have you forgotten? Hey, how was Cancun? Did you wear out that pussy? I would have, that's for damned sure."

Max could be so annoying sometimes. "No, nothing happened."

The other end of the phone went silent for two beats. "Hold on, hold one. What do you mean?"

"Shit!" Explaining what did or didn't happen on his trip wasn't important right now. "Don't change the subject."

"Wait, wait, wait a minute. Are you saying you didn't get any action the whole time you were in Cancun? Was Candice ragging? Tell me you at least got a blowjob."

Tony slumped deeper into his chair. How was he having this conversation right now? "No, dickhead, nothing." Across the hall, Bailey was busy on her computer again. "Look, I don't want to talk about Candice."

"Why?"

"Because... it's not... going anywhere. It never was going anywhere. We're just having fun."

"Holy shit, I think I just grew a vagina."

"Look, I called you because of this thing with Bailey—I'm just saying you don't have to screw everyone you meet."

"I screwed Candice before you guys started going out, and that didn't seem to bother you."

"This is different. Bailey is different."

"How?"

"She just is."

"Okay, okay. Calm down. I'll let you in on a little secret that might be hard to believe, but even I strike out sometimes."

"Then consider yourself benched. We good?"

"We good. Hey, wait, does this include hand jobs?"

"Asshole."

Chapter Fourteen

The images on Bailey's computer screen blended into the fog of her confusion. "This isn't the letter style I wanted." She swirled her mouse over the list to find the right one. Kayla and her bubbly energy skipped into the room.

"Hey." Kayla rolled a chair next to her and sat down, pointing to the screen. "You spelled *desperate* wrong."

"What? Crap. Figures it had to be that word."

"Everything okay?"

"It will be. Let's try this again. Desperate." She punched in the correct letters. "Who calls their farm Desperate Acres anyway?"

"I think it's a cute name for a farm." She cleared her throat. "So, were you able to get a hold of Max?"

Bailey abandoned her search and let out an exasperated breath. "Yeah. Honestly, I thought he'd say no since it was such short notice, but he said he'd happily go to the wedding with me." She leaned back in her chair and picked at the frayed edges around the knees of her jeans. "He offered to have drinks tonight to get better acquainted." Bailey's eyes closed, and she felt really dirty all of a sudden. "Maybe I should've called Doug, but taking him to a wedding? I barely know him...not that I know Max any better." Her fingers webbed along her temples and gathered a fist full of hair. Ripping it out would only make her look more pathetic. "Oh god, Kayla, I hate this."

"It'll be okay, you'll see." She remained quiet—for a whole ten seconds. "So, what did your friend Jordan want?"

Bailey huffed again. "Nothing really. He said he

just happened to be out for a ride and ended up down this way. Which I suppose is possible. We used to ride through the mountains, but never this far. Well, one time we stopped to see Uncle Frank, but—" She stopped her ramble and pulled her hands and hair forward to cover her face. Why did Jordan's surprise visit leave her feeling so discombobulated? She'd never once doubted her decision—*before*.

Muscle memory dragged her gaze where it always went. The veil of her hair didn't hamper her view of Tony enough, and gauging the multiple lines running across his forehead, he didn't seem all that happy either. The urge to yell at him—for no real reason fueled her confusion even more.

"Doesn't Jordan live a couple of hours away?" Kayla tilted her head to the side, fracturing her line of sight.

"Yeah, he does." Now she felt dirty and nauseous.

"Well, that doesn't sound like nothing."

"He brought up Quin's wedding, and I just knew where he was going. That was his way of asking if I was seeing anyone. Jesus, Kayla, I panicked. I—I don't know. I don't want people looking at me, thinking I'm pining away after my ex."

"Well, are you?"

"No. Trust me, I'm not. It's just seeing him right now… It's unsettling." Bailey whipped her hair back and sat up straighter.

"Maybe he came here because he's the one pining away."

Bailey laughed sarcastically. "Did I mention that Jordan is engaged? *And*, his fiancée is actually at the wedding party."

Kayla's mouth fell open. "Really! Ugh, yet he came here to see you. Hum." Her chin lifted higher.

"What a pig...a really good-looking pig, by the way."

Bailey snickered. "I guess." Her shoulders lifted.

"I'll let you get back to work." Kayla stood and rolled the chair under the other end of the table. "If you want to talk later, let me know."

"Thanks, but I'm sure it will be all right."

None of this felt right.

****

Bailey scrambled up the hallway from the shop and handed Kayla two completed work orders. "Okay, I said I'd have this done by Friday, and I've kept my word. The sign for Binnamy Farms is done, and Laz is weeding the vinyl for the Library job as we speak."

"Bailey, it's past noon. You were supposed to leave an hour ago. Heck, you should've taken the whole day off. You definitely earned it."

"I'm going, I'm going. Here, I need you to get this to Max." She handed Kayla a folded piece of paper.

"What's in the note? You're not ditching him, are you?

"No. My phone landed in a sink full of water this morning." *Actually, the toilet, albeit an unused toilet, but... sink just sounded better.*

"You're lucky it didn't land in the toilet."

"Yeah... Anyway, all I had was a box of beef-flavored Rice-a-Roni, and it's still drying out. I planned on texting Max the address for my parent's house later tonight, but can you send him the information for me? I wrote their home number on there, too, in case he'd need to get a hold of me for whatever reason."

"Absolutely." Kayla came around from her side of the desk and threw her arms around her neck. "I hope you have a wonderful weekend, Bailey. And don't worry about Max. I think Tony had a talk with him. He'll behave, that is, if you want him to."

"Kayla, as handsome as Max is, he's not really my type." Bailey's eyes darted to the rear of the shop, shamefully searching for the man who was.

Kayla also glanced toward the shop. "Tony will be upset that he didn't get to say goodbye."

"You can tell him for me. I'll see you Monday, Kayla."

Chapter Fifteen

Bailey stepped from the shower. Condensation blurred the face of the small, ceramic bird clock her mother had sitting on the shelf in the bathroom. She swiped her thumb over the glass to see the time. *Dang it.* With her phone not working, it wasn't until her parents left to buy tomato plants from the garden center that she figured out her dad had never changed the clock in the foyer to Daylight savings time.

Max would be here any minute, and being naked or even semi-dressed in his vicinity was risky. She twisted the towel around her hair, turban style.

Makeup: A light foundation smoothed over her complexion, a smidgen of blush added a warm peach color to her cheeks, and a bit of eyeliner, shadow, and mascara framed her hazel-green eyes. Last was a swipe of lip gloss. There, makeup done. She double-checked her reflection, dismissing the selfish wave of approval. Sometimes it all came together, and sometimes it didn't. Today was a good day. Not that it mattered to—anyone special.

She yanked a pastel yellow sundress off the hanger. The thin shoulder straps didn't fare well with a regular bra, and her strapless bra was nowhere to be found. Fortunately, the material was thick enough that she could go without it. The dress was simple and one of her favorites. The zipper was halfway up when the neighbor's beagle, Remington, started barking near the fence, and a car door closed outside in the driveway. That dog was better than any alarm system. Bailey's chin landed on her chest and her arms contorted to reach the zipper and get it the rest of the way up.

The doorbell rang, and three quick taps followed.

Her parents wouldn't knock, it had to be Max. The main door was already open, and the full-length glass storm door was unlocked.

Bailey cracked the bathroom door and hollered through the narrow opening.

"Come on in. I'll be down in a minute." She yanked the towel from her head, flipped her head upside down, and added some curling product. Her hair curled better drying on its own. She checked the mirror and added a few more scrunches. *Good enough.*

Bailey skipped across the hall to her childhood bedroom. The reception was outdoors, so she opted for wedges since regular high-heels sink into the grass. She grabbed the shoes and bounded down the steps with her bare feet.

When she reached the foyer, no one was there. "Hello?"

"In here."

She turned toward the living room—and couldn't believe her eyes. "Tony?"

Tony, not Max, stood in her parent's living room looking disturbingly more handsome than usual. A light beige summer suit fit his chiseled body perfectly. He even had on a pale yellow tie. What were the odds?

His attentive gaze started at her feet and chiseled a path to the highest damp curl on her head. "You know you're not supposed to outshine the bride, right?"

The hideous girly-girly laugh escaped as the core of her belly clenched. "Why—I mean, where is Max?"

Tony stepped toward her. "I know it sounds like an excuse, but he got called out of town at the last minute. He had to fly to Chicago last night or be out of a job, and trust me, it wasn't an easy decision for him. Apparently, he found out just after you left. He said he tried to call, but it wouldn't go through. Kayla mentioned something happened to your phone?"

"Yeah, I dropped it in the sink." *Toilet.* "But why are you here?"

"Kayla thought it would be good if I took his place. Something about, you didn't want people looking at you funny. I can't wait to meet these people," he said jokingly.

"Tony, you don't need to do this. I'm fine going by myself. I wouldn't want to...upset anyone or cause any kind of confusion."

"Do you mean Candice? Don't worry, it's fine. It just so happens that she's at a wine festival with her friends for the weekend. And, I left her a message to let her know what I was doing."

Tony scanned the room and noticed the photographs sprawled across the mantel. Being an only child, there were a lot, ranging anywhere from preschool pigtails to preadolescent pimples and dreaded braces—with headgear. It was more than a glimpse into her personal life.

Strolling toward the fireplace, he pointed to her high school graduation picture. "Oh my gosh, look at you." Her big hair accurately measured the horrible humidity in the air that day. Right beside it was a photo taken the same day of her and Jordan sharing a loving embrace in their caps and gowns. Tony inspected the photo thoroughly before moving to the next one. Thanks to her mother, at least fifty percent of the pictures so proudly displayed on the mantel included Jordan at some point in their relationship. And Tony studied all of them.

"Tony, are you sure about this?"

He turned and gave her a reassuring look. "Look, Bailey, today, your best friend is getting married. That's all today is about. Nothing else matters. Okay?"

The thought of spending the whole day with Max

had her sick to her stomach since making the call. Knowing Max, or in this case, not knowing him, he probably had the wrong idea of why she invited him in the first place.

Relief in the form of a shiver raced down her spine. At least going to the wedding with Tony, those worries didn't exist as long as she looked at it from his perspective. They knew each other. They got along great and had fun working together—not counting the times when her hands were down his pants, or she was parading around in front of him in just her bra.

Today really was about Quin and Liz. "Okay. Let's go, but I'm driving, and the driver picks the tunes. Those are the rules."

****

Bright pink tulips lined the wavy brick sidewalk of the quaint Methodist church. A few people milling near the entrance had the large oak doors propped open with flower pots.

Two young boys dodged past them.

A woman smoking a cigarette at the base of the steps apologized. "Sorry. They're at that age." She took another puff. "Boys, I don't want you to get—"

The boys dodged around a tree and fell.

"Dirty. Dang it, boys. Where is your father?"

Tony made a bleak face and whispered into Bailey's ear. "Someone's in trouble."

The narrow foyer beamed with colors from tall stained-glass windows. Patrick, an usher and one of Quin's roommates from college, offered his arm.

"Hi, Bailey. You look fantastic."

"Thank you, Patrick." She shot Tony a playful smile over her shoulder.

Entering the main chapel, a white-haired woman who looked to be in her nineties was playing a transformed melody "Sweet Child of Mine" on an ancient pipe organ near the front. Definitely not something you see every day. Her fingers moved pretty fast for her age.

Patrick ushered them up the center aisle of curved pews. A few people turned, sparking a wave of whispers. Bailey scanned the onlookers as more shoulders got tapped and more heads snapped in her direction. The surge raced all the way to the front and found Jordan. His head lifted, and the smile in his eyes disappeared when they shifted to Tony.

Patrick stopped at the second row of the groom's side. "Quin made it clear that you're supposed to be up here with his family." His gaze flitted over Tony. "Maybe later, we can talk some."

She wanted to be polite. "Sure, we'll see." Bailey slid to the middle of the hard wooden pew. It felt cold against her skin, even though the temperature inside the church was plenty warm. It felt like every set of eyes in the church were on the two of them.

Tony sat next to her and casually unbuttoned his blazer. He leaned close and spoke softly. "Wow, and here I thought Kayla was exaggerating. That was quite an entrance. Does that happen every time you walk into a room, or just sometimes?"

Bailey glanced at him. "What makes you think they were looking at me."

"Trust me, I know who they were looking at."

"You'd tell me if the back of my dress was caught in my underwear, wouldn't you?" She laughed silently.

Tony chuckled with her. "Still going with the panties instead of a thong?"

"Honestly, thongs are horribly uncomfortable."

"Okay, panties it is. And yes, I would tell you."

"Good to know." His smile relaxed, and it took everything she had not to fall into the sagey green mist of his eyes. Sometimes four seconds could be an eternity and sometimes, it was heaven.

His brows drew together, all serious-like. "Is that old lady playing 'Bittersweet Symphony' now?"

She snorted, chuckled. "I think so." Her gaze shifted away from his, to reaffirm that today was about Quin. She smoothed out the hem of her dress. "And Tony, thank you for filling in. I don't think I could've handled this day with Max."

"Me neither."

A couple of minutes later, all the buzzing chatter inside the chapel stopped when Quin and his groomsmen entered from a side door. Bailey straightened in her seat.

Right after Quin asked Liz to marry him, he then asked Bailey to be his best woman. Liz didn't seem thrilled with the idea, and Quin was blind to the drama it could cause, so Bailey graciously bowed out to keep things from getting too awkward.

Her best friend looked amazing in an all-white tuxedo. The groomsmen, also in white tuxedos, wore bowties with matching cummerbunds in red, blue, or yellow. The theme of the wedding, primary colors? Maybe? Liz teaches kindergarten, and Quin is an artist.

The music changed to a solo guitarist. He strummed "Pachelbel's Canon" as four bridesmaids paraded down the center aisle wearing royal blue dresses, and carrying mixed bouquets of yellow tulips and red roses.

Everyone stood when Liz and her father entered the chapel. While everyone watched the bride, Bailey turned to catch Quin's reaction. He was about two breaths away from full-on blubbering. Liz was perfect for him, and Bailey couldn't be happier for them both.

When Liz reached the front, the church fell utterly silent. At the altar, a balding red-haired preacher raised his arms. "How do we recognize love?" His smile showered over Quin and Liz. "Is it in her smile? Maybe his laugh? The signs are always there." The preacher addressed the congregation. "Does your heart fill with happiness when that special someone walks into the room? Are you drawn to that person in a way that feels so natural it can't be explained? Love, real love, is all-consuming. It's built on the foundation of friendship and understanding. It's embedded deep in your thoughts, your actions, your words, and your touch. We are here today to understand what it means to love and celebrate it with this union. You may be seated."

Bailey settled onto the pew as those words nibbled away in her subconscious. *The signs are always there.*

Her heart lit up every time she saw Tony. She'd never been drawn to anyone like she had been to Tony. It was as natural as breathing, and they'd built a foundation of friendship.

It'd been there the whole time.

She swallowed hard, struggling to accept what she already knew. She surpassed 'infatuation, attraction, and intrigued' long ago. She was in love with the man sitting beside her. But she couldn't do a darn thing about it.

Tony shifted on the pew and straightened his jacket. He ran a hand down his tie. Bailey studied him from the corner of her eye. A stern look governed his face. *Was he thinking about Candice?* Then, a subtle curve caught his lips, and his gaze shifted to her.

****

The ceremony lasted another fifteen minutes. They stood and sat several times. Someone read, there was a prayer, more standing, a kiss, and then Quin and Liz were married. The guests staying for the reception were directed to the large white tent on the lawn behind the church.

Going through the receiving line, Quin plucked Bailey off her feet and cackled like a total dork. "Can you believe this?"

"I'm so happy for you, Quin."

"Liz was worried that it was going to rain. But you know what they say."

"Hey, you need all the luck you can get."

Quin accessed Tony with genuine interest. "Glad you could make it, Tony." His large hand shot forward. "Keeping her out of trouble, I hope."

Tony shook Quin's hand. "I've found that it depends on how much tequila she drinks."

Bailey's jaw fell open.

Quin leaned toward Tony and lowered his voice. "She cusses when she pukes, and she does this other thing—"

Tony chimed in. "Drunken Sorry Kitten. I've seen it."

Together, Tony and Quin laughed—at her expense. It was almost as if they were bonding...over her. Her head felt weird enough.

Quin pointed them toward the tent. "Hey, we'll be in after pictures. I had Liz put you guys at the table next to ours. It's all the way in the front."

"We'll see you inside." Entering the tent, Tony's hand landed on the small of her back. For today, she'd roll with it. Didn't mean anything.

They found the correct table, and Bailey took her seat. Tony leaned over her shoulder. "How about a drink?"

"Yes, please, a beer would be great, thank you."

"No, Tequila?"

Bailey snickered. "Ha, ha, ha."

He lifted his eyebrows, feigning complete

innocence. "Beer it is."

****

Steam curled from the chafing dishes, filling the air with the thick aroma of grilled meats. The buffet was an unpretentious mix of most of Quin's favorites. Beef brisket and smoked turkey, with sides of spring mix salad, green bean casserole, roasted potato wedges, macaroni and cheese, and German-style coleslaw. The quinoa and artichoke wraps had to be something Liz selected.

After the main meal and cake were served, the DJ announced the bouquet toss. "Okay, folks, let's get all the *single* women lined up." Liz and Quin combed through the guests, searching for prospective candidates.

Through the years, Bailey had participated in plenty of bouquet tosses and even caught a few. The saying goes that the single lady who catches the bouquet will find true love and be the next to marry. Puh.

Someone shoved Bailey from behind. It was Quin. "Get out there."

"All right, all right, all right." Bailey figured that if she didn't go peacefully, he might caveman carry her, and she didn't want that. Tony crossed his arms, clearly interested to see how this played out.

A waft of anxiety gripped Bailey's stomach. She had no intention of catching the stupid thing. She drifted to the outer edge of the huddled women until she felt relatively safe. The mob of women standing directly in the center—like Michele, had much better odds of catching it now.

Perfect!

Liz stood in front of the assembly of single women. When the music started, she turned and tossed the miniature bouquet of red roses and mini daffodils over her shoulder. However, Liz's overzealous throw slammed into the slanted canvas ceiling of the tent, altering its original trajectory.

Instinct forced Bailey's hands out. Before she knew it, she had the crumpled mess of flowers clutched in her hands. "Shit." the curse came out under her breath.

Liz ran to her side and gave her a massive hug. "Well, look at you. It must be a sign, Bailey."

"Great." She forced her grimace into a fake smile and walked away from the dance floor with her 'prize.'

Tony offered his congratulations with a snide smile and an overzealous hand clap. "Did that work out the way you planned?"

"Not even close." Bailey plucked a few petals from the tattered bouquet and threw them at him.

The burlesque ramp barely passed the first four bars before Quin had Liz's garter removed.

"You know what comes next, right?" Tony glanced at the flowers in her hands. "Now I have to go out there and try to save you—again. He removed his jacket and hung it on the back of a chair. "And from the looks of it, I've got my work cut out for me."

Bailey eyed the forming crowd. "Tony, you don't have to do this."

"Oh, no, I'm going. And I'm doing this for Quin and Liz. The way I understand it, the higher the garter goes, the better the luck for the marriage, right?" Wearing a coy smile, he took two steps backward before turning.

Tony joined Quin's single buddies, friends, cousins, uncles from both families, a few older men— probably divorcees, six or seven teenage boys, and Jordan on the dance floor.

The lacey red garter twirled around Quin's index finger as he surveyed the men in the swarming semicircle. They looked like predators ready to pounce, and Bailey suddenly felt like a baby lamb.

The microphone popped and squealed. Everyone flinched before the DJ hit some buttons and made it stop. "Sorry about that, folks." "Whatta Man" started playing. "Okay, Five, four, three, two…"

Quin tossed the red garter over the horde of men. Outstretched arms and hands lunged for the skimpy piece of elastic. The scramble ended up on the floor. One by one, the unlucky participants walked away.

For a baited moment, Bailey held her breath. A second later, Tony sauntered away from the crowd empty-handed.

"I tried, sorry."

Bailey's gaze shot back to the remaining men still huddled together. All the hooting and hollering made her heart thump with anticipation. *Oh god, don't let it be Jordan.*

At last, one arm shot into the air, and the mob finally scattered. Wearing a wide grin, Patrick laced the garter over his wrist and looked at her like the hungriest lion she'd ever seen.

Bailey had no time to react before being escorted to a designated chair in the center of the dance floor.

Patrick knelt in front of her. His eagerness was a smidge unsettling. "I know this is just fun and games, but I've got to admit, Bailey, I would've done just about anything to get this opportunity."

"Oh, well. Okay." That makes one of them. *Quin better appreciate this.*

Marvin Gaye's "Let's Get It On" lit the crowd into a frenzy. Patrick's slim hands snaked the garter around her shoe and over her calf. It took him forever to reach her knee—way more than four seconds.

Patrick eyed her from his crouched position and tucked in his bottom lip. The garter shot three inches higher, no four.

Bailey formed a blockade around her leg with her hands. "That's far enough, Patrick." By her calculations, Quin and Liz would have around eighty good years, and as much as she loved Quin, the rest was on him. She leaned forward and whispered into his ear. "You try to go any higher, and you'll have me, Quin, and my friend over there to deal with."

Patrick glanced in their direction. Quin's raised chin was marred with suspicion. Standing beside him, Tony had crossed arms and his feet set in a shoulder-width stance.

The garter ritual came to a merciful end. *Thank God.*

Chapter Sixteen

When Max got called away on business, Tony actually did a little jig in his office. The thought of Bailey being subjected to Max's shenanigans…well, thank goodness she didn't have to go through that.

Tony took a swig from his beer while Bailey and Quin were at the DJ's table, going through the lists of songs. Quin was a pretty cool guy. He was kind of funny—plus, they had Bailey in common, and despite not really knowing anyone besides Bailey, he *was* having a good time—a great time, actually. Ranked right up there with the day they went hiking.

"They're just friends, you know?"

Tony glanced to his side and found the bride standing next to him. "That's exactly what she told me. By the way, congratulations, Mrs. Chenney." He clinked his bottle to her glass.

"Wow, that's something I'll need to get used to hearing, but call me Liz. And thank you."

Together, they took a moment to observe the duo, now arguing over a Tom Petty song.

"It's so bizarre how they get along," Liz offered. "It bothered me at first because I didn't understand it, and, well, just look at her."

He was. "She's definitely…unique, that's for sure." Tony took another swallow of beer.

Liz scanned the crowd. "I think it's fair to say that you sabotaged some hopefuls today, Mr. Shepard.

"Call me, Tony, please. And whatever do you mean?"

Liz cocked her head to the side. "Some of these guys were probably hoping she'd come by herself. I can think of one in particular." She used the tip of her champagne glass to point toward Jordan. "Heck, some people here still think they'll get back together."

Wait, what? "I'm sorry, I thought he was engaged."

Her brows lifted skeptically. "He is, to my cousin, believe it or not?" Liz visually scoured the crowd and identified one of the girls from the wedding party.

The young woman had brown hair and was pretty but not quite in the same league as Bailey. Well, at least not to him.

"Let me ask you something, Tony. Have you ever looked at a couple and just knew that it wasn't right? When I look at Jordan and Michele, that's what I see, and I think it's because he's still… well. He and Bailey were together for a long time. I'll just leave it at that." She snickered.

Tony cleared his throat with a short cough. "How long exactly?"

"Gosh, they were together in high school, and I think they'd lived together for at least four or five years after that." She took a sip of champagne. "Quin knows the whole story. I only got remnants. Don't get me wrong though, Jordan's not a bad guy, but overall, I think he took what they had together for granted, and it cost him. Bailey told Quin that breaking up with Jordan was the hardest thing she ever had to do."

Tony found himself searching for Jordan. For a fleeting moment, he actually felt sorry for the man.

The first few notes of Adele's version of a Bob Dylan song, *Make You Feel My Love,* began playing. A chill shot down Tony's spine when Jordan sat his drink down—and the man's gaze zeroed in on Bailey.

Was that asshole actually thinking of asking Bailey for a dance? Tony couldn't take that chance.

"Here." With one thing on his mind, Tony handed

his bottle to Liz and set off to save Bailey again.

In front of the DJ table, Tony extended his hand toward her without saying a word. At first, she looked like a deer in the headlights—every bit the stunning, beautiful creature she was, but her hesitation only lasted as long as it took for a smidgen of color to find her cheeks. He led them onto the dancefloor and eased them into the rhythm of the music. He was doing this for her, and there wasn't anything wrong with that.

His hands slid further around her thin waist and sparked a churning inside his chest.

How could it be wrong when having her in his arms felt—right?

So incredibly right.

J. ALISON COLE

Chapter Seventeen

The last note faded into oblivion—the same as every cell in Bailey's body. Tony's jaw slid along the side of her cheek, and her hands slid higher onto his shoulders until the tips of her fingers found the delicate, softer hairs at the base of his neck. In his arms, this close, her senses buzzed from a looming kiss, or maybe it was how much she wanted to be kissed by him.

She could almost feel the tiny whiskers by the corner of his mouth. Why the hell not?

Bailey did the unthinkable, and her lips landed on his. Just a peck like the one he gave her. It won't mean anything to him.

The softest moan escaped from the back of his throat, and his head tilted ever so slightly. The temptation to part her lips unleashed war upon her emotions. If that happened, then what? She couldn't take it back, and she'd never recover.

Bailey summoned strength from somewhere and eased away from the kiss. "Thank you for the dance." Her voice was barely a whisper. Tony shivered, or she did. Heck, maybe they both did.

His gaze bore into hers. "You're welcome."

Weak-kneed and light-headed, she mostly floated off the dance floor.

Tony flirted all the time. He'd kissed her before, and it didn't mean anything. Why couldn't she do the same? A stupid, flirty kiss. That's all it was. Heck, it's not like it was a *real* kiss or anything. Besides, today was about Quin. Nothing else mattered. He said it himself. Tony wouldn't care one way or another.

She didn't have to barter or justify her actions to anyone but herself, period—and maybe Quin.

Quin charged right up to her. *'Wtf'* written all over his face, having witnessed her and Tony together on the dance floor. Bailey shrugged him away.

Quin mouthed, *Really?*

Bailey shrugged again and mouthed, *Don't worry. It was nothing.*

Quin leaned closer. "You looked awful cozy up there. You told me you had this under control. You're just lucky that I want to talk to him, or I'd give you what for."

"Go on, Marian." She used his middle name, hoping he'd let it drop. None of his college buddies knew his middle name. She always kept that threat in the holster.

Quin's lips drew tight, and he turned away. "Hey, Tony, I had a few questions about square foot pricing for manufacturing and retail space. I realize your area is different, but the prices are probably relative to what I charge for the signs I make."

Tony took a casual stance. "Sure, the biggest thing to keep in mind when renting is the length of the lease, what's included, and what's not. Utilities are big: heating, AC, and maintenance, for starters."

Quin crossed his arms and shifted to business mode. "Hey Bailey, could you get us all another beer?"

"Why, of course, Mr. Chenney." Bailey bowed her head and spread her hands like a servant. "You're lucky that today is all about you."

Bailey joined the lengthy line at the open bar. The holdup was a woman at the head of the line who apparently couldn't make a decision. The bartenders repeated the entire list of beers they offered for a second time—and then a third.

The hint of a familiar cologne reached her nose just as the bow on the back of her dress received a hefty tug. A candid glance over her shoulder revealed Jordan wearing half of a grin.

The light gray suit he had on was the same one they'd picked out together for his first job interview after college. He always looked so handsome in that suit, and today was no different.

"Hello, Jordan." The repercussions of the two of them speaking happened in just under a heartbeat. The chatty woman standing behind them hushed her companion. Two people walking by pointed and whispered to one another. The only thing missing was a spotlight.

Bailey tentatively scanned the tent for Michele, but Jordan's fiancée was on the dance floor doing some kind of line dance with about twelve other women.

Jordan took a short breath. "Bailey, I—" Hesitation chopped his words. Something was on his mind, and he was building the courage to say it.

"What? What is it, Jordan?"

A scowl transformed his features, and his eyes narrowed. "Did you fuck him yet?"

Bailey was almost too stunned to react—almost. "Jesus, Jordan." She grabbed his forearm and pulled him away from the line of people to an unoccupied corner of the tent. An audience was the last thing she needed or wanted. When they were far enough away for anyone to hear, she spun to face him. But he raised his hands before she got one word out.

"I'm sorry. God Bailey, I'm so sorry." He dragged a hand through his dark blonde hair. "I didn't think seeing you with someone else would be this hard. But I've got to be honest. It's tearing me up."

Bailey knew him well enough to know that he meant it.

"The thought of another guy being with you—

inside of you—that way, aw Christ." His head fell forward and swung from side to side.

The pain Jordan was feeling was precisely the way Bailey felt—eight months ago. "You'll get over it." *I did.*

His head snapped up, genuinely surprised. "Maybe I don't want to, Bailey."

"What? Please don't do this, not here, not today."

"I don't know what else to do. That's why I came to see you. Quin, let it slip that you had the hots for some guy. That's him, isn't it? I can tell by the way you look at each other." He cast a resentful look at Tony.

She often wondered if Jordan really understood the reason they broke up. All those months ago, he never looked as distraught as he did right now. However, even though Jordan assumed incorrectly that she and Tony were together, he needed to get beyond this.

"Jordan, when I asked you for a little time and space, it wasn't so I could see other people. I told you that." Equal amounts of air and dismay filled her lungs. "I actually hoped that it might clarify our relationship for whatever came next, and you never fought or asked for anything different. You let me go. And after seven years together, it took you—what, a week and a half to find my replacement?" Saying that aloud—left a bitter taste in her mouth. The way he moved on so easily hurt most of all. "I'd call that clarity. Don't you see? If what we had was real, things would've worked out differently."

"How can you say that? It was real for me, Bailey." Unwanted tears brimmed the corners of his eyes, automatically triggering her own. "It still is."

Her calm exterior threatened to splinter. "You're wrong, Jordan." Her voice cracked. "You're wrong."

"I didn't know what else to do. I'm numb without you."

This can't be happening. "Stop. Do you even hear yourself? My god, Jordan, you're engaged to someone else." Her cynical laugh held no humor. "A woman you've professed to love. A woman you're planning a life with. Those actions, those words, are supposed to mean something." Her chin rose, unexpectedly empowered. "The first time *you fucked her,* you weren't thinking of me, and don't pretend otherwise." A rebellious, lonely tear seared down her cheek. Bailey swiped it away. Don't lose it now.

Across the tent, Liz spread her arms in front of Tony and Quin, to keep them from interfering. "Shit." Causing a scene was the last thing Bailey wanted, and deep down, she knew Jordan didn't want that either.

Jordan stepped closer and gripped her shoulders, forcing her attention back to him. "You're wrong, Bailey, because it is you that I see. Every time. I've never stopped loving you, and I don't think I ever will." He placed a gentle kiss on her forehead and then raced around the corner of the church. A cloud of dandelions followed in the wind behind his footsteps, and his unraveled emotions.

A pang of sorrow tugged at her heart. Who's to say what might've happened if he'd felt this passionate eight months ago— *No.* No second-guessing now. Jordan made his choice, and it wasn't her. In the deepest part of her gut, she did the right thing no matter how much it hurt either of them.

Bailey mustered what was left of *her* emotions and headed back to where the others stood.

Tony greeted her at the edge of the dance floor, concern written all over his face. "Everything all right?"

"Yes, I'm fine." Bailey's quick and automatic reply didn't sound overly convincing. Her gaze skirted between Liz, Quin, and Tony. "I'm fine, really. He just had some things he needed to get off his chest. A smile nearly cracked her face. Oh, I forgot your beers, Quin."

"Don't worry about the beers, Bailey." Quin put his hands on his hips, looking past her shoulder to stare down a few drama seekers lurking nearby. "What are you looking at?" He lifted his hands as if to say *'What?'* "We'll get some in a minute."

For the next two hours, Bailey put on a happy face. It felt like the best performance of her life. When it finally came time to leave, she thought she might implode from a needling thought that had planted itself in the back of her mind. And it had nothing to do with Jordan—not directly, anyway.

Walking across the parking lot, Tony inquired—again. "Bailey, you're awfully quiet. Are you sure you're okay?" He reeked with sincerity. *Reason five hundred and whatever.*

Her feet felt heavy, and the ache in her chest doubled in size. "It must've been all that quinoa, but would you mind driving?" She tossed him the keys.

He caught them with ease. "Sure. You may need to help with directions."

"No problem. Can do."

Ten minutes from home, sitting in the passenger seat, the setting sun strobed through the trees lining the side of the road, adding to the pounding in her head. Bailey closed her eyes and let her head flop against the headrest. Silently, she rehashed the words she spewed at Jordan. They, too, applied to the man next to her. Not word for word, but in principle. Tony was involved with someone else. At night, he goes to bed with Candice—and does—other things with—her. If this *attraction* between herself and Tony were real, then things between them would be different. It all boiled down to "Tony *has* a beautiful girlfriend—and *I mean nothing.*"

A gigantic sob burst free.

Tony slammed on the brakes and pulled to the side of the road. The crazy outburst clearly startled him. Bailey sucked in a harsh, shuddering breath, angry and irritated by the inability to reign over her reality and disappointment.

"I'm fine. Really, I'm sorry." Her gaze shot out the window, too afraid to look at him or she'd keep crying. At the very least, he'd think these tears belonged to Jordan. *Let him.*

"Tell me what to do, Bailey?" His voice dripped with concern.

Another sob escaped as Bailey rummaged in the glove box for something to wipe her nose. Searching gave her the chance to calm down and arrange her thoughts. She pulled out a crumpled wad of unused Taco Bell napkins.

The nagging thought that pestered her from the moment she saw him standing in the living room—surfaced. "What did you say in your message?" At this point, she had nothing to lose. Why not sink the knife in deeper?

"What?" Tony flinched, confused by the question.

Bailey turned in the car seat to confront him directly. "Candice. You said you left her a message. What exactly did you tell her you were doing today?"

Tony shifted in the seat. "What does that have to do with anything?"

Her gaze locked with his. "Because I want to know." She dragged the napkin under her nose. A loud sniff marked the punctuation.

The question hung in the air for a lot longer than four seconds. Then, little by little, the creases on his forehead deepened. "I told her—I was helping a friend."

Those simple words buried her. Tony's chin

dropped to his chest, and his mouth opened to speak.

She cut him off. "Thank you. That's all I needed to know. Take me home, please."

Chapter Eighteen

By Monday morning, Bailey's self-destructive revelation had reached the festering stage. No more band-aid to rip off, and no more pretense. Now, for her own sanity and self-preservation, she had no choice but to get over it, *get over him.*

Tony graciously did an outstanding job avoiding any and all unnecessary face-time with her. When he did have something to say, he wouldn't look her in the eye, which served her right. She'd brought this anguish on herself. He was never to blame.

"What the hell happened?" Kayla, ever alert, knew instantly that something was off.

"Everything's fine. It was a beautiful wedding." Turns out that trying to act normal is much more complicated than it sounds. And apparently, she sucked at it. Monday was a long, long day.

Tuesday—more of the same. "Was my brother a jerk to you?" Kayla refused to let it go.

"No, of course not. Did I tell you that they had artichoke wraps? And the cake was gorgeous. Let me show you the pictures."

Wednesday—Kayla buzzed into her workspace like an angry hornet with her tiny, little hands on her tiny, little hips. "Well, something happened because he's acting just as weird as you. I want to know what happened."

Bailey leaned away from her computer. "Tony didn't do anything wrong." *It was all me.* "I promise, and that's the truth."

How could she tell Kayla that she had a full-fledged epiphany, the love she had for Tony wasn't real? As it was, she had no one to confide in, other than Quin.

But he was on his honeymoon for the next week, and Bailey's other friends were also Jordan's, so discussing Tony with any of them would be awkward, especially after his most recent confession. Even her mom wouldn't be any real help. The woman was team Jordan all the way.

"Now, I need to get back to work." *And I need to move forward.*

Kayla hovered beside her for another minute. "Yeah, work, work, work. That's the same reply I got from him. I know something happened between the two of you, and I'll find out what."

"Nothing happened." The bitter reply snapped a little too hard.

And now Kayla was mad at her, too.

Friday afternoon, what should have been a simple design just wouldn't come together. None of the fonts Bailey picked seemed to work. So she tried changing the shape of the sign, but that didn't work either, just like everything else going on right now. Bailey rubbed her temples. How pitiful?

Tony entered her workroom. "Do you have a headache?"

Her hands dropped back to the keyboard. She answered without turning around. "No," How long was it going to be like this?

"Bill Porter just called. He wants to meet on Monday at his office in Leesburg to discuss more work."

Her curiosity got the better of her. Bailey swiveled in her chair to face him. "What kind of work?"

"I don't know. From the sound of it, it might be a good bit. I guess we'll find out Monday. He wants both of us there, okay?"

"Okay." Bailey could be all about business.

"We'll need to leave here around ten."

"Fine." She fired up her inner bitch.

"Dressed for business." He glanced at her t-shirt and jeans, indicating her casual attire with a disgusting shrug.

"Okay! I do own nice clothes." *Go, bitch, go.*

He squared his shoulders and his jaw twitched. "Good."

Bailey swiveled back toward her computer. His lingering presence practically burned a hole in the back of her skull. "Is there anything else?"

A weird growl rumbled from him. "No. That's it." The ghost of his reflection on the glass in front of her finally disappeared, along with all the remaining oxygen in the room.

****

At 4:30, Bailey analyzed the changes she made to the recently unsalvageable design. Using different letters from different fonts combined actually worked perfectly for the eclectic second-hand clothing store. Who knew bitter confrontations could be so motivating?

Her Rice-a-Roni, toilet phone came back to life two days ago. It buzzed in her rear pocket, and she scrambled to answer *without* bothering to look at the number.

"Hello?"

"Bailey?"

"Yes?"

"This is Doug Shellman."

Don, Dan, Doug. How drunk was she that night? She had no memory of giving him her number. "Doug, yeah. How are you?"

"I'm great. Hey, I was wondering if you'd like to get together, maybe do something this weekend?"

"Hmmm." Her auto-search skirted around for Tony. *Dammit!* "Yeah, I'd like that. Tell you what, there's this place here in the industrial park called Brindles, and we're getting ready to head over there for happy hour." She would've preferred to skip the traditional happy hour, but Kayla would only hound her with more questions if she were a complete no-show. "We can get a drink and make plans there if you want?"

"I know exactly where it is." He sounded pleasantly surprised.

"Great, I'll see you in a bit." She stood and shoved the phone into her rear pocket as the computer finished shutting down. When she turned, Kayla was standing in the doorway, slack-jawed.

"Did you just make a date with handsome Doug?"

"I guess I did." Bailey grabbed her purse and stormed past her. "You coming?" She'd done her best to be nice to Kayla, but her mood was still prickly, and yes, she was PMS-ing. So why not add raging hormones to her bitch factor?

Poor Doug had no idea who he was about to meet, and quite honestly, she didn't know either.

****

Lazlo found the last open table, a curved booth that held up to eight people. Brindles' was packed with regulars. All the regulars, including Candice and her Eastwick coven roommates.

Bailey's left eye twitched every time Candice spoke, and for some reason, she seemed exceptionally talkative this evening.

Glass should be breaking right now.

Not knowing how long it would take Doug to get there, Bailey sat on the side, which gave her a good view of the door. As luck would have it, Tony ended up on the opposite side of the curve, straight across from her, which led to a blatant and nefarious stare-down between the two of them.

"Make sure we leave room for Doug," Kayla announced unexpectedly.

"Who's Doug?" Shawna inquired.

"Bailey's friend."

Raven perked up. "That guy from the club. Nice! Let me just say he's quite the dancer."

Bailey always thought there was no bigger bitch than Karma because, at that moment, the same song she and Tony danced to that day in the shop started playing. She swapped glances between Tony and Lazlo and the blob of dried mustard on the table right in front of her. *She hoped it was mustard and not some weird booger.*

Lazlo recognized the song and chimed in. "You know who else can dance? Tony."

Candice hyena giggled, "Like that would ever happen. I've never seen him slow dance, much less fast. You're so silly, Lazlo."

"No, no, no. Tony dances. Him and—"

"Hey, Lazlo," Bailey cut him off. "What was that beer you were telling me about? Didn't it have vinegar in it or something?"

Lazlo's thoughts and voice stuttered. "It-it's apple cider, not apple cider vinegar. I was joking when I said that." He went on to explain, but she had already stopped listening by then. Her goal was to get him to quit talking about dancing.

She gestured for him to follow her to the bar. "Come on, let's go get some." Lazlo climbed over the back of the booth from the center, and they headed to the bar.

It was so busy, they had to wait to be served.

And wait, and wait.

Why doesn't Tony dance with his girlfriend?

Bailey danced with Tony, slow and fast. She should've let him fry. *Yup. Deep fry!*

Bartender Stephon ignored the two guys standing beside her and signaled for her order. That's right, now she knew the bartender by name. *Uh.*

"Could we get a pitcher of the Twisted Apple cider, please?"

Lazlo leaned over her shoulder and added. "And like four mugs. Please." He shrugged at Bailey. "Those other girls won't drink this."

A flash of sunlight lasered off the glass door of the club as it opened—the inner turmoil churning in Bailey's stomach sped up like a car at the starting line. Doug walked inside and stood near the entrance while visually searching the crowd. She tossed a twenty-dollar bill onto the bar. "Here, Lazlo, here's twenty towards this." She scurried toward the front of the club to greet Doug. Would he even recognize her? She wasn't dolled up like before: hardly any makeup, no fancy dress, just plain old jeans and a regular shirt. Not that she was looking to impress him or anyone for that matter, but he might take a look at her and just turn around and walk out. Lord, how long had it been since she'd actually *dated* anyone.

Doug's face lit up when he spotted her. Her slightly impeded memory from that night didn't sufficiently prepare her for the eerie resemblance *he did* have to Tony: same height, darkish hair, and even his smile was close. Only—he was no Tony.

"Hi, Bailey. Wow, you're even prettier than I remember."

"Oh, thanks, Doug." She looked down at her plain attire. Jeans and an emerald-green t- shirt didn't quite add up to Scarlett O'Hara wearing curtains, but... "How about...we sit...at the bar," Bailey stammered. Even though his tongue had been inside her mouth, she didn't know the man. If there were any awkward pauses, she didn't need or want them on display.

"Yeah, yeah. Hey, there are two stools down here."

"Fabulous." Unfortunately, the two available barstools lined up perfectly with the booth. She physically angled her body toward Doug. "I'll be honest with you. I don't remember much from that night, so how about we start at the beginning? Tell me about yourself."

"I know what you mean. Things started to get a little fuzzy for me, too. I don't normally drink that much." He rubbed his hands over his thighs, nervously. "Okay? I'll start with the good stuff."

He talked for five minutes straight. Bailey did her best to listen, but she may as well have been back at the office the way her gaze kept wandering over Doug's shoulder. Tony had his head down like he was brooding over something. *What does he have to brood about?*

"And then I started as a salesman at the Mercedes dealership.

Cars? She knew a little about cars. "I drive an older Audi TT."

"Oh my God, we sell a wide variety of foreign cars, including Audi's. If you ever have any problem, please bring it to our service center. Our guys are the best."

"It could use a tune-up. Maybe I'll make an appointment."

"Just let me know, and I'll be certain—" He leaned closer. "—that you get a discount."

"I'll remember that."

"I hope so."

Candice shimmied around the table and left the booth. Bailey felt mildly alarmed. The *squealing goddess* passed the doorway to the bathroom—and veered toward the bar. *Crap, where was she heading? Oh, she's heading this way? Yes. Holy shit, she's coming this way. And—she's here.*

"Bailey, introduce me to your friend."

Doug twisted the upper half of his torso. He did an abysmal job trying to hide his initial reaction to the beautiful woman holding the back of his barstool.

"Candice, this is Doug Shellman. Doug, Candice Martin."

"Nice to meet you." He shook her slender, perfectly manicured hand.

A giggle followed, sending a spike into the side of Bailey's skull. "I just wanted to invite you guys to the party I'm throwing at Tony's tomorrow. Nothing fancy, around four, if you can make it."

No thanks! They hadn't gotten that far into their plans yet. "I don't know what we're doing yet, so we'll see." Doug looked at Bailey. "Thanks anyway, Candice."

Candice's smile exploded and showcased a complete set of bleached, whitened teeth. The woman should be doing dental ads. "Well, it was nice to meet you. I hope you decide to come. See ya." Candice sashayed away, her butt and boobs bouncing in harmony.

Bailey assumed Doug would be watching the exhibition—only when she turned, his eyes were on her.

"Don't get me wrong, but I think your friend wants to be a Kardashian."

Bailey laughed for real. It kind of caught her off guard. "Right?"

"I mean, sure, she's pretty, but not like you."

Bailey immediately tried to decipher the compliment. Her cynical thoughts surfaced first. Maybe his vision was impaired, or this was his version of a silky come-on, and he was one of those men who'd say anything to get in her panties. Yes, panties. Or maybe he didn't like dark-haired girls with big boobs and bouncy butts. Perhaps he was more of a quirky, curly-haired blonde kind of guy. Then, one last bizarre theory manifested. Maybe, just maybe, he actually meant it.

Nah.

He reached for her hand. "Bailey, I just want to get to know you." This time, when he smiled, his resemblance to Tony was uncanny. Intrigue and a little bit of disgust smacked her at the same time.

Over the next hour, Bailey learned that Doug was thirty-one, divorced with a two-year-old daughter. He grew up in Colorado but attended the University of Virginia in Charlottesville. He could be considered very inimitable with his doppelganger smile and solid athletic build.

"It's settled then. We'll borrow a bicycle from your Aunt and ride along the canals of the Potomac. It'll be great, I promise."

Bailey added her address to his phone. "Sounds like it."

"Great. I've got to leave and pick up my daughter, but I'll see you tomorrow around noon." Doug stood and placed an innocent kiss on her cheek. "Goodnight, Bailey."

"Goodnight, Doug." He and his broad shoulders blended into the crowd and disappeared.

He had potential—if she were genuinely interested. She had to at least try. Give it a whirl, and move on. Maybe this would sever the last tiny thread to the man staring her down from across the room.

****

"Have you been to Sharpsburg, Maryland, before?" Doug unhooked Aunt Trish's bicycle from the back of his Land Rover.

"Can't say that I have."

A dilapidated stone wall edged the parking lot and

funneled visitors down a small hill. Through the trees, flashes of light reflected off the nearby river like sparklers.

Bailey had to admit that this was a brilliant first date. It was more pleasant than a bar, pressure-free because it was casual, and the scenery, and history surrounding the area carried most of the conversation. Nothing felt forced, and it was easy to be herself.

A cool breeze rustled through the leaves of the towering trees that arched over the well-worn, dirt-hardened towpath. The same towpath that horses and carts used to pull boats through the canal. Weeds and downed trees filled the gully now. Doug even pointed out a few of the different landmarks, like the locks and aqueducts along the *one hundred eighty-four-and-a-half-mile* canal.

Either he studied the night before, or he already knew the history from previous rides. They rode at a steady pace for about seven miles.

"There's a place up ahead where we can stop and rehydrate." His cheery smile revealed dimples.

"Sounds good." *Tony doesn't have dimples.*

She grimaced to herself. Probably wasn't the best idea to compare her 'date' to the guy she was trying to get over.

They coasted up to a roadside stand. Bailey found a bench that had a picturesque view of the River while Doug ordered them two mint iced teas.

He joined her on the bench. "You're in great shape, Bailey. I mean physically, of course, your body is…well…I just mean that you have great endurance. You could probably ride me under the fence all day." He handed her a mint tea. "Oh, gawd, that didn't exactly come out the way I intended." His face scrunched. "I'll shut up now."

Bailey found his awkward ramblings sincere and kind of sweet. "Thank you for the tea." She took a refreshing sip.

Doug took a few gulps before setting his drink on the ground between his feet. He plucked four long blades of grass from behind the bench. "I had an aunt who showed me how to do this when I was a kid." Bailey watched his nimble fingers weave the grass into an intricate chain. He finished by making a loop on one end and a knot on the other.

"Here. This is for you."

Subconsciously, her hands drew closer to her body.

Doug caught her initial reaction. He was almost as perceptive as Quin. "Don't worry. It doesn't mean we're married or anything."

Bailey laughed, mostly at herself. She extended her arm and let him secure the grass bracelet around her wrist. "I'm impressed. Do you make one for all the girls you go out with?"

Doug blew out a small laugh. "Trust me. Since my divorce, I could use one hand to count how many dates I've been on." A flash of sorrow streaked over his features. "I tried hard to save my marriage, but I guess it wasn't meant to be, and it took a while to get over, but now I am." He straightened the bracelet and then wrapped his hand around hers. "My friend Mitch had to drag me to the club that night. I can't tell you how glad I am that he did."

So, handsome Doug was crafty, sensitive, and romantic. He could almost be the perfect man.

"I like you, Bailey, and I just want to get to know you better."

Bailey squirmed, suddenly uneasy. She should like him, right? "Tell me more about your daughter." She needed a distraction.

"Oh, I've got some pictures." His phone lit up with a dozen or more photos. *He* lit up in full animation, talking about her. "I never would've thought something so small could have that much power over me, but she does. When she cries, it breaks my heart, and when she laughs, there's nothing better." He put his phone away and studied Bailey for a moment. "My marriage was already rocky when our daughter came along. She wasn't exactly planned. But I've learned that plans have a way of changing whether you want them to or not. Sometimes, they work out for the better in the end."

Boy, if that didn't sound familiar. Doud had suffered a different kind of heartache and survived. It left no visible scar, but Bailey could sense it, and she could totally relate. Perhaps it was for that reason she opened up.

"If my first plan had come together, I'd be married by now, looking forward to the first of two beautiful children."

"Only two? I'm from a big family, so I'm thinking five. Minimum."

Bailey laughed. "Five? Is that counting the one you already have or addition to?"

"Depends on what I can talk you into." He had charm.

"You don't think it's a little early for this conversation?" She tossed him a playful look.

"I'm a terrific salesman, and besides, you did agree to wear my bracelet." His arm stretched over the back of the bench behind her. "So, what's your new plan?"

Well, it was moving to Virginia and starting a new job. "Right now, I don't know." Falling for her boss definitely wasn't part of it.

His fingertips brushed the top of her shoulder. "There's always the 'One day at a time.' Then we can start on the five kids."

They both laughed, and as the laughter faded, she could almost predict what came next. Doug leaned in for a kiss.

Unlike the horny, liquor-laced kiss from the bar, this kiss was very measured. His tongue traced the edges of her lips before slipping into her mouth. Bailey waited to feel something—anything.

When the kiss ended, Doug veered away and whispered. "I've wanted to do that since I saw you yesterday."

Bailey had no reply because, as sweet as he was, the kiss hadn't stirred her. She had no new plan, but even if she did, and try as she might, she couldn't see him in it.

****

Bailey rolled Aunt Trish's bicycle into their garage beside the Tahoe. Music from the party at Tony's house drifted through the trees and across the yard. She wanted to get the heck out of here.

Doug stood beside the front fender of his SUV and pointed toward Tony's house. "Hey, someone's waving at you."

The groan inside her head was much louder than the one that came out. A *conservative* glance revealed Kayla leaning over the front railing, her arms flailing about, motioning for them to come over. Bailey waved back, hoping that would be the end of it.

Doug eyed Bailey over the top of the hood. "Let's stop by real quick."

"Oh, I really should get home. I'm all sweaty from riding and not really dressed for a party." Kayla must've been waiting there like a hawk.

"They're your friends. I seriously doubt they care.

And you look fabulous, by the way." He came around the front of the vehicle and held out his hand.

It didn't feel right to leave him hanging, and she'd have a hard time convincing Kayla that everything was 'fine' if she ignored the zealous invite completely. "Okay, but can we just say hello and then get going? I really don't want to stay long. I'm…kind of tired after all that riding."

"Sure." His large hand enveloped around hers.

Anxiety clawed away at her gut with each step. This must be what it felt like to walk to the gallows.

The front door flew open, and Kayla threw her hands into the air. "Come on in. I'm so glad I saw you guys, and so nice to meet you, Doug. Beautiful flowers, by the way. Bailey loved them." She shot Bailey a discreet wink.

"Thanks. Kayla, is it? You know, you look really familiar. What kind of car do you drive?"

"Hah, don't tell me you're a used car salesman."

"W-well, actually—" he stuttered.

Why yes, he is a used car salesman.

Kayla swiped a hand toward him. "I'm just kidding." Next, she started pointing in all directions. "Beer and drinks are in the kitchen. The living room's in there, and the bathroom is down that hall on the right. Why don't you guys go to the living room, and I'll grab you a couple of beers."

Doug grabbed Bailey's hand again and led her toward the living room. "We'll be in here."

Fifteen or so people were milling around in the ample space. Bailey's automatic sweep for Tony left her breathing a little easier. He wasn't here.

She scanned the room a second time and noted the layout and its similarity to Uncle Frank's home, which also had lots of rustic wood and glass. The décor, however, was an interesting mixture of contemporary and vintage pieces. On the shelves, Bailey spotted a collection of books and unusual knickknacks. She hated herself for wanting to inspect them closer. For all she knew, they belonged to Candice. Or worse, they'd accumulated from his string of abandoned girlfriends as mementos left behind. But, to be fair, the room, in many ways, was a reflection of Tony: attractive, energetic, and comfy. It was freaking gorgeous.

Max was sitting on one of two dark brown leather sofas. A woman with strawberry-blonde hair was trying overly hard to keep his attention trained on her bosoms. She must not have known that she didn't need to try so hard. She was probably a second tier witch with a name like Trixie or Cinnamon.

Lazlo and Sherry stood across the room by the large picture window, but they hadn't seen her yet. Bailey figured they'd work their way over, say "hello," and then they could get the hell out of here. As for the other people standing around, they must be friends of Candice. What was the average size of a coven?

Kayla fluttered back into the room with two beers. "Here you go. What a beautiful day for a bike ride. Did you guys have fun?"

Doug spoke up. "The views alone are outstanding. You might even say, spectacular. " His smile stayed on Bailey for an uncomfortable length of time.

She forced a polite nod.

Somewhere on the second floor, a door closed— exceptionally loud. Bailey's gaze shot upward in time to see Shawna strutting along the open hallway toward a staircase.

Doug dismissed the ruckus and turned toward the fireplace behind them. "Wow, that's beautiful. Look at that." He pointed with his bottle.

Bailey was mid-swig as she turned.

Beer spewed from her lips. Some may have even flown out of her nose. "Holy shit—"

Above the fireplace mantel, magnificently displayed—was *her* large painting of the meadow.

Doug thumped on Bailey's back a few times as she coughed and cleared her throat. Her first full breath came just as Tony appeared in an archway from a connecting room. His eyes, more jade today, met hers with laser accuracy, as well as a snide smile that marred his normally handsome face. He marched directly toward her.

Fuming with rage, Bailey's eyes motioned toward *her* painting. "That's mine."

"I have a receipt that says differently." Perfectly poised, Tony's underlying smart-ass reared its not-so-ugly head. *Surprise, surprise, he's actually prepared for this.*

She was not. "I told you I wanted to keep it. Why would you go and buy it?"

" I knew I had to have it the moment I saw it."

Every comeback Bailey could think of made her feel childish, but she had to say something. "Give it back."

"No." Beaming with confidence, Tony lowered his chin. "I've become rather attached."

"Well, maybe I don't want you to have it." *Really? What am I, twelve?*

He shrugged nonchalantly before glancing at Doug. "Oh, it's mine, and I plan on keeping it."

"I'll give you your money back."

"It's not for sale, and I'd have paid three times as much, so keep your money."

Doug interrupted the conversation. "Wait? You painted this, Bailey?"

Her eyes slammed shut at the sound of Doug's voice. "Yes." She answered him with more agitation than he deserved.

Kayla scampered into their circle and took Doug by the arm. "Bailey's a wonderful artist. There's another piece over here. Let me show you." She led him past the sofas and pointed to a small group of paintings on the wall.

Bailey's head dropped another inch to the side. Tony had not one but two of her paintings. Flustered and embarrassed—of all things, she blurted the only thing she could think of. "You *are* an Asshole." If she didn't get away from him right now, her head and heart might explode.

Raven and three other people had the front door blocked, so Bailey raced down the hallway, through the kitchen, and out the sliding doors to his rear deck. It was empty, thank god.

An eternity of no more than four seconds passed before the door opened and closed again behind her.

Bailey kept her gaze directed to the woods behind the house as Tony eased into her peripheral and joined her at the railing. His mere presence dragged her gaze toward him.

It took five long breaths before Bailey could say anything. "Why are you doing this?"

He searched her eyes. "Come on, I think you know why."

His answer slammed into her chest. What was he saying or not saying? The gleam in his eyes ignited. Did she know why? Four more breaths filled the silence. It was hard to think straight and even harder to look away.

Tony veered closer, and his heated gaze drifted to her mouth. "You know exactly why."

Her battered defenses disintegrated under the fiery

stare. And she was done fighting.

His lips claimed hers. Softly at first and satiny smooth, his tongue traced the crease before coiling into her mouth. Her arms laced around his neck, holding him close. The kiss deepened, and everything else melted away: no party, no music, no people, just Tony and the burning passion that consumed her. The gravity holding her soul on this earth loosened and put her back on that special plane of existence. Somehow, she'd known it would be like this.

Tony broke away from the kiss. His nostrils flared as hunger filled his eyes. He looked as overwhelmed as she felt.

Bailey struggled to catch her own breath as he leaned in to revive the kiss—but realization beat him to it.

What did she do?

"No." Bailey pushed away from Tony. Why did she let him—no...why did *she* go that far. A spasm of guilt and stupidity kicked her square in the gut. She'd kissed someone else's boyfriend—knowingly. What did that make her? What did that make him? What if someone saw? Can she still work for him? What happens now?

For a second, she thought she might vomit.

"I need to get out of here." Bailey raced back inside to find Doug. He was near a bookshelf, still chatting with Kayla. "Can you take me home now?"

Tony followed her inside, right on her heels. "Like hell." He stepped onto the coffee table and made an announcement. "The party is over! Get out!"

Uncle Frank's house wouldn't be far enough away. Bailey pleaded with Doug again. "Please. Can we leave now?"

Tony stepped down from the table. He seemed

amped to argue his case.

Doug stepped back, even more confused. "What is going on?"

Max intervened. "Hey, now, it's all cool." He stepped in front of Tony. "Bailey, why don't you and your friend go ahead and leave." Max gave her a quick nod. He was the last person Bailey expected to help, but she'd take it.

She charged toward the front door, shouldering through the slow pokes, not bothering to look back. Doug caught up to her halfway up Uncle Frank's driveway. His jaw was set, and his lips were drawn into a thin, flat line.

Bailey felt compelled to apologize. "I'm sorry, Doug. I just needed to get out of there. Please, let's just go."

He nodded.

The ride to her apartment remained quiet, but in her mind, the tension—roared. *Omigod,* How could she have kissed Tony like that?

Doug tapped the steering wheel while they waited at the red light a block away from where she lived. "Can I ask you something?"

Bailey managed a guilt-ridden smile. "Sure."

The light turned green, and they proceeded through the intersection. "If I'm not mistaken, that was the guy from the club. Right?"

Bailey shook her head.

"Are you involved with him?"

"We're not involved." It felt like a vicious lie the moment it left her mouth.

Skeptic lines crinkled over his brows. "I get the feeling that's not entirely true."

Bailey flushed. "I don't know what we are." That was an honest answer.

Doug turned into the complex and parked in front

of her building. He turned the vehicle off and fiddled with his key fob. "Look, I don't want or need to get in the middle of any kind of drama you got going on, but can you promise me something?" His soft blue gaze reached for hers. "Promise me that if it doesn't work out, you'll at least give me a chance. I really would have liked to have had that."

"I'm sorry, Doug, I didn't mean for any of this to happen." And she didn't. "I guess that things are a little crazy right now. But thank you for—today and for bringing me home." Bailey tried to lighten the mood. "Do you want your bracelet back?"

He chuckled softly. "Nah, I'd rather you keep it, just in case. I can always make another one."

Bailey leaned over and kissed his cheek. "Goodbye, Doug."

****

Bailey stretched out across her bed and tried to unravel the past hour. She thought being around Tony before was hard, but now...how could she face him? What was she going to do? And what about the paintings? He bought her meadow painting, knowing full well that she wanted to keep it. But being angry over that wouldn't save her from—herself.

The front door of the apartment opened and closed. A wave of panic and guilt settled in the base of her spine. Well, that's it. She'll probably wake up with an upside-down pentagram carved into her forehead. It's over.

"Bailey, hey, Bailey, you here?" Raven called. There was a quick tap on her bedroom door before it opened. "The party sure ended in a hurry. Probably a good thing since—hey, everything all right?"

Bailey shrugged. If Raven knew or saw anything that happened between herself and Tony, she wasn't acting like it. In truth, Raven was the one roommate she kind of got along with. But for now, it felt best to keep her indiscretion to herself.

"Raven, how did it work out with you and the guy at your job? The one you had feelings for but was married. How did you end it?"

Raven sat down on the end of the bed. Her cheerful mood and persona took an immediate nosedive. "Not good. I see him day in and day out. I've put in a request, hoping to get transferred. I don't think I'd survive seeing him at the company picnics with his wife and kids. It hurts to know that I was just some erroneous fling." She blew out a deflated breath. "But, even if he had left his wife, I'd never be able to trust him. He cheated on her, so he'd probably do the same to me."

Bailey's situation differed slightly. A kiss wasn't exactly the same as a torrid fling. Still, it would be challenging to be around Tony day after day and pretend nothing happened. She needed to purge her misery. "I could use some ice cream. Do you want to come with me?"

"If ice cream cures heartache," Raven sounded newly motivated. "I am so in. Let's go."

J. ALISON COLE

Chapter Nineteen

Tony flopped onto Max's long black sofa.

"So explain this to me again. You kissed Bailey, and then she took off."

"Yes."

"And you're completely done with Candice."

"Yes. I told you Candice and I officially broke up last night after we got home from Brindles. It was amicable. But she had already planned the party, and I told her that was fine. I didn't care. I just didn't know that Bailey was going to show up with Mr. Bicycle Man."

"I must admit, I've never seen you this out of sorts over a chick. I think you might be losing it, man."

"I feel like I lost it weeks ago."

Max's face crunched with interest, and he kicked at his feet. "Do you want my advice?"

Tony shot Max an incredulous glance. "Your advice? No, thanks."

"I'm serious. What did you expect to happen? That she'd fall to her knees and suck your dick right then and there. Maybe Bailey needs to sort through her feelings, you know, give her some space."

Tony laughed. "For fuck sake, have you been watching old episodes of Oprah?"

"Hey, all women need space sometimes."

"Bailey's not like other women." Tony's gaze drifted toward the ceiling. "She's not like anyone I've ever met. When she's working and really concentrating, she does this thing with her bottom lip. The way it juts out makes me want to...nibble on it. It's so fuckin' adorable." Max had the weirdest look on his face, but Tony didn't care. He slid further into the cushions. "And don't get me started on her body. I mean, well, you saw some of it anyway." He crossed his arms over his chest. "You can't imagine how perfectly she fits against me. It's so easy being around her, and I like it. It's like something was up the first time we met."

"That was your dick." Max snorted.

"No, Max, well maybe, but it wasn't just that. You wouldn't understand. She makes me want—more."

Max choked and pounded on his chest with a curled fist. "Oh, sweet Jesus." His eyes opened extra wide to swallow the thought. "I think they call that love. And for your information, I've been in love. I know exactly what it feels like."

Tony's lip curled up on one side, genuinely surprised. "Now I'm calling bullshit."

"Look. Trust me, I've been in love, but I didn't get the happily-ever-after. She went off and married someone else." Max retreated into his own thoughts for a second. "This is a first for you. I get that. But have you considered that she may not feel the same way about you? Because if she doesn't, you just opened the door for a case of sexual harassment? I know because I'm an HR guy.

"She wouldn't do that."

"How do you know?"

"I know."

"What if she quits?"

The thought of Bailey walking away never entered his mind. "No, Bailey won't quit either. She has too much pride, especially the way work is going right now. Plus, I know she has feelings for me. The first time I saw her walking down the hill from Frank's, she had this look in her eyes that damned near devoured me. I catch her at least ten times a day with that same look, and it steals my breath every time. Plus, she kind of told me. She was drunk off her ass, but..."

"I hope you're right, Tony."

"I am. I can feel it." He *would* give her a little space—and then all bets were off.

J. ALISON COLE

Chapter Twenty

Just once, Bailey wished it was in her to call out sick. But blowing off the meeting with Bill Porter because of her ludicrous love life wasn't something her work ethic would allow.

She turned the corner to the rear of the building. Her grip on the steering wheel tightened. "Dammit." She was half an hour early, but both Tony and Kayla still beat her to work. She liked it better when she was the first one to arrive.

She parked and grabbed a tote from the passenger seat. The tote held a change of clothes for after the meeting. Her business attire consisted of navy blue dress slacks, a plain white blouse, and heels. Simple, direct, and professional. She ran a hand down the front of her shirt. Thank goodness she didn't have to "dress up" for work all the time. She'd take "ordinary" clothes over pencil skirts any day.

Right as she reached for the handle of the shop, the door opened, and Tony stepped to one side with a dramatic sweep of his arm to usher her inside. She rushed by, managing to avoid any direct eye contact. But the memory of their kiss instantly flooded her senses and turned her ankles into mush. Why didn't she wear flats instead of heels?

She made it halfway across the shop when Tony called to her. "After you put your stuff down, I need to see you in my office."

"Sure." Some type of confrontation was inevitable. However, this time she *was* prepared. She'd spent the night before, wallering in a pint of Chip Happens flavored ice cream, working on a list of possible excuses he might use. Number one, he was drunk—only he seemed perfectly sober to her. Number two, he had another fight with Candice—but if that was the case, she wanted no part of his *relationship woes.* Those two topped the list, while all the other excuses felt too far-fetched: A case of mistaken identity—*this wasn't a soap opera.* He tripped, and his lips accidentally landed on hers—*yeah, right.* Lucky for him, she was able to stop his fall with her tongue.

It all boiled down to, if he asked for forgiveness, she would give it and vow to never let it happen again. What else could she do? Quit? No. Life goes on. No matter how confusing, how messy, or how incredibly unforgettable it may be, she would get past this. At Quin's wedding, he said, *'He was helping a friend.'* That's all she was to him, and she was done playing the fool thinking otherwise.

Bailey tossed her belongings onto her desk, pumped her veins full of ice, and ventured across the hall. Standing in the doorway of Tony's office, she braced her feet physically, and her brain mentally. "Is this about the meeting with Mr. Porter?"

"Come in and close the door. And no." When she didn't move fast enough, Tony casually rose from his chair and ushered her deeper into the room—with his nearness. "Please, have a seat."

Fine. Bailey would sit down and hear him out. He closed the door behind her, and she took a calming breath. He should apologize for his behavior, and explain why he purchased her paintings behind her back. Her spine was ramrod straight as she pinched at the crease of her slacks.

Helping a friend.

He sat down and scooted his chair closer to the desk, all official-like. "I've had most of the weekend to think about this."

Here it comes.

"And believe me when I tell you, I'm not sorry, Bailey. I'm not sorry for any of it: buying the paintings, the kiss, or for wanting you."

Bailey squinted to drown out the bizarre buzzing inside her brain. She couldn't believe her ears. *That* was not on the list. "Are you serious?"

"As a matter of fact, I am."

"I mean, it's bad enough that you snuck behind my back and bought my paintings, but the way you... Well, there was nothing innocent about how you kissed me. It, it...was beyond friendly and well past flirty."

His eyes lit up with amusement, and his smile grew. "That is so true, but let's be fair—you kissed me back."

Smartass. "I suppose you have no intention of telling Candice, and I get that. But, I'm surrounded by her friends, and if anyone saw... Do you realize the kind of position you've put me in? I'm not that kind of person. I don't sleaze around with guys who have girlfriends."

"We didn't sleaze anything. And just so you know, Candice and I officially broke up on Friday night. It'd been headed that way for a while, and you can ask Kayla if you don't believe me."

"Yeah, right."

"It's the truth."

Bailey probably blinked five or six times in rapid succession. *He broke up with Candice Friday night.* When she finally found her voice, it was to say something truly profound. "So."

"So—kissing you was after the fact. Look, I know you want this as much as I do. And as far as the position I put you in, well," he snorted playfully. "I can think of a few." He tried and failed to contain a wicked smile.

Bailey scoffed—loudly, shaking her head at his

slightly twisted comment. "Really?"

"I didn't mean it like that." He dragged a hand over his face to hide his grin. "I mean, well, yeah, I have thought about it, but it's not what I was referring to just now. It just kind of came out that way."

How is he so adorable? "You and Candice broke up, so what? You know, if her friends thought I had something to do with your breakup, I'm not sure I'd have a place to live. It will be hard enough working here— knowing what..." *...your lips feel like on mine.* "I've got a lot to lose, Tony—a lot." Her heart, most of all.

"You think you're the only one." He spread his hands over the desk and stood, his arms taking the weight as he leaned forward. "I'm staying with Max until Candice can find someplace else to live. I'm trying to do this, right?"

"Well, maybe I could make it easy and swap places with her? Would you like that?"

His sexy smile made a brief appearance. "Yes, I would, actually." Her face soured, causing his smile to vanish. "I'm sorry. Hey, you're the one who said it. Kind of sounded funny, that's all." Nothing he was saying *should* be working in his favor. *What is happening?* "Look, Bailey, I honestly didn't think I'd have to fight you for this, but I can, and I will."

What? Her thoughts scurried for any thread of reasoning she had to grab. "For how long?"

"What do you mean for how long?" He straightened and crossed his arms.

Bailey rose from her chair and challenged him. "Until someone else comes along, two, three, maybe six months from now. Isn't that what you do? How many women have you lived with anyway? Honestly, you seem to be very fickle when it comes to relationships."

"Fickle?" His eyes narrowed. "And it's not that

many. Who told you that anyway?" He rolled his eyes and scoffed. "You can't listen to Kayla. Look, you know this is different. It's been different from the beginning, so don't pretend it's not."

Bailey made a colossal mistake and looked directly into his eyes. Her determined mindset faltered, trying to remember that she had to protect herself. *Protect her heart.* This was happening way too fast. Right now, staying angry was all she had. "I'm not pretending, and...and I am mad at you."

"Okay. But don't think for a minute that this is done." He moved to the side of the desk and propped his hip on the edge. "I'll give you all the time you need. Just let me know when you're not mad anymore."

Bailey wanted to cave that minute, and she had the feeling that he knew it. *Dammit.* She darted toward the door to make her escape. When it swung open, she found Kayla plastered against the other side.

"Um, sorry." Kayla cringed and resorted to doe eyes, trying to feign innocence.

Bailey tromped back into her workspace. So much for being prepared. Her brain felt like scrambled eggs. A distraction might help. Aha, she'd put together a list of what they needed to take to the meeting. Unfortunately, the paper stayed blank as a different list ultimately formed in her mind.

One, Tony broke up with Candice. Wtf? He said it's what I wanted, too. Yeah, maybe, but not like this. How can guys move on so fast?

Two, he's staying with Max until Candice finds somewhere else to live. What a gentleman. "Augh."

Three, he said I wasn't the only one with something to lose. Is it solely business for him? He values her work. Or does he mean something more significant, like his heart?

Last but not least, he said he would "fight" for this, fight for her. Kayla said he wasn't a fighter.

What was she going to do?

At ten minutes 'til ten, Bailey gathered the folder she'd compiled for Porter Industries and a sketch pad to take notes. Stepping into the shop, Tony was going over a work order with Dylan.

Earlier in Tony's office, she'd refrained from doing her routine head-to-toe inspection of him, but now, she had an unobstructed view of Tony in his meeting clothes. Charcoal-colored dress slacks and a black shirt made him look more GQ than Abercrombie Fitch. Black was a good color for him. It played well off his dark hair and tan skin. And, if that wasn't enough, he must've added a splash of his cologne. Despite knowing better, she inhaled again.

Tony's eyes shifted without lifting his head. The sweltering look in his eyes held her captive. She wouldn't last long at this rate.

Bailey opened the folder in her hands, pretending to review the information inside. *So, it's come to this.*

A wave of static energy fell over her, followed by the shadow of Tony's imminent presence.

"It's Polo Black. I know how much you like it."

Bailey lifted her chin, determined to stay tepid as her wayward resilience melted. "Umm."

"Are you ready for this?." His dialed-up confidence added more pressure.

No. "Yes. I'm ready for the meeting." How long could she last in the truck? "How far away is Leesburg?"

"Not that far."

Sitting in the truck was sheer hell—or heaven, depending on how she chose to look at it. Not only did he smell and look luscious, he had his damned wrist draped over the steering wheel. Why did she find something like that so sexy? Freakin' ridiculous is what it was.

They rode in blissful silence for a full ten minutes before Tony shattered it. "You look really nice, by the way." He did a quick study of her "meeting" clothes.

Bailey struggled to keep her eyes trained on the scenery outside the window.

"That's a compliment. It's a small one, but still a compliment, and remember what Quin said. You're supposed to say, 'thank you.'" Was he trying to fire her up—on purpose?

She caught his reflection in the side mirror. The smug bastard was grinning. "Thank you," The reply tasted like acid. She just shook her head.

"Aren't you going to tell me how I look?"

"Oh my gosh, are you seriously fishing for compliments?" Like he needed to.

"No. I just wanted to know if you thought I should wear a tie. I brought one if you think I need it."

Bailey cleared her throat. "You look—fine." *Too fine.*

That ended the banter for another twenty minutes. Tony reached for a button on the dash and changed the music. He stopped when he found "Animals" by Maroon 5.

Bailey reached for the nob, but he swatted her hand away. "Driver picks the tunes. Those are the rules."

Smartass.

He sang along with the song.

Dammit. Of course, he sang well.

They passed a sign along the side of the highway welcoming them to Leesburg. According to the GPS on the dash, Porter Industries' large office complex was just ahead. At least now, she had a legitimate distraction from Tony. She could focus on work.

Tony parked in a visitor spot near the entrance

and waited for her by the front of the truck. Walking toward him, his gaze blistered a path from her toes to her head. If anyone else had looked at her that way, she would have slapped them. Hard! But, because it was Tony, it took everything she had to keep from throwing him to the ground and leaping on top of him. He said he would give her all the time she needed, not that he would make it easy.

Bailey strutted past him with an imaginary sense of control. Tony followed a step behind but reached around her to open the door. Only he didn't open it right away. She looked up. Big mistake. His green eyes sparkled with mischief.

"What?" she asked quietly.

"Nothing, I just like to see you blush."

Jerk.

He pulled the door open, and somehow, her feet carried her to the reception desk.

"Good Morning," Tony addressed the woman behind the desk. His totally relaxed and calm persona made her want to scream, or maybe smack him upside the head. "We have an appointment with Bill Porter. Tony Shepard and Bailey Jazincski." His charm had no limits.

The woman gave Tony a coy smile. "Take the elevator to the seventh floor. I'll notify Mr. Porter's assistant that you are on your way up."

"Thank you." They joined a small crowd of people waiting for the elevators. As a few more people gathered, Tony's hand landed on the center of Bailey's back. It felt like a hot iron pressing against her clothes. She reached around and brushed his hand away.

The spotless, mirrored elevator doors opened, and the people from inside scurried off before the waiting crowd squeezed inside. Bailey found herself shoulder to shoulder with strangers near the back corner of the tight space. Somehow, Tony ended up against the wall directly behind her. He touched either side of her waist and pulled her closer when three more people crammed in at the last second. The doors closed.

Tony always seemed to catch her off guard. *Let me change my shirt in front of you. Let's dance so you can see how sexy I am. I like to see you blush.* Just once, she'd like to shatter that calmness and surprise the shit out of him. See how well *he* holds it together.

When the cab jarred into motion, she found her chance. Positioned as they were, her backside bumped against him. He sputtered and cleared his throat, so she nudged against him with a tad more vigor. *Take that.*

The elevator stopped on the third floor. The exchange of people seemed endless, but the available space stayed the same. Bailey used the shuffling of people to *graze* against his nether regions again. Her vengeful playfulness stopped abruptly when a noticeable firmness nudged her back, and it was not the keyfob.

Tony's hands gently bit into her waist when the elevator jolted back into motion.

Oh gawd, her plan had backfired horribly. *Okay, okay, that's enough.*

Bailey tapped the shoulder of the man in front of her, hoping to create a smidgen of much-needed space. But—Tony held in place and pressed his hips against her bum.

The elevator skipped the fourth floor but stopped on the fifth and sixth. All but two other people evacuated on this floor. With more space, Tony gently shoved her forward and plucked the folder from her folded arms to discreetly cover himself.

She caught his reflection in the semi-polished chrome interior of the elevator. If her goal was to bother him, then mission accomplished. He was bothered all right—hot and bothered, and she'd never been so turned on.

The doors opened to the seventh floor, and they walked down a short hallway toward another foyer. He paused at a set of glass doors and looked her square in the eye.

"Seriously, what did you think was going to happen?" He handed her the folder, grinned victoriously, and marched to the seventh-floor receptionist.

Chapter Twenty-One

Tony's dick needed a proper adjustment. So did his thoughts. If Bailey was trying to rattle him—she succeeded. And nothing could've surprised him more. He was about to have the most important meeting the company has ever had, and she got his dick so hard he could barely think straight.

"Please, please have a seat." Bill waved them toward the lush set of chairs surrounding a solid glass-topped table. "I can't tell you how pleased I am with the Plumbing vans. Now, we need to upgrade the other two locations. I'll have about fifteen box trucks and roughly twenty-odd vans. That shouldn't be a problem for you, should it?"

"No, sir, not at all."

"Fabulous. As you may know, I own a few other businesses and properties." Bill tapped a stack of folders next to him. "These are the ones I want you to start with. I have a small line of dump trucks that I rent out. Maybe twenty, twenty-five." He leaned back in his chair. "They come in handy for maintenance for the apartment complexes. The newest complex is supposed to be finished in about three months. It has a lake, a park, a... what do you call it... A piazza. It's very hip."

And then, I have plans for two open-air malls that will go beside two specific industrial parks. One where you're located and another outside of Restin. I'm considering having a bakery and a deli in each." He leaned toward Bailey. "I got the idea of the deli from you. It shouldn't be this hard to find a decent pastrami. My wife suggested the bakery, and I do like the smell of freshly baked bread."

Bailey's face lit up. " That sounds like a

wonderful idea, Bill."

"I think so. It's all in the early planning stages, so this one isn't pressing—yet. Maybe in a couple of weeks, we can start on this."

"Are you thinking of bringing in a chain for the bakery or something else?" Bailey's pencil was moving a hundred miles a minute, taking notes.

"Well, that's the same thing my wife asked. It just so happens that I have a cousin who knows a thing or two about operating a bakery. We're in negotiations to see if he'd be willing to relocate from St. Louis to Virginia. Between you and me, he'll do it because I'm his favorite cousin—and he'll make a lot of money."

Tony just sat back in awe. Bailey had Mr. Porter, *Bill,* wrapped around her little finger, probably just like every other man in her life. He didn't see himself as being any different. She really was magnificent.

Roughly two hours later, after a complete series of questions and answers, Bill Porter stood. "Now, I know it might seem like a lot, but I'm headed to Chicago this coming Saturday, and I was hoping to be able to go over any drafts you have time to put together to take with me." He handed Tony the stack of folders. "But, no rush."

What Bill was really saying: *Have everything ready by Friday.*

Bailey's hand shot forward. "I've got some ideas brewing already. Is your trip to Chicago for business or pleasure?"

"Somewhere in the middle. I'm going to see my grandson, the one I told you about." Bill's wiry gray brows lifted. "But I can see that he's late once again. You're a damned lucky man Son. Treat her right."

Bill's innocent observation made Tony smile like a fool. Bailey, not so much. "Yes, sir, I will."

"I'll walk you to the elevator."

Unlike the crowded ride up, Tony and Bailey were the only two going down.

She retreated to the opposite side and gave off a vibe that said, "Stay where you are." It made him want to pull the emergency stop and— Aw man. Waiting was going to be way more challenging than he expected. And probably require a lot of extra showers.

J. ALISON COLE

Chapter Twenty-Two

What in the world made Bailey think that stunt in the elevator was a good idea? It totally backfired, and now she was beyond aroused. However, the drive back was mentally exhausting because two things kept tumbling around in her head.

First, she'd never been so happy to have her period. Period sex needed to be in the shower. At least, that's where she and Jordan did it. Anywhere else was too messy. Not exactly how she envisioned having sex with Tony for the first time. Equally bizarre was the fact that she was *considering* her obstacles of having sex with Tony—right now. *Oh, Gawd.*

The second nagging concern, crazy as it was, probably carried more weight than the first. The little voice inside her head had resurfaced, repeating the name Michele. A while back, it didn't take much for Bailey to find out from Quin, who found out from Liz that Jordan and Michele hooked up the very first time they went out. Bailey didn't want to be *Michele*, the sex-charged replacement.

For all she knew, Tony and Candice were sharing the same bed three days ago, doing god knows what. The sickening thought gave her an instant headache. So, what was a reasonable time frame? Pretty sure it was more than three freakin' days. How could anyone fall in and out of relationships so quickly?

Tony turned into the industrial park and pulled behind the shop. The truck came to a stop. He kept both hands on the wheel, and took a deep breath, preparing to say something.

Quin's ringtone blared from her purse. *Saved by the bell*, or in this case, the theme song to Hawaii Five-O,

Bailey scurried from the cab, and charged through the rear door of the shop, digging her phone out of her purse.

"Quin. Oh my god, hello."

"Hey—" Quin's astounding perception interrupted his cheerful greeting. "Bailey?"

Dang it, Quin. "It's so good to hear from you. Are you back from your honeymoon?" She raced into her office and began separating her "regular clothes" on her desk. *Should have brought panties, too.* Even with a tampon, they had to be a mess between her period and juicing over Tony.

"Yeah, yeah. We made it back in one piece. Hey, what the hell is going on? You sound all flustered."

"Oh, we just got back from a meeting. I literally just walked through the door a moment ago. We might've picked up a whole lot of work. You'd be jealous..." Bailey had hopes of distracting him. In the process of kicking off her high heels, she looked up. Standing in her doorway, Tony, unbuttoning the cuffs of his shirt. His smile defined suave.

"Tell Quin I said hi." He started on the top button of his shirt.

Bailey's eyes followed his hands, and she caught a glimpse of the tiger-eye necklace. It laid below that little divot under his Adam's apple. Her breath shuddered, not having the willpower to look away.

He winked and walked away. Her lady parts— quivered.

"Bailey? Bailey?" Quin's voice was a hundred miles away on the other end.

She mentally crawled back to the phone. "Tony says hi." *Ha, ha, ha.*

****

Kayla glided into Bailey's office. "It's already past five o'clock, Bailey, time for Brindles."

Bailey pressed the button that shut her computer down. "Trust me, after this week, I almost drank that tequila sitting on my desk." The mountain of sketches took the entire week to get done.

"You should be proud of the proposal you and Tony put together. It really is impressive."

Bailey had to agree. Her creativity had skyrocketed to a whole new level. She tweaked, modified, adjusted, combined, and finessed a whole line of versatile ideas. She'd knocked it out of the park no matter what Bill went with, whether it was for the trucking company, the existing apartments, or the signs needed for the new complex with the piazza. The coolest part was how she used a ghosted "P" somewhere in the various designs to identify them as part of Porter Industries. It was some of the best design work she'd ever accomplished.

And all that hard work was the only thing that saved Bailey from herself—and Tony.

"Hopefully, Bill will think so too."

"Tony showed me the numbers. Six figures for a few months of work with a fabulous profit margin for a company of our size. I'm glad he opted to deliver the package in person. But I thought he'd be back by now."

"Yeah, me too."

Tony had given her plenty of breathing space all week long. But, as he left for Leesburg, the look in his eyes said that reprieve might be over. Oddly enough, she was okay with that.

Walking into Brindles, Kayla stood on her tiptoes. "Do you see any tables, Bailey?"

"I see one table toward the back. We can steal some stools."

"Oh, it's the last one too. Should I order us a pitcher?"

"I think I'll start with a vodka tonic."

"Oh, feeling wild tonight, are we?"

"You could say that." Now that Porter Industries' proposal was out of the way, it felt like all the obstacles between her and Tony were also. So yeah, she was feeling something. The first drink went down relatively quick. Within the same hour, the second followed. Waiting for Tony had her ripe with anticipation. Jumping the gun or not, Bailey had never been this horny in her entire life, and she concluded that seven days were better than three.

"You know, we'll probably need to hire more people." Kayla prattled to Sherry. "If I become office manager, we'll need a new receptionist for sure. You know Bailey, you and Tony make a great team. With your artistic ability and his business savvy, you really are a perfect match. " Kayla's gaze shifted in the direction of the door. "Finally, he's here." Bailey glanced over her shoulder.

Tony was scanning the crowd, and even this far away, when their eyes met, the connection was instant. Her adrenaline spiked, and her heartbeat ramped to match the fast tempo of the music playing in the club.

Instead of dress slacks and his standard polo from earlier, he'd changed into a faded pair of worn jeans, a plain white vee-neck, and his dark blue zip-up hoodie. Perhaps that's why it took him so long to get here.

Tony made his way across the club and shimmied next to the pub table. He shoved both hands into the pockets of his hoodie. He looked as anxious as she did.

His longing gaze peppered her face, triggering that warped sense of gravity that lifted her stomach.

She waited a few seconds before stepping down from the stool. "I'm letting you know."

Without a flicker of hesitation or so much as a

single word, Tony grabbed her hand and traversed through the mob at Brindles, like the parting of the Red Sea. He was a man on a mission, and *she* was the mission.

Outside of Brindles, his Mustang was parked not far from the door. The top was down, so she climbed over the side and buckled up.

When they hit the main road, a ripple of goosebumps nipped at her skin, but the cool night air had nothing to do with it. She'd dreamt of this, longed for this, and now it was going to happen. It seemed right. And even if it wasn't, she didn't have the strength or slightest inclination to fight it any longer.

Tony's grip on the wheel wasn't his usual sexy pose. Fixed and full of determination, he held the wheel like a racecar driver on the final lap. The streetlights created dashes from the shadows over his governed expression. She had the urge to reach across and touch him, maybe run her hand up his thigh. *No.* She might not be able to stop.

A few minutes later, his blinker lit up, the car slowed, and he turned into a neighborhood of trendy townhomes.

They made it as far as the front door of what she assumed was Max's townhouse. Tony pressed his body against hers, spreading her arms flat against the door above her head. His hungry kiss slowly devoured her lips and then blazed a trail down the side of her neck. Her skin was on fire. She arched into him when he mouthed her hardened nipples through her white cotton blouse and bra. Holding onto his head was the only thing that kept her upright.

He came up for air. "God, Bailey. I want you so bad it almost hurts."

Bailey felt the same. She pulled his lips to hers.

He tasted like sweet brandy, intoxicating on so many levels.

Tony fumbled with the keys to unlock the door, never fully breaking away from the desperate and feverish kiss. Inside, Bailey unzipped Tony's jacket. It disappeared from there, just like his shirt.

Coiled together, he walked them backward toward a set of stairs. Midway up, Tony tugged her shirt free from her pants and started plucking at the dainty white buttons. She was ready to yank it apart right as it fell open. A groan left the back of his throat when he spotted her lacy black bra. His fingers ran along her ribs and around her back. A second later, the clasp released, and the bra slid higher. One step above him, Bailey wove her fingers into his silky dark hair, drawing him to her exposed breasts. Wetness from his tongue lapped over her nipples, drawing each pink tip into his mouth, sucking and tugging softly. The sensation turned her legs into mush, and she melted where they stood.

Tony claimed her lips and climbed on top of her. His belt clicked and snagged against the front tab of her jeans. Not even the thick denim was enough to hide his massive erection grinding against her pelvis. He rode her body, building and coaxing her desire even more.

Bailey burrowed one leg between his and quickly worked on the buckle. The button on his jeans and the zipper followed. It took a few desperate shoves on the waistband, but his cock was finally free. Tony quivered and released a carnal grunt.

Bailey wrapped her fingers around him, and his hot shaft throbbed against her palm. She ran her thumb over the satiny tip to spread his dew.

He shifted to one side to unfasten her pants. Then his hand eased down the front and underneath the elastic of her panties. He worked her jeans from side to side, caressing her skin and urging her pants lower. She helped by shimmying and lifting her hips, and they gained another step in the process. When her jeans made it to her knees, she kicked her legs free.

Tony's hand cupped over her folds before he slid a finger into her slick center. "You're so wet."

She tightened around his finger and thrust her hips higher. She wanted him deeper. "Augh." Air rushed from Bailey's lungs in the form of a dense, wanton moan, and her back arched away from the stairs. A second finger slid inside, sending a shockwave through her limbs. In and out, again and again, her body pulsed to his rhythm as his thumb worked her sensitive clit. "Oh, my god, Tony." His cock bucked in her hand.

In one motion, he withdrew his fingers from her core and kneed her legs wider. "We're not going make it upstairs, Bailey. I need to be in you now." He scrambled for a condom in the back pocket of the jeans, bunched halfway down his thighs.

Grappling with the same urgency, Bailey took it from him and ripped it open. "Let me do it." She rolled it down his length and positioned the tip of his penis against her opening.

Staring into her eyes, his breathing and his body shuddered against her, pausing for only a second before he sank into her.

Bailey's body vibrated from the initial plunge. The sensation, too immense, as all of her inner muscles clamped around him.

"Jesus, Bailey." He drew air through clenched teeth and pumped a second time. A savage kiss, and he thrust again—and again. Her hips lifted to meet his until his pace lengthened and increased exponentially like a train building speed.

Bailey's orgasm slammed unexpectedly. Her

mouth fell open, but no sound came out. She exploded—tumbled, her insides splintering with mini convulsions. The tremors reached Tony, and the muscles along his back turned to stone. He drove into her, harder and deeper, and his upper body arched and jolted with his release.

Breathless beneath him, she floated from her orgasm with him. Tony eased his weight onto his elbows and kissed her again—a slow kiss laced with emotion. She'd never felt so worshipped.

When the kiss ended, she whispered. "Wow."

"*Wow* is right." Tony withdrew from her body and rolled onto his back beside her on the stairs. He sighed in the form of a laugh. "I almost shot my wad in your hand."

Bailey lifted her head and semi-rolled onto her side. "That's...so incredibly *not* romantic to hear." She teased. "Or is that your version of dirty talk?" Her brows lifted.

His grin was both tantalizing and ornery. "Well, the lack of romance is all your fault. You got me too excited. And if you think I'm apologizing for anything that just happened, you're crazy."

Bracing against the stairs, he lifted his hips and yanked up his pants. He didn't bother to zip them up.

Bailey's body was still tingling when she swung a leg over his hips to straddle him. "What's the matter, not how you pictured our first time?"

He propped himself onto his elbows before stealing a quick kiss. "The *wow* definitely, just maybe not the place. You do realize we just fucked on the stairs—at Max's."

"We're on the stairs because, apparently, you couldn't make it any further."

"Oh, and you could?" he said with a hint of good-humored humiliation. "But the night is young, and I like a good challenge." His hands landed on her knees. "I've got to prove that I can be romantic and last longer than seven minutes." They laughed.

Bailey spread her hands over his bare chest. Desire consumed her. "Well, so far, that was the best seven minutes of my life." She kissed him again, a long, passionate, and probably the best kiss of her life.

When his lips left hers, he scooped her into his arms and carried her to the top of the stairs.

"The Bathroom is the second door, and the room I'm staying in is the last door on the right. I'll get us something to drink. Because if I don't do this now, we may never make it off the stairs."

J. ALISON COLE

Chapter Twenty-Three

Tony discarded the used condom in the downstairs bathroom and cleaned himself up. Staring at his reflection in the mirror, the smile on his face felt permanent. "Holy shit!" Sex always felt good, but *never* that good. *What the fuck?*

The refrigerator in Max's kitchen looked like the empty shelves at the grocery store before a snowstorm. The top shelf held half of a bottle of ketchup, a partial block of sharp cheese, seven eggs in a bowl, and, surprisingly, an entire bag of purple seedless grapes. The middle shelf sat empty. Sitting alone on the bottom shelf was a six-pack caddy of Samuel Adams Lager with two bottles already missing. In the door was an unopened bottle of Zinfandel and a bottle of Crown Royal whiskey. Tony opted for the wine because out of the three, wine symbolized romance, plus he liked a good Zinfandel. He grabbed a wine opener from the drawer and searched the cupboard for—*wow, Max actually has wine glasses.* He grabbed two and took the stairs a couple at a time.

Entering his temporary bedroom, he found Bailey leaning against the dresser opposite the bed. She had turned on a small light sitting on the nightstand. It cast a warm glow around the room—and her. Her white shirt was crisscrossed instead of buttoned. If she figured *why bother,* she'd be right. As it was, the bottom of the shirt barely reached the top of her gorgeous legs. With her mass of long curls gathered over one shoulder, she looked like a siren. He was definitely under her spell.

"I found some wine."

Bailey glided across the room and took the bottle and opener from him. It was all he could do to hold the glasses still while she poured. He was thirsty all right, but not for wine.

"Cheers." Bailey touched her glass to his and took a sip. "Wine was a good choice." She licked her lips afterward, and then her devouring gaze—enslaved him.

He tipped his glass, maintaining eye contact. "Yeah, I thought so too." He corralled her to the foot of the bed. "Why don't you have a seat?" Her lips curved into a smile, easing onto the foot of the bed. Her shirt fell open, giving him an enticing glimpse of her supple, well-rounded breasts and naked body. Her confidence was as sexy as her. He dropped to his knees and urged her to lie back with feather-light kisses down her neck and stomach.

"Now, hold still." Carefully, he poured a small amount of wine from his glass onto her midsection. It formed a puddle in the firm, flat area below her navel. The soft intake of her breath sent blood racing to his dick. She propped herself onto her elbows to watch him lick along the edge of the puddle, where it threatened to spill down her sides.

Tony shifted lower, and her smooth, shapely legs opened for him. He dribbled a small stream of wine onto a neatly groomed strip of her pussy. Her mouth fell open as the chilled wine seeped into her crevice. Tony guzzled the remaining wine in his glass and set it aside.

Bailey drained her glass and then tossed it onto the pillows at the head of the bed. A glimmer entered her eyes.

He didn't know who was turned on more. He'd dreamt of this almost as many times as he'd beat off over the last month.

Tony placed kisses along her inner thighs as he positioned her legs over his shoulders. Slowly working his way up, he reached the apex of her body. He nuzzled into the delicate pink flesh of her dainty folds. The wine mingled with her sweet taste and the noises she made—somewhere between a sigh and a moan. A more beautiful sound didn't exist. He sucked, circled, and lapped against her until her head fell back and her chest heaved.

Tony's hands eased beneath her hips as she quivered against his tongue, taut, ripe—ready. Two more long swipes, then he pummeled her clit with his tongue. She launched like a rocket. Her heels dug into his shoulder blades, and her body jolted and bucked against his face.

Watching her come was as gratifying as coming himself.

J. ALISON COLE

Chapter Twenty-Four

Bailey's orgasm unraveled with a series of sporadic twitches. The bed shifted from Tony's weight as he climbed up and collapsed beside her. Basking in the lingering effects, she rolled onto her side to admire him. Tony was sprawled on his back with his arms above his head. His eyes were closed, and his cheeks and lips were glistening. Seeing her wetness on him only enhanced the intimate knowledge of how it got there.

His body was a combination of fit muscles and a sculpted torso. The spray of dark hair on his chest trailed lower to a line of finer hair below his waist. His unzipped jeans beckoned not only a glimpse into the shadows—but her hand.

Bailey's fingers combed into the small, wiry patch of hair to discover that he was fully aroused—and ticklish.

Tony rolled onto his side to face her. "Do you ever think we'll get all the way naked?" He flexed his hips against the hand she had down his pants.

"I can if you can." Bailey sprung to her knees and peeled away her shirt. She'd never felt so seductive. "Your turn."

Tony flopped onto his back and shimmied from his jeans and underwear. His pants ended up at the end of the bed, inside out and twisted. One final kick knocked them onto the floor before he stretched out beside her. His gaze held her captive while his whisper-light touch consumed her through his fingertips.

"Bailey, I've never wanted anyone the way I want you."

"I know how you feel." Bailey placed a soft kiss in the hollow under his ear. His skin felt hot against her lips, and his alluring appeal ignited her senses with a yearning to taste and discover him the same way he just did her.

She shimmied lower and pushed him onto his back. Her fingers swirled across his chest as she nibbled over his ribs and down to his hip bones. Her unruly hair made a veil over his abdomen as she wiggled herself nicely between his legs.

Bailey slid one hand down his hard shaft and cupped his balls with the other. She flattened her tongue and ran it against his throbbing penis. Then, she dipped lower and mouthed the velvety skin of his sack, sucking each ball into her mouth.

"Holy hell, Bailey, that feels so good."

"It's about to get a whole lot better." She gripped the base of his cock and gently primed the engorged mushroom tip with her tongue. Then she took his dick deep into her mouth until it hit the back of her throat. "Um." With the base of her tongue, she pressed and tightened her lips around him. The suction held until her lips released from the top with a pop. She went down on him again, her head bobbing up and down on his smooth, thick rod. Her tempo increased, and his hips bucked in unison with her rhythm.

"Bailey, you need to stop." Pleading, he touched the top of her head. "I'm going to come."

"Mm." Bailey moaned with desire, increasing her pace and adding pressure against the thick vein. She hollowed her cheeks to finish him.

Tony's body went rigid, and his climax gushed into her mouth. Bailey swallowed his creamy essence and lapped his dick clean.

His eyes were still closed as she dragged a thumb over her lips, marveling at his sheer masculinity. Being an artist, she could appreciate his nude form, the shadows created by his muscles, and the dark contrast of hair in his armpits and between his legs. Lying there, with his arms flopped above his head, Tony was a piece of art.

His breathing evened out, and he propped himself onto his elbows. "Jesus, Bailey."

She retrieved the bottle of wine from the end of the bed. "Was that okay?" She filled her glass and then offered the bottle to him.

Tony took three big gulps directly from the bottle. "That was more than okay." He quietly studied her. She did the same to him.

They needed this silent, unhurried deliberation to absorb one another.

"Tell me everything, Bailey. I want to know every part of you."

****

Bailey lost track of how long she talked, listened, and laughed. They covered birthdates, middle names, likes and dislikes, music and movies, places they've been, favorite foods and colors, first cars, pets, and pet peeves. Tony's voice was filled with a tremendous amount of love and sadness when he talked about his family and the loss of his brother. By the time he finished, Bailey felt as if she knew Aaron and mourned him, too.

"He sounds like he was a wonderful man. I think I would've liked him a lot."

"Oh, I've no doubt about that. Everyone loved him. You would've succumbed to his irresistible charm in a heartbeat." Tony scooted closer and nuzzled at her neck.

"Charm?" She chuckled. "You must have inherited all of his then, because you have entirely too much for any one man to possess."

"Well, I can't apologize for that." Tony's hands

skimmed along her hips before trailing to the sensitive skin near the inside of her thighs. Her body responded to his touch in an instant. His lips found hers for a lengthy, passionate kiss. Not a peck, not a friendly, *how are ya,* but a real kiss.

Somehow, she always knew it would be like this. The kiss was smooth yet hungry, full of wonder, yet somehow knowing. Every tilt of her head, every sweep of her tongue, anticipated and rewarded. She'd never tire of kissing Tony.

He broke away from her lips. "I want to make love to you."

Bailey couldn't find the words to say how she felt. What they did before was urgent, needy sex necessary to get to this point.

Tony reached over the end of the bed to retrieve another condom from his jeans. Watching his muscles flex along his shoulders sent a ripple of heat straight to her core.

"You seem awfully prepared." She poked his ribs playfully. "How many of those do you have?"

He clambered next to her, smiling. "I'll be honest, I put one in my pocket hoping—but not expecting anything." He raised his hand innocently. "But I'm really glad you were ready because I don't think I could have held out much longer. Max shoved two more into my pocket right before we went inside the club."

"And what happens when they're all gone? I'm not on the pill—right now."

"Just so you know, I'm very vigilant when it comes to protection. I've always worn one when it comes to intercourse. So I guess we'll have to get creative." He eased closer for a kiss. His hand slid between her legs, fueling her hunger and sparking her juices.

Bailey rolled to her back and opened herself to

him. Tony mounted above her, resting his hips against hers. Her arms entwined around his back as their bodies merged. Tender and sweet, this time, they made love.

****

Bailey stirred awake, nestled in the crook of Tony's arm. Lying face down, the sheet was below her waist, but the heat from Tony's body was keeping her warm. The last round had drained her, and in this surreal moment, Bailey gave in to the tempting thought that this was how she'd like to wake up each and every morning for the rest of her life. She couldn't imagine ever feeling different.

Careful. The voice in the back of her head whispered the worthless warning. And a soft, giddy chuckle escaped.

Tony's fingers massaged into her scalp.

Bailey's hand snaked further around his waist. Knowing that he was awake made the butterflies in her chest dance.

A door closed somewhere downstairs. She lifted her head.

Tony leaned up too. "Must be Max. What time is it?"

Bailey squinted at the boxy green numbers displayed by the clock setting on the nightstand. "Three-thirty."

"Are you hungry?" Tony inquired.

"God, yes."

"I'll get us something to eat." Tony rolled *over her*, making a point to roguishly smear his body against hers. She loved it. He haphazardly hopped into his denim jeans. "Be right back." At the door, he darted back toward the bed just to give her a quick kiss.

After Tony left the room, Bailey sat up and hugged her knees. Her thoughts drifted again to her intense yearning for this to be real and forever. *And ever.* The sound of muffled voices drifted through the open crack of the door from downstairs. Tony and Max were probably doing that *guy* thing, but she didn't care, not in the slightest.

What felt like an hour was perhaps no more than five minutes before Tony reentered the bedroom carrying a bowl of grapes, some crackers, and a bottle of water underneath his arm. He set everything on the table, removed his jeans, and climbed back into bed.

Bailey snatched the bowl of grapes from the table. "So, what did you guys talk about?" She knew perfectly well what they were talking about. She took a handful of grapes.

"I told him that he needs more wine." He picked up a grape and popped it into her mouth. The smile on his face was the same one that had captured her from the very beginning.

How was she able to resist him for as long as she had? She polished off a handful of grapes to cure her hunger, but her appetite for Tony wasn't filled yet.

He was sitting up, propped against the headboard. She placed the bowl onto the nightstand and then straddled his waist with a wicked smile. She ground her hips against him, sparking the results she sought. Tony handed her the last condom.

Bailey pressed his bare shaft against her folds, gyrating and prodding him against her core as she ripped the foil wrapper open. Air wheezed through his teeth as she ever so slowly rolled the condom onto his full erection.

Bailey rose to her knees to position over his penis. Then slowly, she lowered, wanting to feel every nuance of him entering her body—the stretch was amazing. Once she took him deep inside, she lifted, and started the whole process again. Her pace, measured at first, increased to meet the burning need inside of her.

Her rhythm came to a crashing halt when the headboard slammed against the wall. "Oh my gosh," Bailey tried to contain a startled giggle. "Do you think we woke Max?"

"Max, the neighbors, the man down the street," Tony said with a smile.

"I'm serious. The bed must have shifted. Should we stop?"

He blew out a breath and enticed her closer for a reassuring kiss. "God, no."

Bailey's hair made a tent around his face. "I'm so glad you said that." She whispered against his lips and resumed her rhythm. If it banged again, so be it.

Tony lifted his hips to hers, pounding into her from below. His fingers seared a path along her upper thighs, massaging and rubbing. His thumb found her clit and sent her over the edge.

Bailey's spine arched, and head whipped back, spraying her hair like a fan, and nothing could suppress the brazen sound that erupted from her mouth.

A second later, Tony bolted upright against her. He pressed down on her hips and burrowed his face against her neck as he shuddered.

"Fuck—me—" The words tumbled from his lips. After the final tremor, he collapsed onto his back, spent, just like her. "Jesus, Bailey." He scrubbed his chiseled face and ran his fingers through his hair. "What the hell are you doing to me?"

Bailey flexed her inner muscles around him one last time. "Well, if I have to explain it, then I must not be doing it right."

"Oh, trust me, I've never been done this right before." Bailey caught his boyish grin. "That one hit me hard. You're amazing."

Tony quickly disposed of the used condom and returned to bed, gathering her close.

Falling asleep in his arms was the most natural thing she'd ever done.

****

Bailey rousted from a peaceful slumber. The block-green numbers on the clock showed the time as five in the morning. Something hard nudged against her back. She rolled over and saw a glimmer in Tony's eyes.

"Are you going for some kind of record?" Bailey asked.

Tony's brows lift curiously. "What is your record—for one night?"

"Ew, that's not something I would think you'd want to know."

"I'll tell you mine."

"Now that's something I definitely don't want to know—"

"Three. And before you ask, yes, the same girl. And it was a long, long, long time ago."

"Three?" Bailey looked at him suspiciously. "Huh, probably more like thirty."

"Thirty? I'm not a machine, and I don't think that's physically possible." He lifted his chin. "Now, tell me yours."

Bailey imagined bringing Jordan into her thoughts here and now might make her uncomfortable. Remarkably, it didn't, so she pondered his question.

Years ago, she and Jordan went to an outdoor concert. They did it once before leaving the house, a second time at the show underneath a blanket, and then again on their kitchen table when they got home. However, the third time, only one of them tripped the light fantastic, and it wasn't her.

A look of worry captured Tony's features as she sorted her thoughts. So Bailey purposely exaggerated the calculations by checking off all of her fingers.

His chin dropped open. "You're right. I don't want to know."

"Can I just say that you've shattered all the records in the record book tonight?"

Even though Bailey was tired from lack of sleep and copious amounts of spent carnal energy, she wanted Tony again. Her gaze traced over his features. She loved his little widow's peak and the spattering of whiskers just under his chin. The darkness in the room helped to define the perfect shape of his lips. Sometimes, when he smiled, the crinkles near his eyes made him look extra ornery. But now, his deep-set eyes reflected the same longing and desire she felt.

With a great deal of zeal, Bailey inquired. "So? How creative are you? I know you said that you don't pull out. But…"

"Ha, ha, ha. Wait, you'd let me do that? You'd trust me to pull out?"

The look he gave her was sexier and more daring than any she had seen from him before. It made her appreciate that she still had much to learn about him. "I understand if you don't want to."

"Oh, I want to." Tony made a noise that sounded like some kind of happy guttural hum. "You know, we could go full out, kinky."

"No! Not that just yet."

His eyes widened. "Oh, but maybe someday."

"Yeah, maybe—someday." Feeling like a cat in heat, Bailey perched onto her hands and knees. "I trust you, Tony."

"You really are perfect." Tony maneuvered behind her and caressed the small of her back before gradually slipping one hand between her legs. "Sweet Jesus."

It seemed that all she had to do was look at him to be slick and ready. He rubbed the head of his penis through her wetness, grasped her hips—and slowly entered her from behind.

Bailey's senses were already super heightened from their previous *record*-breaking encounters, but the feel of him inside her without a condom escalated to a new level.

The friction of skin on skin generated a more pronounced and enticing degree of pleasure. Tony amped into fuller and more zealous thrusts. A type of euphoria gripped Bailey's body. Her arms trembled, and she dropped to her elbows. The new angle allowed him to go deeper. "Oh god, Tony. Aw, god." The cadence of his skin slapping against hers revved to a new speed.

Her body seized around him with an explosion of pure bliss.

"Ugh." Tony's rhythm faltered, and his grip on her hips tightened. "Ugh—god." He plunged two more times and then jerked free of her body.

His hot release spilled over Bailey's lower back. She found it curiously erotic and completely satisfying. No one had ever come on her before, and she liked that it was him.

****

It was well after nine when Bailey woke again, and she was famished—but this time for food. The few grapes she'd eaten hardly substituted for the dinner she'd skipped the night before. Tony's lying on his back, still asleep, and every part of his body is exposed. The sheet was twisted and bunched near the foot of the bed. Good thing since he used it to wipe off her back. Biting back a smile, she admired his sleeping form. The length of his member, even flaccid, was still quite impressive. Her CSI skills weren't too far off. She had the urge to touch him but decided against it.

Climbing from the bed, she scanned the floor. The empty wine bottle was on its side next to the glasses, and several grapes scattered across the rug. How did that happen? Her shirt was nowhere to be seen, and she left the rest of her clothes on the stairs. She hoped there was something in the dresser that she could wear.

The drawer squealed open, and she found an ash-gray tee. Holding it against her body, she opened the door a crack and made a beeline for the bathroom.

After a considerably long pee, Bailey stepped into a warm shower. Muscles that have gone unused for quite some time gradually loosened as she washed away Tony's luscious scent and a mixture of their bodily fluids.

She toweled dry, and pulled the t-shirt over her head. It's long enough to reach her mid-thigh. Good thing because her panties were MIA.

Bailey tip-toed downstairs to the kitchen. In one cupboard she found two boxes of sugary sweet cereal but—no milk in the fridge. However, there were some eggs in a holder and a bag of shredded cheddar cheese. *Omelets it is.* Rummaging in a few different cupboards she located a mixing bowl, season salt, and much to her surprise, a very fancy frying pan. *This won't be so hard after all.* This was a better breakfast than she normally ate, which only seemed right, since she'd had the best night ever.

Basking in happiness in front of the stove, waiting for the eggs to firm up, two large hands crept around her waist. The warmth of a body pressing against hers radiated down her back, igniting a smile along with her memories.

"Yum," said someone—who was not Tony.

Bailey nearly jumped out of her skin. Wielding the wooden spoon, she spun, ready to strike.

Max veered away, palms raised defensively. "Alright, alright." His gaze snaked over her body, freakishly fast in a nonthreatening, but sleazy-Max kind of way.

Suddenly, the shirt didn't feel long enough. She gave the bottom another yank, just to be safe. His attire— or lack thereof registered. Skimpy, black Calvin Klein boxer briefs barely met the low rise of his breaching man pubes.

"You need to put something else on." Bailey lifted her chin to keep her gaze above his waist. "And what are you doing awake?"

"Me?" He scoffed. "Jesus, how are *you* awake? Is Tony okay? I mean, is he still alive? Christ almighty, I can't believe some of the sounds I heard coming out of that room. I half expected the neighbors to call. This is a townhouse, you know."

Her eyes narrowed, but she was too happy to care, and besides, Max wasn't serious. If anything, she would almost guess that he was happy for his friend.

Bailey lowered the spoon and turned back toward the stove. "I used all the eggs you had. Would you like some breakfast?"

Max craned over her shoulder but wisely kept his hands to himself. "Hell, yes, I'm starving, and that's the least you can do since you kept me up all night. I didn't get a whole lot of sleep either."

From behind them, a shrill voice practically slashed her brain in half. "Max, you're such a scoundrel."

Bailey and Max turned at the same time to see Candice standing at the corner of the couch.

"Oh shit," Max said it first.

Bailey, second. "Oh, shit." Awkward didn't even

come close to this situation, but Candice just stood there smiling. Bailey glanced at Max to absorb the scene. *She and Max snuggled close at the stove, barely dressed, laughing and making breakfast. It told a story, just not the right one.* Candice wrongly assumed that she'd hooked up with Max.

Max cast Bailey another quick look. "Candice. This isn't what it looks like." He'd obviously come to the same conclusion. "I—don't think you understand."

"What's there to understand?" Candice's bright white smile expanded. "I'm just surprised that it took this long."

Bailey didn't care for the insinuation. "What the hell—?"

Footsteps bounding down the stairs drew everyone's attention. Wearing only his jeans, Tony came to a dead stop near the bottom when he saw *three* people in the kitchen. "Oh, shit."

Now there were four people exchanging glances, and Candice was the only one wearing a happy smile.

"Tony." Candice's blissful ignorance maintained her loving tone, and Bailey wanted to smack *her* with the spoon.

"Candice, what the hell are you doing here?" Unease filtered into Tony's voice.

"The door was unlocked. I texted, but you didn't answer. I needed to see you, and it can't wait any longer."

"This really isn't a good time, and you need to know something."

Candice stepped toward him. "When you came by yesterday, it reminded me of how great you are, and why I liked you from the beginning."

Tony was with Candice yesterday. The harsh mental slap quickly summed up why he took so long to get to the club—and he was wearing different clothes.

Tony's gaze darted across the room to find Bailey's. "I only came by to get some clothes, that's all." His raised eyebrows sought her understanding.

"Yes, but what you said meant the world to me. You said you wanted me to be happy."

"I do. Look, Candice, I really can't—"

"I'm late, Tony." She cut him off.

The room fell silent. It mimicked the sound effect in movies when a bomb goes off, a loud nothingness.

Bailey stood frozen in the silence until Max pierced the span with a long, drawn-out exclamation. "Fuck."

Bailey imagined those simple words, *'I'm late'* were every single guy's nightmare. She knew what they meant. Max clearly understood what they meant. And it took another long moment and maybe a boatload of powerful wishful thinking, but Tony asked anyway.

"Late?"

Candice looked at him and smiled—lovingly. "Yes, Tony. I'm late."

Bailey's grip tightened around the spoon.

"That can't be." Tony's chin lowered.

"Oh, it can, and it is."

He snatched his hoodie from the back of a chair. "I'll figure this out." He took Candice by the arm and led her out the front door, and just like that, he and Candice were gone.

A thin haze fogged Bailey's vision of the front door. *What's that smell?* Her brain must be fried.

The smoke detector went off. Max snapped out of his stupor first, grabbing the pan from the stove. He tossed it into the sink and waved a dish towel at the smoke detector. The beeping stopped, and the eerie quiet returned.

Max dragged his hands down his face. "Bailey—

just—Tony will figure this out."

A hollow, emptiness filled Bailey. "Not a whole lot to figure out," her voice cracked. "Tony's a good guy."

"He is, so remember that. He'll do the right thing." Max quickly realized what he said and how it sounded. "That's not what—I meant he'll do what is right for everyone." Unfortunately, those words aren't any better.

A cynical and deranged burst of laughter cut loose. "One more day, that's all I needed, one more day."

"Let's just wait. You don't want to do anything you'll regret, Bailey."

She snorted. "Regret? You have no idea." Bailey stormed by him, following the path she and Tony had taken the night before. She collected her scattered clothing and raced upstairs. She found everything but her panties. *Dammit.*

It was the fastest she'd ever gotten dressed, but when she opened the bedroom door to leave, she came face to face with Max standing on the other side. He'd thrown on sweatpants and a wrinkled polo.

"You need to give him a chance," he pleaded.

Max was trying to help his friend, but Bailey needed him to help her instead. "Can you take me to my car? Or, I can call an Uber."

"Fuck, Bailey. Don't do that, and don't ask me to do that. Please, just wait."

Salty tears brimmed to the edges of her eyes. "If I had waited, I wouldn't be in this position. Look, Max..." Her voice disintegrated into the first distraught sob. It seized her entire body all the way to her soul. "You know his father wasn't around. Tony will want to be a good father. You said it yourself, he'll do the right thing." Building pressure fractured her voice. "He will figure this out, but—I can't be here when he does." Her lip quivered, and her stomach filled with nausea. She'd never felt so hopeless and helpless. "It—was—just—one—night." In the deepest trenches of her gut, there was only one thing she could do. The last pillar of her willpower broke and the emotional dam burst. Tears flooded down her cheeks.

Max caved instantly. "All right, let's go."

Chapter Twenty-Five

"Jesus, Max! Why did you take her anywhere?"

"You didn't see her. Christ, Tony." Max, severely hyped up on coffee, paced across the room. He never could handle caffeine. "Is it true? Is Candice really knocked up?"

Tony levered his head up and down. "You know, I can't even remember the last time we were together. And I always used protection with her."

"Maybe it ripped."

"I...I don't know. But, I made her take another test in front of me. It matched the first two she took. She couldn't get a real appointment with a doctor for another three weeks." Tony didn't need three weeks to understand that his life would never be the same.

"So, how late is she?"

"Like two weeks."

Max's cheeks ballooned full. "Fuck. Is that even enough time to know for sure?"

"Apparently." He asked Candice the same question, and she answered in the same annoying way.

"Is there a chance there was someone else?"

"She says no. And that question went over *real* big."

Tony collapsed onto the black leather sofa in Max's living room. His hands balled into fists over the ache in his chest that wouldn't go away. He felt like his heart had been ripped out. Maybe because it had.

If he tried to call Bailey now, she probably wouldn't answer, and he couldn't blame her. She wasn't at the apartment or her uncle's. He already checked. He was confident that she had gone home to Pennsylvania, and all he could do was hold onto foolish hope that he'd see her Monday.

****

Monday came, and no Bailey.

Tuesday, Wednesday, and Thursday were the same. He tried calling Bailey for the first time on Friday, but her number was no longer in service.

Kayla and Max have been offering advice all week long. Of course, they're only trying to help, and he hasn't been very nice to either of them, and for that, he felt terrible.

Focusing on work was impossible. His desk had a stack of calls waiting to be returned, and he had a meeting scheduled this afternoon for another new potential client—a referral from Bill Porter. Tony checked the time on his phone. It's 11:30. He tried giving Bailey time and space, but now it's time to talk.

"Fuck it. I'm going to Pennsylvania." The moment he stood up from his desk, his phone rang. It's a number he didn't recognize. *It could be her.* He scrambled to answer it.

"Hello?"

"Tony? It's Raven."

Disappointment hissed out of him like a flat tire. "What is it, Raven?"

"I thought you'd want to know they're coming to get Bailey's clothes and stuff." Her curt tone appropriately vilified him.

"Her stuff? At the apartment, when?"

"She told me noon."

"Shit. I'm on my way, and—thanks, Raven."

Tony raced from his office, and jumped into his truck, but he couldn't start it. He had an entire week to figure out what to say to Bailey and still didn't have a clue how to fix this. He wanted to be honest about his feelings and tell her everything. Just like he did with

Candice.

He and Candice agreed that doing something like getting married because of a baby wouldn't magically fix their relationship or make them a couple. But he gave his word that he would be there for everything. Candice moved out of his house that day, and he hadn't spoken with her since the earlier part of the week.

I wish Aaron were here.

A sharp tap on the truck window jolted him back to the present.

Kayla tried peeking into the cab of the truck. "What are you doing?"

Tony lowered the window. "Raven said they're moving Bailey's things today."

Kayla raced around the truck and jumped in. "Okay, let's go."

Well, Kayla was the closest thing he had to Aaron and the one person who knew about heartache and loss. Not a day went by when he didn't see the sadness in his sister's eyes from losing Jason.

But right now, he caught a slight glimmer in her eyes. Hope. And it was for him.

****

Tony spotted Quin carrying two dresser drawers toward a red pickup truck outside of Bailey's apartment.

He parked in an open space not far away and hopped out. Quin practically threw the drawers on the tailgate and charged toward him. In some ways, Tony felt like he deserved what was coming.

"You son-of-a-bitch." Quin grabbed a handful of Tony's shirt and drew back. Only he didn't swing. His fist levered a couple more times—before Quin shoved him loose. "Fuckin' asshole. You goddamned fuckin' asshole, Tony."

He couldn't disagree. "Is Bailey here—with

you—now?"

Quin snorted with disgust. "No." He adjusted the ball cap on his head before placing his hands on his hips. "She fuckin' cried nonstop for days." Quin twitched and swiped at his nose, obviously reliving the uncomfortable vision.

Someone else came out of the apartment building carrying a small desk. Now, Tony wished Quin would've knocked him out.

Jordan slid the desk onto the back of Quin's truck. The blatant grin on his lips landed like a cinder block on Tony's empty chest.

"Motherfucker," he spewed from under his breath.

Quin glanced over his shoulder just as Jordan disappeared back into the building. "Yeah, that's right. And guess what, he broke off his engagement right after my wedding. It's been over nine months since he and Bailey broke up, and now he's dead set on getting her back." His eyes narrowed. "Do you want to know why they broke up in the first place?"

Part of him didn't want to know. But no matter what he said, Quin was bound and determined to tell him.

"I'll enlighten you because it's probably not what you think."

Tony didn't have a clue.

"About a year and a half ago, Jordan's best friend, some guy they went to school with, was getting married. Bailey said all day long, people kept asking them when she and Jordan were going to tie the knot. She said he told them all the same thing. 'Yeah, soon.'" Quin crossed his husky arms to make sure Tony was listening. "You see, apparently, it wasn't what he said that bothered her. It was how he said it. She told me it almost sounded resentful and left her wondering if he really wanted to get married or if he'd only do it because that's what people expected to happen next. She thought if they just had a little bit of time apart, it might give them a new perspective or maybe even rejuvenate the relationship and the feelings they had for one another. But the fucked up part, Jordan jumped at the opportunity to be free and started dating other people right away." He scoffed. "Figures the first guy she really liked would screw her over royally. No pun intended, and yeah, I know everything."

"I didn't hurt Bailey on purpose."

"No, no." His lips flattened and he shook his head. "She actually defended you. But she's devastated just the same. And nothing can change that now." Quin spun and stepped away.

The thought of losing Bailey forever filled him with panic. "Help me, Quin. How do I make this right?"

Quin stopped and turned. "Help you? Jesus, I wouldn't know where to begin. Christ, Tony, you're having a baby with your ex-girlfriend. Do you really have the balls to ask Bailey to be a part of this fucked up situation? And before you say yes, put yourself in her shoes. I mean really. What if it was the other way around? What if she—" He nodded over his shoulder, indicating Jordan. "—was having a baby with someone else? Would it really be so easy to ignore, or would you be willing to step out of the picture to give them a chance?"

"I didn't even get to talk to her."

"What could you possibly have to say?" An angry scowl distorted Quin's face. "I've never seen anyone that upset before."

"I don't want to let her go."

"Don't make this harder on yourself. And if you do care about Bailey for real, then think about what's best for her." Quin mustered one last sympathetic smile. "She said you're a good guy, Tony, so prove it. Prove it by doing the right thing—for her." Quin turned and marched back into the building.

Tony stood there for a moment before he climbed back into the truck with Kayla.

"What did he say?" Kayla's voice still carried hope.

Hope, that he just lost. "He told me what I needed to hear."

Chapter Twenty-Six

Retrieving her belongings midday on Friday was way better than waiting until the weekend. Thank god Raven agreed to meet Quin. And since Jordan offered to help, she didn't have to risk seeing Tony. Her heart was shredded to ribbons, and if she saw him now, there would be nothing left.

From the next street over from her parents' house, the recognizable squeal from Quin's front axle echoed through the neighborhood. Quin rounded the corner and backed up to her parent's garage. She stepped off the porch and headed down the sidewalk.

He clambered from the truck and rushed past her. "I need to pee."

"You know where it is."

Jordan lowered the tailgate, perched his backside against it, and crossed his ankles.

Bailey's emotions may be raw, but she could still be civil. "Thanks for helping Quin and—me."

Jordan leaned back, braced on his arms. "Five hours alone in a truck with Quin, heck Bailey, I'd do anything for you. You know that." He patted a spot on the tailgate beside him.

A soft laugh trickled through her lips. Even though she and Quin had so much in common, Jordan and Quin had never really gotten along.

Bailey hopped onto the tailgate beside him. "I'm sure you had lots to talk about."

His head shook, no. "He barely said two words the entire time—but I'm assuming he knows why you're back home. I think maybe he feels it's not his place to tell."

"He's a good friend."

"I was your friend, too, once upon a time." His kindness was sincere as he reached for her hand. "I'd like to think I still am."

She studied Jordan. His hair was longer and shaggier than before. But something else was different. He seemed to have grown, not physically but emotionally. Bailey liked that, not for her so much, but for him. The last thing she saw was a whisper of hope in his soft blue eyes. It forced her to look away.

Quin charged out of the house. "Shew, I feel better. Let's get this shit unloaded. It ain't gonna take itself off the truck. Come on now, I've got to meet Liz at her parents' house for their anniversary. She doesn't like it when I'm late."

It didn't take long to unload two dressers, a double bed, one fold-up round chair, a corner lamp, and a vanity she used as a desk and nightstand. Oddly, it's all the same furniture she and Jordan had used over the years—and divided after the split.

Quin shoved one of the dressers closer to the wall before giving her a quick kiss on the cheek. "I've got to get going, Bailey." He lowered his voice and leaned closer. "Give me a call later. Okay?"

Bailey reached up to hug him before he had time to step away. She turned, expecting some type of goodbye from Jordan, but—he didn't move, even when Quin's truck started.

"Aren't you going with him?" she asked.

Quin stuck his head from the window. "Sorry, Bailey, but I'm headed in the opposite direction. I was hoping you could give him a ride. Is that okay?"

If Bailey said no, she knew Quin would go out of his way and take Jordan home. But he'd already helped enough. "Yeah sure, and thanks again." She waved goodbye, and turned to find Jordan studying her. "I'll get my keys."

From what Bailey understood from her mother, Jordan had moved out of the apartment that he shared with Michele right after Quin's wedding. Which just happened to be their old apartment. She slung her purse over her shoulder and bounded from the porch toward her car. "I just realized that I don't know where you live."

He laughed sheepishly. "I'm renting a house outside of Greencastle. I can tell you the way, or I can drive."

If he drove, she might get lost coming home. "No, I'll drive, but thanks for offering."

The roads were unfamiliar, and the drive was quiet even with the radio on. Eventually, Jordan pointed to an upcoming road.

"It's up here on the left. The second house."

She turned onto the driveway of a small white cape cod. His motorcycle and Acura, ILX, were parked underneath the side portico.

"Come inside for a minute," he chirped.

Bailey followed him through the side door into the kitchen, not really knowing why. But the moment she stepped inside, her old life cued up like a movie, all because of a coffee mug sitting on the counter.

The cup was brown with a bluish-green edge. She'd always liked it because it was extra tall and held twice as much coffee. It belonged to a set she and Jordan had purchased when they first moved in together—so many years ago. The mug was the last surviving piece. Bailey picked up the relic—remembering.

Jordan ventured into the next room. She set the cup down, and followed him into a narrow living room. She recognized a brown paisley chair from his parents' house and a side table that they made from a wooden crate and some Plexiglas. His television was mounted to the wall, but the tools were scattered on the floor as if he'd just finished and hadn't had time to put them away.

But what really caught Bailey's attention was the forest-green sofa. It held more memories than the mug. So many memories…

Jordan rested his hands on his hips and surveyed the room with her. "So, what do you think?"

Thinking was the last thing Bailey wanted to do. She stepped in front of him and placed a hand on the center of his chest. His heart raced beneath her palm as she searched his face. His head lowered, and his lips landed on hers.

Chapter Twenty-Seven

Waiting the last three weeks to accompany Candice to her appointment have been the longest three weeks of Tony's life.

The plastic orange chair he'd been sitting in for the past hour has only intensified his discomfort. Anatomy posters covered every wall, and depicted the various stages of pregnancy with close-up views of the reproductive organs. Fair to say, he might not look at vaginas the same way ever again. The room felt sterile and cold, but not in a good way. And every time Candice moved, the paper crinkled under her. She was as restless as he was, perched on the end of the exam table in a dingy-looking hospital gown. She didn't want him to be here, and in truth, he'd rather be anywhere else. But he wasn't a complete asshole. And he was part of this, whether she liked it or not.

A quick tap on the door came right before the doctor entered the room. The man had a folder pinched under his armpit and used his foot to maneuver a stool on wheels from the corner. He plopped down and rolled toward them with an overzealous push.

"Good afternoon. I'm Dr. Azeia. Sorry if you've been waiting for very long. I don't know about you, but I've already had a busy day: four deliveries starting about two o'clock last night and possibly a few more before the day ends. Must've been something in the water nine months ago." He laughed at his own joke.

There was another tap on the door before a nurse popped her head inside the room. "Excuse me, Dr. Azeia, it's an emergency, Mrs. Packson. An ambulance is taking her to the hospital as we speak. You need to leave right now."

"Oh, okay. I'll be right there." He spun to face them. "Well, Ms. Martin, I apologize, but we'll need to complete this exam at a later time. Which is probably better. As it is, I haven't had the chance to thoroughly review your test results." He flipped the folder open. "I did, however, notice that your hormone level is exceedingly high, which isn't necessarily unusual. All pregnancies are different, and it doesn't mean that there's anything wrong with the baby. " The doctor exchanged glances between him and Candice, waiting for smiles that weren't there. "From the blood we drew, I'll set up the proper prenatal plan with vitamins, and then we'll do some other tests to monitor your iron and sugar levels. It's extremely early to do any kind of ultrasound, but perhaps by your next visit. I'm sure everything is fine. Before you leave today, I'll have the nurses put together some information you can read over. Don't worry, you have plenty of time. I'd say about eight months, give or take." He was the only one who laughed. "Any questions?"

Tony's grip on the plastic chair turned his knuckles white. Somewhere in the back of his mind, he thought maybe it was all a mistake.

The doctor stood and waited for a second longer. "Congratulations, being a parent is a blessing. You'll see." His smile faded. "I'll be in touch in a couple of days."

Chapter Twenty-Eight

The phone in Quin's shop rang again. He gave Bailey one of his *Wtf* looks and asked, "Are you going to get it or not?"

"Need I remind you that I don't work here? It's just so boring at home." Bailey felt extra snarky today.

"Well, you've been here day in and day out for weeks now, so that's the least you can do." He sat his paintbrush down and grabbed the phone. His tone went from crabby to pleasant in the blink of an eye. "Good afternoon. Chenney Signs."

Bailey tuned him out and flipped through the mail lying on his messy desk. Most of the envelopes had the same yellow label from the post office that forwarded his company mail to his new location. She had to give Quin credit. He did a great job finding this place, and the new shop wasn't far from where they used to work. His sign company should do well here, but it would still be a while before he could offset any new overhead, pay himself—and afford her.

Bailey tossed the mail aside and drummed her fingers on the clutter. The mess wasn't confined to his desk. Everything was in disarray, but Quin made it clear that she was not allowed to move or straighten anything. He liked his stuff this way.

The front door chimed. Quin tucked the phone under his chin and rolled his eyes, silently asking her to handle the customer on the other side of the petition.

"Fine." Bailey branded a fake smile on her lips and headed around the corner to greet his patron. Only it wasn't a patron. Standing in his dismal reception area was a sprite of a woman with lavender streaks adorned through her dark-cropped hair. They matched her metallic shirt and unicorn covered leggings.

Bailey stared for a good ten seconds, unable to move. "Hi, Kayla."

"Hi, Bailey," Kayla used her bill-collecting voice.

Bailey ventured to guess why she was there—and wasn't happy with any of the reasons she conjured. Her stomach soured and churned for good measure. "May I help you?" Sarcasm saturated her voice, reflecting how she felt.

Kayla took full advantage of Bailey's cynicism, which served her right. "As a matter of fact, you can."

Her bitch skills were slipping. "How so?"

"You can hear me out, for starters." Kayla stepped closer, and her smile softened. "You need to come back."

The air in Bailey's windpipe exploded in the form of a huff/grunt/snort. "That's not going to happen."

Kayla shoved a handful of papers toward her. "Look at these."

Bailey glanced at a thumbnail sketch on top. It kind of looked like a block of some sort. "What am I looking at?"

"This is what Dylan designed for Bill Porter's bakery. It's supposed to be bread."

It looked more like a gigantic turd. The few sketches underneath weren't any better.

"Bill didn't see these, did he?"

"No! Thank goodness. We've been so busy, Bailey, trying to keep up with everything. Tony hasn't had time to hire a new graphic designer or train someone new to help in the back. Ajak's needs you. I need you."

"You?"

Her gaze shifted to the floor. "He won't ask, but I will. Just help us get caught up until we can hire someone. Look, I know a lot of shit hit the fan, but I'm asking you from a business point of view. You left—

without any notice at all." Her tiny chin lifted. "This company is just as important to me as it is to Tony."

Leave it to Kayla to make her feel guilty.

"Just give me a couple of weeks. Please."

Bailey shuffled through the turd sketches again. "Kayla—I don't know if I can."

"Look, if you're worried about seeing Tony, he's almost always out of the office. I'm sure your Uncle wouldn't mind if you stayed with him since it's temporary, or if that's too close, you know, you can stay with me." Kayla followed her to the counter. "You won't see Candice either. She and Tony, well, she doesn't live there anymore, but I'm not going to get into that. That's not why I'm here."

Where was Candice?

"Two weeks, Bailey. You owe me that." Kayla's stern, bill-collecting voice kicked back in. How was someone so small, so intimidating? Was there such a thing as a *bad* pixie?

"She's right, Bailey." Quin, no longer on the phone, was standing in the doorway behind her. "You need to finish what you started."

Quin's comment came as a surprise. She'd told him everything—absolutely everything. He knew how hard she fell for Tony, so he had to realize this wouldn't be easy.

Bailey turned back toward Kayla. "And what about Tony?"

"What do you mean?" Kayla's head fell to the side.

"You said he wouldn't ask. Does *he* want this?"

Kayla crossed her arms stubbornly. "He can barely think straight. Between all the work and how it all happened with Candice. I just don't know what he'd do if the business faltered too."

Bailey braced herself against the counter. Kayla added to her argument. "Look, Quin told me you don't have another job yet."

Quin! Bailey's chin dropped, exchanging glances between the meddling duo.

Then Kayla threw him the rest of the way under the bus. "I called him yesterday to get directions. He told me I'd have better luck in person."

"Ugh. You guys!"

"Please, Bailey," Kayla begged.

She wanted to be angry, she wanted to tell both of them to go to hell, but she couldn't. "Fine. Two weeks, Kayla, and I'm gone whether you find someone in that time or not."

Kayla clapped her fingers together. The highlights in her hair sparkled as she jumped. "Great. I need you to start first thing tomorrow morning."

****

That evening, after dinner, Bailey shared her short-term plan with her parents. Her father seemed more concerned with the baseball game that just started on television. But her mother remained strangely quiet before disappearing into the kitchen to wash dishes.

Bailey retreated upstairs to her old bedroom. If she set out early enough in the morning, the traffic wouldn't be too crazy. It only took her a few minutes to gather a new garbage bag of the clothes she'd need for her temporary stay in Virginia. She sat the bag by the door, and it slumped on the floor like a deformed pillow.

All throughout dinner, she couldn't stop thinking about the drafts Dylan had put together for Bill Porter's bakery. She flopped across her bed to doodle some renderings of her own.

Two ideas came to mind right away. The third idea took a little extra tweaking but quickly became her favorite.

From downstairs, her mother's laugh welcomed a visitor. A moment later, the oak stairs creaked under the weight of footsteps, and Jordan's reflection appeared in the mirror hanging over her white princess dresser.

She looked over her shoulder. "My mother called you, didn't she?"

He entered the room and sat on the corner of the bed. "As a matter of fact, she did." Determination covered him like a heavy sweatshirt. Only it was warm outside, and he was wearing shorts and a thin tee. "She told me you were going back to finish some work. Is that all it is, the work?"

Bailey closed her sketchbook and shook her head instead of answering verbally. Work was the only thing there for her.

He stretched onto his side beside her. "Why don't I believe you?"

Bailey tossed the sketch pad on the floor and rolled onto her back to stare at the ceiling. She knew why Jordan didn't believe her, and it had everything to do with the last time she saw him and what happened, or more accurately, what didn't happen.

The day she drove Jordan home, the kiss that started in the living room made it to his bedroom. Their shirts were the first to go before collapsing onto his bed in a heated knot of arms and legs, groping and pawing one another. She grabbed the tab of his zipper.

****

"Bailey, tell me you want this." He whispered in her ear.

"I want—this."

He rolled on top of her, kissing her throat. "Say it. Say you want me."

"Jordan—I—" She kissed him harder and shoved

at the waist of his pants. She almost had them down far enough.

But his kiss fizzled away, and his head lifted away from hers. "Bailey, stop." He pulled her hands away from his body and held them firmly on either side of her head. "Open your eyes. Look at me, Bailey."

She did, hoping he wouldn't see her true feelings or lack thereof.

"You know how much I want you, but I need to hear it from you. I need to know that you're doing this because you want me and not because you're trying to forget—someone else."

Bailey lifted her hips against his solid erection, hoping to persuade him that it didn't matter.

He responded with a firm grind. But it still wasn't enough. He was offering his body—and his heart, but she had to take both.

The shimmer in his blue eyes faded and cooled when he realized she couldn't say what he needed to hear. He rolled away from her, hurt and frustrated in more ways than one.

****

One small lie on her part might have drastically changed the outcome of that day. Bailey studied him, lying next to her now. But it wouldn't have fixed anything.

He propped his head up with one hand and leaned against her. "Bailey, don't go back to Virginia. Please."

"I'm only going to help them catch up and hire another graphic artist. It's strictly work. Jordan, I'm not staying. It's not possible, trust me."

Jordan draped his free hand around her waist and swayed against her. "Prove it." His head dipped lower in search of a kiss.

"Don't." Bailey turned her face away from him.

His fingers crept under the edge of her shirt in search of skin. "That's not what you said the last time we were together."

Bailey stopped his hand from going any further. "You were right to stop me then."

"Maybe that was a mistake." His growing erection pressed against the side of her hip.

Bailey closed her eyes. "Jordan, it wouldn't be fair to you."

"Oh, Christ, Bailey." He rolled flat onto his back, the bulge of his cock easily visible against the fabric of his thin shorts. Sheepish disappointment filled his laugh. "After all of this, I still can't figure you out. You're lucky I'm a good guy."

No wonder he was confused. Bailey had done a complete one-eighty since the last time they were together. Now she felt sorry for both of them. "You are, you know—a good guy." Bailey's voice lifted softly as a way to apologize.

Jordan's gaze fixed on the ceiling before turning toward her. "Not good enough, it seems." His lingering stare traced over her features. "Bailey—what you and I had, it was good? Wasn't it?" The tenderness in his voice was honest and pure.

"Yes, it was."

"Do you think either of us will ever find something that special again?" His openness tugged at her heart.

Bailey turned on her side to face him. "I hope so."

"I'm sorry—if I hurt you back then." His compassion triggered a quiver on her lips. Jordan lifted his arm and offered his shoulder. Bailey curled up in the comfort of his embrace. "And I'm sorry that—he hurt you now."

Unable to form the words, she nestled against him

as a river of tears streamed down her cheeks.

Chapter Twenty-Nine

Tony's phone pinged with another text message. He glanced at his phone.

Kayla: **Tony, where are you?**

It wasn't nine o'clock yet, and Kayla had been hitting up his phone for the last half hour. A sense of dread washed over him. He had a sneaking suspicion that Kayla's panic probably had something to do with Bill Porter. The business mogul has called every day for the last week, wanting to see the logo designs for his bakery. But Tony has nothing to show him. Then, two days ago, Bill asked to speak with Bailey, and Tony couldn't bring himself to say she was gone. It's been four weeks, but it felt like a lifetime.

Navigating the last turn to his shop, his suspicion was confirmed. Parked right in front of the door of Ajak's Signs, a shiny silver Lexus belonging to Mr. Porter. Tony parked next to it and rushed inside, still strategizing the best way to tell him the truth.

Kayla rose from the chair behind her desk as Bill Porter cheerfully bellowed from further away. Then, someone else laughed. Tony stopped in his tracks. What the hell?

"I like the last one here. It's perfect. Get it neatened, and send it to me this afternoon." Bill Porter veered into the hallway from his office. "Oh, look, there he is." He extended a hand. "Good morning, Mr. Shepard. How nice of you to join us."

Tony searched past Mr. Porter to see the other part of 'us' and his heart nearly stopped.

J. ALISON COLE

Chapter Thirty

Bill Porter's car pulled away, and the tension in the air prickled over Bailey's skin like a bad case of poison ivy. *Two weeks and I'm out of here.* The second she turned, her gaze not only locked with Tony's, she fell down the rabbit hole unable to look away.

A tick in his jaw tightened, and fury pinched the corners of his eyes, which he unleashed on his sister. "Are you out of your fuckin' mind, Kayla?" He stormed into his office.

Kayla sprung from her chair. "I'm trying to help you," she screeched after him.

Bailey dashed into *her* workroom and fired up the computer. The lethargic swirling dots on the screen weren't enough to drown out the shouting across the hall.

"Jesus, Kayla—what the hell are you trying to do to me? I told you a week ago to hire someone, anyone— Fuck! How could you do this—to her?" The misery in Tony's voice landed in the pit of her stomach.

"This is *our* company. We need Bailey right now. And if you haven't noticed, she's not easy to replace."

Bailey did the unthinkable and lifted her gaze away from the screen. Tony stood behind his desk, his head hung heavy between his shoulders. Dark circles rimmed his eyes, and no remnants of his glowing tan remained, leaving his complexion pale by comparison. He wore his cloud of misery the same way she wore hers.

Tony's head lifted, and he met her gaze. Slowly, he veered around his desk and came into her room. His first guilt-ridden look fell to the floor. Guilt he didn't deserve. His second attempt succeeded, and his eyes hardened to steel. "Thank you for doing this. Hopefully, we can find a replacement quickly." Then he left quicker than she could blink.

****

Bailey handed Kayla six completed work orders for billing. "Here, Kayla. Lazlo and I were able to spit these out." She received four new work orders in return. At least she had made some progress. "Did you hear from anyone today?"

Kayla's dainty brows lifted. "I heard from a lot of people today."

"I mean—about the position. Any applicants?"

Kayla's gaze skirted over her desk. "I got two phone calls. I set up both appointments for tomorrow. One had some experience, and the other just got out of school. I guess we'll see."

"Okay, that's good." Bailey shook her head.

"Hey, since you're staying with me, are you about ready to leave?" Kayla tilted her head.

Bailey glanced at the clock, surprised to find it was well past five. The day had flown by. The large bay door in the back of the building rattled, and the setting sun poured further across the floor as the door rose higher. Tony and Dylan were back.

"Yes, let's go." Bailey grabbed her purse and headed to her car.

She followed Kayla to a small brick rancher five miles from the shop. The outside of the house looked so *average*, and the inside was no different. The walls were a simple light gray. No bright colors or shelves full of fairy figurines anywhere. Her living room had a black tweed couch and two gray barrel chairs. Not at all what Bailey envisioned for her quirky friend.

But one thing stood out. Mounted over the sofa was a sizable, black and white portrait of what appeared to be Kayla's wedding day.

Bailey recognized Aaron, Tony, and Kayla. The

fourth man in this photo had one arm wrapped around Kayla's waist and the other over Aaron's shoulders.

Aaron, Jason, Anthony, Kayla. AJAK's.

"Your Wedding day?" Bailey asked.

Kayla looked at the picture as if it was the first time she'd seen it in years. "Yes. That was my Jason."

The man in the photo had a long, slim face and shoulder-length hair. "He was handsome."

"I thought so," she laughed softly. "Although he hated his nose, he always thought it was too big. But, I loved it, and him, nose and all." Kayla sighed. "He could make me laugh every single day." Memories that only she could see silenced her for a brief moment. "The way he looked at me, made me understand what love really is. It was almost tangible. You know what I mean?"

Bailey understood precisely what she meant.

Kayla flopped on the couch and tapped the cushion beside her. Bailey sat next to her. "I was young and very naive before Jason managed to sweep me off my feet. You see, before Jason and I got close, I was head over heels in what I *thought* was *love* with someone else—a gorgeous hunk of a man who never looked at me twice. Jason helped me realize that I deserved to be seen and treated better. He made me feel like a queen. So, after I graduated from school and turned eighteen, I wanted to get married right then." She smiled shyly. "Even though they were all friends, Aaron and Tony weren't as thrilled about it. They thought I should wait." Kayla's gaze drifted across the room. "I'm so glad I didn't." She took a somber breath. "The accident happened not quite a year after that picture was taken. They said Jason died on impact, but Aaron actually lived for a day. He managed to say one thing before he died. He said, 'All you have to do is follow the signs.'" Her voice thickened. "Aaron was…philosophical in some ways." Kayla pulled her feet closer to her body, and sat like a pretzel. "And if you look, I mean really look, there's always some kind of sign."

Bailey pondered for a moment. "I guess."

"You guess? It's like following your gut. It applies to everything, and I'm not saying that because we have a sign company. It's much more than that. But honestly, it would make a cool neon sign for the office. Don't you think?"

"Sounds to me, you're more like Aaron than you realize."

Kayla's fluttering laugh filled the room. "I suppose, in some ways, that's true. Aaron was the dreamer and got a lot of credit for starting the company. Still, without Tony, it would've never happened. Tony was the anchor for Aaron when he couldn't make the hard decisions. Kind of like the one he has to make now." Kayla gave her a sympathetic smile. "I want to thank you again, Bailey. I know being here is difficult for you. But you should know, it's not easy for him either."

Bailey's voice rattled before she could bury the distress. "Well, things have a way of working out the way they're supposed to."

Kayla smiled. "They always do."

****

The first applicant, Edith Winters, was a fifty-year-old woman with twenty-two years of experience making signs. The second applicant was a twenty-one-year-old college graduate with no hands-on experience—and he wanted top-dollar to start.

Bailey and Kayla scanned over both resumes.

Kayla stretched in her chair. "The guy was kind of cute."

"Kincaid?" Bailey laughed. "He said it like it was his first name."

"It's not?"

"No, it's Morris." Bailey snorted. "What's wrong with Morris?"

Kayla crossed her arms. "I had a cat named Morris. So, who do you think can do the job?"

"I think they both have qualities that could work."

The phone rang. Kayla picked it up, "Hold, please." She cupped her hand over the receiver to address Bailey. "Tony will want to discuss this with you when he gets back."

"Oh." A discussion with Tony required speaking face-to-face. The thought twisted Bailey's insides into knots. "When is he expected back?" She needed to prepare.

"He's supposed to be back by two." Kayla brought the phone from under her chin. "Ajak's Signs, can I help you?"

It was ten minutes past one o'clock. Bailey strolled down the hallway in a daze. That was nowhere near enough time to patch together the pieces of her heart.

Two o'clock on the nose, the steady rumble of Tony's truck hummed outside the rear entrance. The big door rose a moment later, and he stepped out of the truck. Exhaustion clung to him like the mud that covered his boots and the cuffs of his jeans from a messy install.

Bailey scanned the shop for Lazlo, but he'd disappeared, the coward, and Dylan was still outside by the truck. She was alone in the shop with Tony.

He marched inside with his head down and his gaze fixated on the floor. "How did the interviews go?"

The static energy between them filled the air like smoke. "They each have some potential. The woman has more hands-on experience, but the guy might offer newer techniques."

A brief glance followed his woeful breath. "Good. Which one could start the soonest?"

"Both said, two weeks."

"Not any sooner?" His voice held a twinge of desperation.

"I'm afraid not." A bereft silence followed.

A mixture of turmoil and empathy grew in his eyes. His chest swelled with a full breath. "Bailey—"

Whatever he was about to say, was drowned out by the distinct tap of heels on a concrete floor.

Chapter Thirty-One

He was about to tell Bailey what their night together meant to him, but Quin was right. He couldn't drag her into the shit show mess he was in. She deserved better. That's when every bit of color drained from Bailey's face from the sound of someone entering the shop. Tony turned, hoping it was somebody else, but no.

Candice paraded across the open space. *Jesus. Perfect!*

He met Candice in the middle of the room. "What are you doing here? The appointment isn't until three, and I told you I'd meet you there." Tony tried to sound less perturbed than he felt.

Candice's dark eyes turned coal black. "I've already been."

"What?" Tony's brain tripped with confusion. "Let's go into the other room." He held out his arm to lead her out of the shop, but she side-stepped him.

"No, I'd rather tell you here." Her gaze shifted toward Bailey. "Everyone may as well hear what I have to say."

His gut twisted with anxiety from the peculiar way Candice was acting. "Is something wrong? Is the baby okay?"

A scornful snicker sputtered from Candice's lips. "Define wrong because, in some ways, I have to think this is right."

"Just tell me what's going on, dammit."

Candice's expression cowed, and the sarcasm in her voice faded. "The doctor finally had the chance to review my tests, so he called me this morning. He said my HCG levels were not just high but abnormally high, and he wanted to do another test and try an ultrasound.

"You should have called me. I thought it was too early for an ultrasound. And what the hell is HCG?"

"It's the hormone that a woman's body makes. They drew more blood and did a few more tests, comparing them to the previous results. They were the same, only…" Her gaze fell to the floor.

"Only what?" Tony's patience unraveled.

"The ultrasound revealed an ovarian cyst about the size of a tennis ball. It's responsible for my hormone levels being so high."

"What exactly does that mean? Does it hurt the baby?"

"It means I'm not pregnant, Tony. I never was."

The words piled up inside Tony's head like a collapsed building. *Candice isn't pregnant. It was all a mistake.* Oddly, the first emotion he felt was *loss*, followed by a slim and skeptical margin of relief. "I'm so sorry, Candice."

Her contemptuous laugh reached the rafters of the metal-framed building. "Really? Because I'm not. I didn't want a baby to begin with, but the thought of having one with someone who—someone you're not meant to be with—well, you know."

"Are you going to be alright? Is there anything I can do?"

A single tear ran down her cheek. He and Candice had agreed to do this together. It seemed only right that they would end it the same. "Come on, let's go talk."

Chapter Thirty-Two

Tony and Candice walked out of the shop together, leaving Bailey glued to her spot like a statue. She had no idea where they went, how long they'd be gone, or what to expect next.

Candice was never pregnant.

Questions crept into her mind. Should she offer Tony congratulations? Does this change things between them? What happens now?

Tony is free.

Kayla skipped into the shop. "Whoa-whoa." The smile on her face was too big to measure. "So, what do you think about that?"

"I don't know what to think."

Kayla gave her a comforting hug. "We'll figure it out. I think this calls for a celebration. I'll make us something special for dinner tonight."

****

Pots and pans clanked on the stove, and the thick smell of Oregano and garlic filled the air. "I'm making my special spaghetti. I hope you're hungry." Kayla hollered to her from the kitchen.

She wasn't. "Sounds great." Bailey's appetite hadn't been right for weeks. Sitting on the sofa in the living room, her mind hovered in a fog of—elation, anxiousness, and, most of all, doubt. Tony was free. He just dodged a huge bullet. The dust hasn't even settled, so why would he jump right into something new with someone else? Even if it was her. *He wouldn't.*

Gnawing on the side of her thumbnail, she called Kayla. "Did you need any help?"

"No, no, no. I've got this." The doorbell rang, followed by the crash of a pan hitting the floor. "Oh, shit." Kayla veered around the corner, "Could you get the door, though?"

Bailey hopped from the couch. "Sure."

The door swung open. Max did a double take, clearly surprised to see her.

"Hey, Bailey. So you're staying with Kayla. I heard you were back." Max shouldered past her and entered Kayla's house.

"I'm not... back, I'm—helping out."

Kayla's head popped around the corner of the kitchen. "Oh, it's you, Maxwell."

"I just heard the news." Max sashayed into the kitchen. Bailey followed a few steps behind. Curious to hear his take, she leaned against the archway between the dining room and the kitchen.

"How did you find out? Did Tony call you?" Kayla cautioned Max out of her way. "Move." She headed toward the sink to drain the hot water from the pasta.

He sidestepped the scalding pot. "No, I heard it from Raven."

Kayla veered away from the steam billowing from the colander. "Figures you'd call her."

"Hey, she called me," he countered defensively.

Bailey's back pocket vibrated right before it rang with a standard factory ringtone. Her pulse launched into hyperdrive, recognizing the number. Only a handful of people had her new number. Up until now, Tony was not one of them.

Kayla.

Bailey took a long breath before answering. "Hello?"

It took an equally long moment before a response came from the other end. "Hi, Bailey." The sound of his voice triggered her pulse.

"I was wondering if I could come by, and maybe you and I could talk."

Bailey moseyed away from the kitchen. "I...I—" Her roller coaster of emotions left her speechless. The doorbell rang again. "Hold on, Tony. I'll get it, Kayla." She flung the front door open. "Oh my god." It never occurred to her that Tony would be the person standing on the other side.

His phone lowered from his ear. "Hey."

Max peeked from the kitchen. "There's the luckiest son-of-a-bitch I know."

Kayla's cheerful face appeared around his shoulder. "Oh, hey, come on in. You're just in time. I made lots."

Did she invite everyone? Bailey stepped away from the door as Tony came inside.

For the most part, he still looked drained but *at peace* in a weird kind of way. "Thanks, Kayla, but I'm not hungry."

"Nonsense. I can't imagine you've eaten today with everything that's happened. Max, if you're staying too, you need to set a few more plates at the table."

"What the hell?" Max grunted. "You could say please."

"Please," Kayla droned.

Bailey hugged her arms around her chest to keep from trembling. It was hard enough for her to get her head wrapped around what happened, but trying to imagine what Tony was going through was impossible.

"Well, it's ready. Everyone can take a seat." Kayla placed a large platter of spaghetti on the center of the table and began mounding each plate. "Sit, sit, sit before it gets cold." Max sat down first, then Kayla. Bailey eased into a chair across from Tony, followed by the elephant in the room.

Max loaded his fork and took a hefty bite. "Damn, Kayla, I didn't know you could cook like this?"

Kayla swirled her fork with noodles. "What the heck does that mean?"

"I mean, it's actually good."

"You're a dick," Kayla snorted. Then, the room fell silent other than the clank of silverware scratching on plates.

Bailey took a small bite of spaghetti, but it knotted in her stomach like a hunk of rope.

Kayla interrupted the awkward quiet. "So, Tony, where did you go this afternoon? Unless you'd rather not say."

Tony swallowed and wiped his mouth on a white paper napkin. "No, I'll tell you." His gaze ricocheted around the table. "Candice and I went to the doctor's office together. I wanted to hear it for myself. I didn't want any more surprises."

"And what did they say?" Max asked sarcastically. "Sorry, we almost fucked up your life."

Tony semi-choked. "No. He said it's a rare condition but that it happens sometimes. It wasn't done on purpose." Tony's focused stare found Bailey. "It was no one's fault. It was just a big mistake." His gaze lowered to the plate in front of him, and the room fell silent once more.

Kayla jumped up from the table. "Oh, I almost forgot the bread." She pulled a tray of toasted bread from the oven, tossed it into a wicker bowl, and brought it over to the table. "By the way, Tony, I have a doctor's appointment on Friday."

"What kind of doctor?" Max inquired with a full mouth.

Kayla took a piece of bread, visibly perturbed by his nosey question. "If you must know, Dr. Evans is a gynecologist/OB."

"Ha, ha. Damn." Max laughed. "Just as long as he's not the same one Candice used. Hell, if anyone should've been pregnant, it's Bailey." One more laugh slithered out before a forkful of food silenced him. Then three sets of eyes landed directly on her.

Bailey's chin lowered to her chest, and her gaze zeroed in on her plate. *Wow, this is a massive plate of spaghetti.* "I'm—I'm not." She raised her head to reassure them. "I'm not." But looking up was a mistake.

Tony offered a timid but endearing smile, instantly sparking the memories of their night together.

Max stopped eating. "Wait, so why are you going? Is it just a checkup or something else?" He leaned back in his chair, waiting for Kayla's answer.

Her brows lifted satirically. "What's it to you?"

Max's shoulders sagged. "Are you dating again? Christ, are you pregnant?" Now, all eyes landed on Kayla.

"Oh my gosh." Kayla shook her head. "No!" Her voice lowered. "People typically need to have sex to become pregnant." Kayla dismissed Max with a smug smile. "Bailey, did you want any bread?"

"No, thank you," Bailey politely ignored the bowl Kayla shoved under her nose. Tony did the same.

Max snagged a piece of bread as the bowl zoomed past him. "Are you going on the pill? Screwing the doctor? What?" Max pressed on.

"Don't worry about it. And maybe I want to screw the doctor!" Kayla shot back.

Tony set his fork down, and caught Bailey's attention. He nodded toward the other room.

She couldn't force herself to eat anymore, anyway.

They left the table virtually unnoticed by the

bickering pair and stepped outside onto Kayla's small front porch. A robin flew from its nest in the soffit to a small tree in the front yard. It hovered close by.

Bailey gripped the railing for a sense of stability.

A few feet away, Tony took a similar stance. "After Candice and I left the doctor's office, I took her to her parents' house. The rest of the afternoon, I did some soul searching, but even now, I still feel like I can't catch my breath. I don't know how to figure out what comes next."

"I can't imagine."

Tony's voice grew soft, no doubt, smothered under his drained emotions. "I know it's been weeks since ah—things got messed up." He took a lengthy pause. "If I could change it, I would." His focus stayed on the tree. "You don't know how much I'd give for that, but Aaron always said you can't un-ring the bell."

"That was a pretty big ding," Bailey tried to lighten the tremendous weight of the conversation.

Tony snickered. "My ears are *still* ringing." His head turned just enough to see her from the corner of his eye. "Bailey—"

The Hawaii Five-O theme song—buzzed from Bailey's rear pocket. With a huff, she hit "Ignore" and shoved it back into her pocket. "Sorry."

"That morning, there were some things I never got to say." Tony released the railing and stepped closer. A shiver seized most of her body. His chest expanded, preparing to speak.

A ding sounded from Bailey's phone, alerting her to a new text. And it rang again, interrupting Tony a second time. Bailey was going to kill Quin.

Tony glanced at her hip. "Maybe you should answer it."

"It's just Quin. Sorry." Bailey grabbed her phone,

ready to give Quin what for, when she saw the text: **911-911-911! Need you Now!** Her knees nearly buckled from under her for the *second* time in one day.

Bailey took his call immediately. "Quin, what is it?"

"It's Liz. She's been in an accident. They took her in the Medi-vac to the hospital. I don't even know if she's alive or dead." Quin sounded nothing like himself.

Bailey's free hand covered her mouth. "Dear God."

"Bailey, please come. Please."

Her eyes lifted to meet Tony's. He'd heard Quin's frantic pleas, and nodded with understanding. "I... Yes. I can leave now."

"Hurry, Bailey, what if—what if she's—" Quin bawled into the phone.

"You can't think like that, Quin. I'm leaving now." Bailey shoved the phone back into her pocket. "I'm sorry, Tony. I have to go." She darted into Kayla's house and gathered her car keys and a few things from the spare bedroom.

Max and Kayla stood next to Tony in the living room. The worried look on Kayla's face suggested that Tony had filled them in on what was happening.

Tony stepped forward. "Are you okay to drive?"

"I'll be fine." She'd only been back for two days and was leaving again. "Kayla, I have to do this, and... I hope you understand."

"She does." Tony took her plastic bag suitcase from her. "I'll walk you out." He tossed the bag onto the passenger seat of her car and bent lower to see her through the window. "Be careful, okay?" He tapped on the side of the door.

"Hey," Bailey caught him before he stepped too far away. "Tony—"

"It's—okay, Bailey. Go help, Quin." He turned and walked away. No backward steps, no lingering glances, not even a wink. He entered Kayla's house, and the door closed.

Chapter Thirty-Three

Liz and her cousin Michele were part of the nine-car pile-up on Turnpike 81. It was all over the radio how they shut the road down. Quin called every ten minutes, making Bailey's drive to the Trauma Center in York, Pennsylvania, feel like days versus hours.

When Bailey got to the hospital, she found Quin in the lobby, sobbing like a baby. His weight collapsed onto her shoulders, and she feared the worst. "Tell me what's happening, Quin." It was all she could do to keep both of them upright.

"We only know that she's still in surgery."

"Well, let's take that as good news, okay?" She navigated them to the surgical waiting area. There, rows of teal-colored chairs created a maze with a few sofas in the center. Sporadically mounted on several of the walls were three relatively small televisions playing the cooking channel with no sound. Near the back of the room, behind a desk, was a larger television displaying color-coded listings of doctors and the various surgeries and stages they were in. It updated every three minutes but seldom changed. Plus, they had no idea of the name of the doctor operating on Liz.

Liz's mother sat quietly in the corner with a magazine. Her father paced nearby on a visible path of trampled Berber carpeting.

Others waiting in the room, clung together in clusters, each claiming their own territory. Each time someone new entered, they'd join their appropriate tribe or form a new one.

Jordan burst through the doors and joined theirs. "Do we know anything yet?"

When no one spoke up, Bailey answered. "No,

there hasn't been any news."

He looked at her sheepishly. "I, uh, thought someone should be here for Michele. Her parents are in Montana. I'm not even sure they know what's happening, and I can't seem to get a hold of them."

"It's good of you to come, Jordan. We may be in for a long night."

****

The first report came right after midnight. Liz and Michele made it out of surgery. Liz suffered a collapsed lung from three broken ribs. Glass and metal had sliced her hand open. But the most severe injury was a huge knot and deep abrasion along her left temple. They were monitoring the swelling and the pressure it might put on her brain.

Michele's injuries, though severe, weren't as life-threatening. She'd survive with a mild concussion and a broken femur. It would still be a few hours before either one could receive visitors.

"God, I need some coffee." Quin scrubbed his hands down his face.

"I'll get it for you." Bailey rose from the teal pinstriped sofa, and stretched her neck. "Would anyone else like anything?" She made the offer to the others in their prospective group.

Sitting across from Quin, Jordan rose. "I'll come with you."

The snack room was down the hall from the waiting area. The lights flickered on when they entered. Three of the soda machines took cash and cards, but the coffee machine was older and only took quarters. The change machine on the wall had a handwritten note taped over the dollar bill slot that read: *Out of Order*.

Great.

Bailey sat her phone down and emptied her

pockets onto the table, rummaging for enough change. Thirty-seven cents wasn't going to cut it.

"I don't have enough change, either." Jordan only had bills and plastic.

"We passed a nurse's lounge. Let me see if I can get some from them." She grabbed a five-dollar bill from the table. "Watch my stuff. Go ahead and get some snacks for Quin and the others. I'll be right back."

J. ALISON COLE

Chapter Thirty-Four

Moonlight filtered through the skylight into Tony's bedroom. After all the shit that went down this afternoon, he still couldn't find any real rest, much less sleep. It felt like a merry-go-round racing around and around, and now that it stopped, he was too dizzy to think straight.

Finding out that Candice wasn't pregnant filled him with relief that made him happy and mad at the same time. Happy because he wouldn't be tied to a woman he didn't love, and mad because even though he was vindicated, there was no magic reset button or a way to turn back the clock like it never happened. It did. And it cost him dearly.

Up until a couple of days ago, Bailey had been gone for weeks. She wouldn't have returned now if Kayla hadn't forced her hand by guilting her into it. And what good did it do? *She's gone—again.* Was the universe trying to tell him something? *Well, fuck the universe.*

Tony rolled over and opened the drawer of the nightstand. Last week, he came across the file that contained the photos Bailey had taken that day on the ridge. He angled the picture to capture the available light from the overhead skylight, the one of him leaning over Bailey. A tightness squeezed around his heart. He'd been a fool and too afraid to see what was right in front of him the whole time. He should have broken up with Candice that very day, and maybe none of this would've ever happened.

Tony grabbed his phone. Yeah, it was the middle of the night, but if anything, he could make sure she made it there in one piece. He pressed Bailey's new number.

"Hello?" A man answered.

Tony's brain skipped a beat, not expecting to hear someone other than Bailey. He glanced at the number. Yeah, he'd pressed the right button. "Quin?"

"No, this is Jordan. Who's this?"

All the oxygen left the room. "Umm, this is Tony. I know that it's late. I just wanted to make sure Bailey got there safely. How is Liz?"

After a lengthy pause, Jordan replied. "Bailey made it here okay, and Liz is out of surgery but being monitored. She may have a long recovery."

"That's good. I mean, I'm glad Liz is going to be all right." Another span of silence followed.

"Look, Bailey left her phone here to go up the hall to get some change. I'll let her know that you called."

"That's okay. She needs to be there for Quin."

"Yeah, he's a mess. She's the only one who can calm him down. Look, man, I know she was supposed to help you for a week or two, but that may not happen now."

A sinking feeling washed over Tony. He was never going to see Bailey again. "Just tell her that…" *That I didn't want this.* "Just tell Bailey to take care of Quin. Tell her not to worry about…Ajak's."

"Sure thing. That's probably for the best." The phone call ended.

Tony stared at his phone. When the light went out, he threw it across the room, and it shattered against the wall above his dresser.

Tony flopped onto his back, letting the ceiling become a blank slate for his emotions. He stayed like that until a whisper of morning light replaced the darkness surrounding him. As much as he would've liked to stay home and sulk, the company was the one thing he had left, and he couldn't lose that too.

Chapter Thirty-Five

"Really, Bailey, I can't thank you enough for helping me these last few weeks." Quin reversed an old wooden chair beside his desk and sat down with his elbows propped on the back."

Liz had called Bailey every day since her release from the hospital, begging her to get Quin out of her hair. This was his first full day back at Chenney Signs.

"No problem. Don't forget about the deliveries coming in tomorrow, and you still have a couple of calls to return from yesterday. I wrote the numbers down along with some information you'll need to give them prices." Bailey pointed to the notepad on the desk behind him.

He studied the message, "Tony's Place, really?"

"It's a pizza joint," Bailey clarified in a harsh tone.

"Wow." He scoffed and eyed her warily. "I'm just saying."

"Well, don't. Just...don't say anything." Bailey silenced him with a *not-so-friendly* smirk.

Quin took the hint. "Hey, have you thought about what I ask you?"

"Sure, I thought about it." Quin hinted that she should stay on. She peaked at his books. Even though he was busy, the workload wouldn't support two people—yet, and would drain his bottom number.

As usual, he read her thoughts. "If you did come to work with me, things would pick up, maybe double."

"And if it doesn't?" She gave him another smirk. Tanking Quin's business was the last thing she would allow. "No, Quin. I'll help out here and there until I find something else."

"Well, I don't want you working for the enemy."

"I wouldn't do that. Look, you don't need to worry about me. I'll figure it out."

He grunted and tossed the notepad back onto the desk. "So… Have you heard from anyone else?"

Who he meant by *anyone* was clear. "No."

"Not even Kayla?"

Bailey shrugged. "No one. I tried calling…him the morning after Liz's accident, but he didn't answer. So what good would it do to talk to Ka-Kayla." Her voice wobbled, and the silence of the room grew along with her discomfort.

"Okay." Quin popped up from his chair. "Hey, would you mind closing again this evening? I have a prescription to get filled for Liz, and the pharmacy locks their doors right at six."

"Sure, go ahead."

"You know, I actually think she's getting tired of me being around, and get this, she doesn't like my cooking. I'm a way better cook than her." He paused. "Never tell her I said that."

Bailey conjured a smile even though her heart wasn't in it. "I won't, and that's crazy. You're a great cook."

"I know, right." Quin stopped next to the door. Worry pinched the corners of his eyes. "Are you really—okay, Bailey?"

She tossed a pen at his head and scurried from behind the counter to shuffle him along. "Get going, go home, and take care of Liz."

"Hey, that could've hit me in the eye." Quin ambled through the door.

Luckily, he left before the tear rolled down her cheek. The fact that she had any left came as somewhat of a surprise.

An hour later, Bailey locked the door of Quin's

sign shop and headed to her parent's house.

****

Went to play cards with Leo and Ginger.
We may be late, so don't wait up.
    If you have time, can you clean the pool for
Dad?
Love, Mom.

    Bailey crumpled the note she found on the kitchen table. She had the sneaking suspicion that her father only opened the pool to keep her from slugging out on the couch. She opened the fridge and searched around the *two* half-empty jars of mayonnaise. The third was probably hiding behind the pot roast her mother made yesterday. But nothing sparked her appetite. The door thudded closed, and she headed upstairs to change into her swimsuit.

J. ALISON COLE

Chapter Thirty-Six

Tony put the Mustang in park and killed the engine. Bailey's car was the only one sitting in the driveway. He'd stewed over this long enough. Was this a mistake? Probably. He may never have closure, but he had to do this to be able to live with himself.

A dog in the yard next door started barking, and before he reached the front door, someone hollered from the rear of the house.

"I'm still cleaning the pool. Hey, can you bring me the round brush next to the front rail? I'm almost finished."

Tony followed the stepping stones to the rear of the yard. The water splashed, and then all went silent. He entered the gate around the pool and spotted a round brush propped on its side.

Bailey was a blurry shadow in the corner of the deep end. He knelt down beside the ladder right above her.

She jetted to the surface and took a massive gulp of air. Matted hair and water streamed down her face. She swiped the water away from her eyes. "When did you get flip-flops, Dad?"

"I've had them for a while. And I'm not your dad."

Bailey's gaze lifted, and her hand groped for the top edge of the pool. "Oh my god. What...?" Her hand slipped off the edge, and the water choked more than her words. She cleared her throat. "Tony?"

Tony straightened to his full height. "There's something I need to say to you."

Bailey swam toward the ladder. Coming out of the water, she was a goddess in a white bikini. Water trickled down her smooth, narrow waist and glistened off her skin. She was every fourteen-year-old boy's fantasy, only she was real and walking toward him.

Tony closed his eyes, drawing on his inner strength to get through this without falling to his knees. He took a long, deep, breath.

"Let me start by saying I didn't come here to cause you trouble or mess with your head. I know things got screwed up, and I have to live with that, but if I don't get this off my chest, it will hang over me for the rest of my life." His nerves prickled, and his throat tightened.

"Bailey, you once asked me what I was afraid of—well, it's this. Finding someone that I truly care about, only to lose them. You're more to me than just my friend, and not just because you can throw a football way better than Max. You're funny and beautiful, you get me, and when you walk into a room, my world lights up. I knew you were special. I knew it from the beginning, but it scared the hell out of me. Bailey, I fell for you, and I just didn't realize it until it was too late. I-I wanted...no, I need you to know that the night we spent together meant something to me. It was—more real than anything I ever experienced before."

There! He'd said what he needed to say. His chest was ripped open and his heart was in his hands, completely exposed. He took what felt like his first full breath since this all started. Bailey remained quiet and just stared at him. His knees balked with a jerk. "You don't need to say anything, Bailey. I just wanted you to know."

Bailey pulled the round brush from his hand and tossed it aside. Her gaze reconnected with his. "What are you going to do with that?"

His brain skidded to a halt. "Do you mean...the brush?" Semi-confused, he glanced to see where it landed.

"No." Bailey's smile ignited—her big, beautiful smile and Tony thought his heart might explode.

She stepped closer, and her palms landed on his chest. "Is that a star bit in your pocket, or are you just happy to see me?" She gathered a handful of his shirt and proceeded to yank it higher over his head.

Tony freed his arms from his shirt and gathered her in for a kiss. Lavish and hungry, her passion met his. But then, Bailey ended the kiss, walked backward toward the water, and jumped in. His jeans and flip-flops landed in a disorganized pile on the concrete, as he followed her into the pool.

The water was calm compared to the uproar of emotions strumming inside his body. Bailey circled him in the water like a predator lurking in the brush. Water masked the lower half of her face, but he recognized the look in her eyes.

"You know everything I just said and did, by the way, was extremely romantic."

Bailey's brazen smile surfaced, pretending to contemplate his statement. "So." She spewed a perfect stream of water past his head. "You looked a little flustered to me." She made another tantalizing circle around him. She was absolutely stunning—and ornery.

"Here, I've professed my love, and apparently, all you saw was my dick. Not the most romantic thing I expected to hear."

The water swallowed her chuckle when she submerged and swam toward the deep end of the pool. Her long hair flowed like a spray of grace following her. She surfaced with her back against the sidewall, spreading her arms like wings to grip the edge of the pool. "You still haven't answered my question."

Tony pushed off the bottom and launched under

the water like a torpedo. He breached the water directly in front of her, staying afloat by holding onto the edge on either side of her head. "I love you, Bailey." He'd never said those three simple words to anyone and meant them the way he did now.

The gleam in her eyes set him on fire. "I love you too."

He sought her lips, and the water lapped and splashed around them like a tidal wave of desire.

Her slender legs locked around his hips as she kissed and nibbled on his bottom lip. "I want you Tony."

He veered away from the kiss. "I don't think I've ever had sex in a pool before."

"Well, I never had sex on a set of stairs. So, I guess there's a first time for everything."

"Bailey, I don't have a condom. And god help me, I don't think I'd have the strength to pull out this time."

The top string of Bailey's swimsuit slithered down her neck, exposing her breasts. She kissed him again, and her legs tightened pressing her core against his erection.

All the signs pointed to one thing, and Tony was going to follow them. "You know what? There is a first time for everything."

Chapter Thirty-Seven

Bailey's phone buzzed. The number on the screen triggered a ripple of excitement in her belly. A quick glance across the hall—Tony on his phone, wearing his panty-melting smile. She answered. "Hello?"

"Bailey?"

She swiveled her chair back and forth, playfully. "Yes, this is Bailey. Who is this?"

"Oh...man. This is Tony. You may remember me. We met a few months back."

"Tony... umm... yeah, I think so."

"Come on, you helped me install a sign in a shopping center once. Anyway, I was hoping you're free tonight. We could go out, maybe have a nice dinner somewhere that's not Brindles, then head back to my place."

"Tonight? I don't know." She offered him a cynical pout through the glass walls. "I just started a new job, plus I moved yesterday into a small room at my Aunt and Uncle's house."

"I know of a bigger place." He added the wink.

"Yeah—yeah, that would probably be really nice, but..."

"But what?"

Six days ago, Tony's declaration next to the pool made Bailey's return to Virginia inevitable. The more challenging decision was where to live. Moving in with him felt rushed. Realistically, they hadn't even dated. What if he hoarded mayonnaise too? In all honesty, she didn't care.

The space felt appropriate with everything that happened over the last few months. They would get there when the time was right.

Kayla entered Bailey's workroom carrying a small rectangular box. "Here, this just came for you." She set the box on the desk and left.

Tony straightened in his chair. "What's that?"

Panic seized her brain, remembering the time she received another delivery. What if this was from Doug? How did he know she was back? "I don't know. There's no card on the outside of the box."

Tony stood. "Maybe you should open it."

"I'll wait."

"No, go ahead."

"Why, is it from you?"

"You tell me." He smirked.

Bailey set her phone down and tore the shiny red paper away from the box. She opened the lid. Inside, dangling from a silver chain was a polished star-bit pendant.

Bailey's gaze shot across the hall, but Tony's standing in her doorway, arms crossed, leaning against the side, drenched in the au jus of all his beef-cakey-ness.

Sauntering toward her, without saying a word, he removed the necklace from the box and secured it around her neck. "Do you like it?" A shit-eating grin adorned his face.

"You're so cheesy. But yes."

"It's the same one, just in case you were wondering. I took it to a jeweler."

"I see. How very thoughtful of you. Thanks."

"It's for when you go on installs with Dylan, but you won't need to wear it if you're with me."

Bailey leaned forward and kissed him softly. "I'll remember that, and yes, I'd love to go out with you tonight."

Chapter Thirty-Eight

It's been two months, and this morning, Bailey agreed to go with Tony to check out the larger space for rent that's three doors up from where they are now.

"It's got two bay doors in the rear, and the rent isn't much higher for the square footage we're gaining." Tony walked ahead of her, carrying a seemingly heavy box.

"I don't suppose knowing the owner of the complex and being on his good side has anything to do with that."

He smirked, "Let's hope so. Keeping Bill happy is part of your new job description. He likes you the best." They reached the locked door.

Tony propped the box against the glass and struggled to keep it from falling. "Hey, can you get the key for me?"

"Where is it?"

He hoisted the box again, trying to maintain his grip. "Where do you think?"

"Oh, really, you've got to be kidding."

"Come on, it's not like you haven't done it before."

Bailey scanned their immediate surroundings and parking lot. No one was in the vicinity. She sidled next to him. "You could always put the box down."

He jostled the box again. "I could...but I'd rather not. I'm afraid the bottom will fall apart if I keep lifting it up and down."

"Alright, hold on." Bailey situated herself behind his left shoulder. Her hand eased into his front pocket and over his hip with *unmistakable* intent, and it wasn't to find the key. "Well, well, well," She groped and rubbed the front of his thigh. "I don't feel anything. Oh wait, now here's something." She fondled the side of his penis." He flinched, and laughed—seemingly at himself.

"Now come on, Bailey. The box is kind of heavy. You can play with *'Big Tony'* once we get inside."

"Fine." She gave his penis one last brush before collecting the contents in his pocket. "Let's see. Here's your truck key, a pack of gum, a few loose coins, a ring—

In the middle of her cupped hand, the sun sparkled off the multi-cut facets of a princess-cut diamond ring.

"Did you find it?"

"Tony?" She looked up and saw his coy smile. He sat the box down, plucked the ring from her palm, and dropped to one knee. Her mindless giggle trickled loose.

He captured her gaze. "I know this is all happening fast, but I don't want to wait any longer. I want you by my side forever. I want us to start a family—me and you. Bailey, you brought me to my knees a long time ago. Will you marry me?"

Kayla, Edith, and Lazlo burst from the front door of Ajak's. They scurried and shoved one another back inside after seeing him still kneeling before her.

"You're getting really good at this romance stuff."

"Thanks, I've been kind of inspired lately." He took her left hand in his and slid the ring into place.

"Yes, by the way."

"I figured as much. Besides, I wasn't going to take no for an answer."

The End

Epilogue

An early autumn painted the trees near the top of the mountain with every fiery color imaginable. The meadow, holding onto a few subtle shades of greens, made the sunset ceremony something right out of a fairytale.

Lights strung along the fence around Tony's yard cast a unique glow on the newlyweds sharing their first dance in the center of the yard.

Kayla stood next to Max. "What a perfect day." She'd never seen her brother this happy. "It's hard to believe it's only been a month since Tony asked Bailey to marry him. And you know, after everything they've been through, they deserve this."

Max handed Kayla a glass of champagne. "You're right. It's pretty amazing."

"Can you see how much they love each other?" She took a sip.

He leaned closer. "Yeah. You can almost feel it, too. Must be in the air."

Kayla gave him a stern, sideways look. His astute response actually surprised her.

"So—can I tell him now?" Max lifted his eyebrows.

Two nights ago, Kayla did the unthinkable and caved by accepting a dinner invitation from Max. Her one condition was to not say anything to Tony until after the wedding. News of his sister going out with his best friend might cause some ruckus. Plus, Max wasn't just any friend. He was—the infamous cock monster, to boot. However, other than one reserved kiss at her door, he didn't try any slick moves or "assume" he was invited in for a "drink" afterward. In fact, he was totally respectful. She wasn't prepared for this, *Max*, and it kind of threw her for a loop.

Max downed his sparkly, then took the champagne from her hand to lead them to the center of the yard to join the happy couple.

"I like having you in my arms." His smooth, velvety tone could've churned the flutters in her belly into butter.

"Huh." Kayla tried to muster as much nonchalance as possible.

"I'm serious." The warmth of his hand penetrated the fabric of her dress and reached the curve of her lower back. "You know, when we were younger, I didn't always come over to your house to see Tony."

Kayla looked into Max's ridiculously gorgeous brown eyes. The same brown eyes that haunted all her adolescent dreams from the age of twelve to seventeen. And now, against her jaded better judgment, she had to admit how much she liked being in his arms. "Oh, really? Did you have a thing for my mom?"

His square jaw jutted to the side. "Don't get me wrong, your mom was hot, but—no." He bit his bottom lip. "You're the one that lit my fire." Something weighty entered his eyes. "Kayla, I was arrogant and stupid enough to think you'd always be there. I'm not going to make that mistake again." The cocky, self-assured Max transformed right there in front of her into someone she remembered from a long time ago: her brother's shy friend. "I know it's taken you a long time to heal from losing Jason, but if you're ready, I want to be part of this new chapter of your life."

The music ended, but they kept dancing.

EVERNIGHT PUBLISHING

www.evernightpublishing.com